"I want you more than I've wanted any woman in my entire life."

His words hit Elise like a blast of cold water, and effectively doused the flames raging within.

Want.

Not *need.*

Not *love.*

Want.

Trembling from the aftershock of Dev's overwhelming kisses, and from that harsh dose of reality, Elise drew back, pushing his hands away. Trying to regain some semblance of dignity and control, she ducked her head, unwilling and unable to meet his gaze.

"Elise..." he protested, reaching for her again.

"No, Dev." She drew a deep breath, willed herself to look up, to meet those smoldering green-gold eyes. She touched her mouth, sore and swollen from his kisses, while his gaze followed the path of her fingers. When he would have gathered her close, she put up her hands in warning. "No. No more. We have to talk."

Dear Reader,

Welcome to Silhouette **Special Edition**, where each month, we publish six novels with *you* in mind—stories of love and life, tales that you can identify with.

Last year, I requested your opinions on our books. Thank you for the many thoughtful comments. I'd like to share with you quotes from those letters. This seems very appropriate now, while we are in the midst of the THAT SPECIAL WOMAN! promotion. Each one of our readers is a *special* woman, as heroic as the heroines in our books.

We have some wonderful books in store for you this June. *A Winter's Rose* by Erica Spindler is our THAT SPECIAL WOMAN! title and it introduces Erica's wonderful new series, BLOSSOMS OF THE SOUTH. Not to be missed this month is *Heart of the Wolf,* by Lindsay McKenna. This exciting tale begins MORGAN'S MERCENARIES.

Wrapping up this month are books from other favorite authors: Gina Ferris (*Fair and Wise* is the third tale in FAMILY FOUND!), Tracy Sinclair, Laurey Bright and Trisha Alexander.

I hope you enjoy this book, and all of the stories to come!

Sincerely,

Tara Gavin
Senior Editor
Silhouette Books

Quote of the Month: "Why do I read romances? I maintain a positive outlook to life—do not allow negative thoughts to enter my life—but when my willpower wears, a good romance novel gets me back on track fast! The romance novel is adding much to the New Age mentality— keep a positive mind, create a positive world!"

—E.J.W. Fahner
Michigan

TRISHA ALEXANDER

WHEN SOMEBODY WANTS YOU

Published by Silhouette Books New York
America's Publisher of Contemporary Romance

This book is dedicated to my first grandchild, Kaylee Ann Howard, who is destined to become a heartbreaker and the apple of her grandmother's eye. Welcome to the world, sweetie!

A special thank-you to Heather MacAllister and Alaina Richardson for always being there for me, and to Joni Turner, who gave me so much help in researching Lafayette.

SILHOUETTE BOOKS
300 East 42nd St., New York, N.Y. 10017

WHEN SOMEBODY WANTS YOU

Copyright © 1993 by Patricia A. Kay

ISBN: 0-373-09822-7

First Silhouette Books printing June 1993

TRISHA ALEXANDER

has had a lifelong love affair with books and always wanted to be a writer. She also loves cats, movies, the ocean, music, Broadway shows, cooking, traveling, being with her family and friends, Cajun food, *Calvin and Hobbes,* and getting mail. Trisha and her husband have three grown children and one grandchild and live in Houston, Texas. Trisha loves to hear from readers.

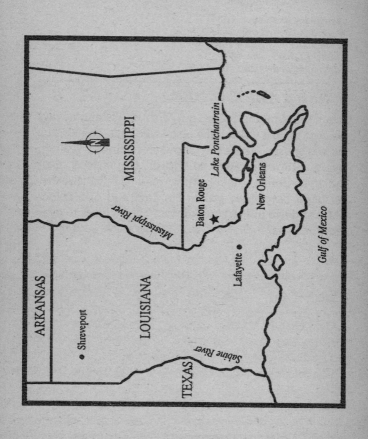

Prologue

He liked everything about her.

Her hair. The way the dark, glossy curls bounced when she walked.

Her head and the way she held it. Chin up, so that his view of her profile and her sleek neck was unobstructed.

Her graceful movements. The flash of her long, tanned legs as she strode past him.

The length of her skirts. Not too short. Not too long. Just brushing the tops of her knees so that she looked ladylike and innocently sexy all at the same time.

The colors she wore. Cool colors. Soft colors. Feminine colors.

This was the third time he'd seen her. Every afternoon he sat on a bench at Cypress Lake and ate the lunch Daisy had packed for him that morning. And all three times, about ten minutes after he'd arrived, the woman entered the pathway that circled the lake, walked past him as he sat on his bench munching his sandwich, and proceeded a few yards down to a bench that sat directly under one of the cypress trees. Once there, she'd sit and open her big book bag, remove a sketch pad and quietly draw for about forty minutes. Then she'd put her sketch pad away and walk quickly back to the main campus.

Dev knew she was a University of Southwestern Louisiana student, although she looked as if she were in her late twenties or early thirties—much older than usual for a college coed.

She never looked at him. Or at any of the other males who eyed her as she walked along the path. Dev liked that about her. He liked that very much. It reinforced his idea that she was someone special, a woman without vanity or wiles. An honest woman.

Of course, he wasn't the romantic type, but this woman brought out something in him....

He even gave her a name.

Ann. In his imaginings, he'd called her Ann. He'd always liked the sound of the name Ann. It was clean. Pure. Simple. And old-fashioned. No parents named their daughters Ann anymore. Like Mary, Ann was a forgotten name, belonging to a bygone era when women were happy and eager to make a home for their families. When they thought it was the most important work a woman could do to keep house and cook meals and care for children and wait for their men to come home from the wars.

She had an aura of innocence about her...a sweet, straightforward integrity that drew him...that caused him to think about her at odd moments throughout his day.

He wondered what would happen if one of these days when she approached his bench, he spoke to her. Just said ''Hello'' or ''Isn't it a beautiful day?''

He imagined her voice: soft, low, cultured. Never strident. Never shouting jingo. Never argumentative.

He imagined her smile. Gentle. Sweet. A little wary. Because she wasn't the kind of woman who would feel comfortable talking to a strange man—even on a college campus—but she also wasn't the kind of woman who could be deliberately rude or cruel. Dev wasn't sure how he knew that about her, but he did.

Yet something held him back from speaking to her. He told himself that he didn't want to do anything to make her feel uncomfortable or cause her to stop coming to the lake. He also told himself it wasn't a good idea for a teacher to make an overture to a student—even an older student.

But he knew these were all excuses. Because in his innermost thoughts, deep where his darkest secrets lay, Dev admitted that to speak to her, to force her to respond to him, might destroy all his illusions about her.

Chapter One

"Thank you, Ms. Cantrelle. I hope your stepmama, she likes the scarf."

Elise smiled at the motherly Cajun salesclerk.

Ms. Cantrelle.

She savored the sound of the name.

Cantrelle. Her father's name.

And now it was hers.

Elise accepted her charge card from the clerk at Abdalla's, her favorite place to shop in Lafayette. She signed the charge slip and took her package, which contained the silk scarf—a gift for her stepmother, Lisette—whose birthday was on Sunday.

The smile remained on Elise's lips as she exited the store and headed for the parking lot and her Toyota. The July sky was clear and bright, and even though it was only a little after nine-thirty in the morning, the air held the promise of another hot Louisiana day.

Elise was filled with a deep contentment. Her life was so different than it had been only a few years ago. During the past three years she'd made so many positive changes: she'd left an abusive husband and gotten a divorce, she'd been reunited with the father she'd never known and been made his legal heir, and she'd enrolled at the University of Southwestern Louisiana.

She smiled as she unlocked her car and tossed her package in the back seat. Next January, after the fall semester, she would have her degree in psychology. Then, if all went as she hoped, she would join the full-time staff at the women's shelter.

Elise sighed with satisfaction. Soon she would even be financially independent—a goal she used to wonder if she'd ever reach. At thirty-one, her future seemed bright—the possibilities that lay ahead of her limitless. It was hard to believe that so few years back she had felt almost completely alone and without hope. Now she had not only found her father, but she had friends, she had goals, she felt useful and in control of her destiny, and she had been welcomed into her father's large and wonderful family without reservation.

As she started her car, she glanced at her watch. Nine-forty. She had plenty of time. She wasn't due at the St. Jacques Women's Shelter until ten. For the past year and a half she'd worked three days a week—Tuesdays, Thursdays, and Saturdays—at the shelter, doing whatever needed doing. She'd worked behind the reception desk, helped sort and catalog donations in the Thrift Shop, assisted in food preparation in the kitchen, organized field trips, tutored children and taught their mothers simple skills, gone through the training necessary to man the hotline, and now she led group therapy sessions as well.

The work was by turns enormously satisfying or deeply frustrating. Sometimes it was even frightening. The workers at the shelter fought a constant battle to stay as objective as possible. Meg Bodine, St. Jacques's director, had warned Elise of the danger of becoming too personally involved with any of the women and children. "They'll break your heart, sweet pea, if you let them," she was fond of saying. "Teach them, help them, listen to them—but don't take their troubles home with you. Not if you want to survive."

Elise smiled as she thought of Meg, who, in addition to being a woman Elise admired and respected and hoped to be like someday, had also become a friend. She wondered if Meg was back from the symposium she'd attended in Boston. She'd been gone a week, and the shelter just hadn't seemed the same without her brand of breezy goodwill and down-home common sense.

A few minutes later Elise's question was answered when she pulled into the shelter's parking lot and saw Meg's sporty red Miata in its covered parking slot—the only perk Meg guarded like the crown jewels. Elise chuckled every time she saw the spiffy little car, which reminded her of an Easter egg. It was such an incongruous form of transportation for Meg, who was tall and big-boned, cared nothing about clothes or how she looked and routinely donated large chunks of her salary to the shelter's coffers.

"Hi, Elise," said the young woman sitting behind the reception desk as Elise entered the two-story building.

"Hi, Kim."

"Meg wants to see you."

"Oh, okay." Elise headed straight for Meg's office, poked her head around the open doorway and peered inside. Meg was shuffling through some papers on her desk. "Welcome back, fearless leader. How was Bean Town?"

Meg looked up and grinned. "Bean Town was great. I wowed 'em at the symposium, of course."

Elise returned her grin. "Well, of course. I expected no less."

"I also ate too much, as usual." The grin faded, and Meg's bright blue eyes filled with some nameless emotion. "Come on in. I want to talk to you for a minute."

A tentacle of fear crept along Elise's spine. "What's wrong?" She walked into the small office and perched on the edge of the black leather chair centered in front of Meg's desk.

"It's Penny," Meg said.

Now the fear turned to alarm. Elise swallowed against the sudden dryness in her throat. "Wh-what happened?"

"Last night her husband went on another drunken rampage. He hurt her bad."

Elise fought to keep her voice steady. "How bad?"

Meg shook her head. "They don't know if she's gonna make it."

"Where is she?"

"St. Elizabeth's Hospital."

"What about the children?"

"They're okay, thank God."

"Where are they?"

"Here, temporarily."

"Temporarily?"

Meg nodded. "Penny's sister, you know...the one who lives in West Virginia...she finally said she'd come and get them. She'll be here on Saturday."

Elise fisted her hands in her lap. The alarm had been replaced by anger, an anger so deep and so strong, she was trembling with the force of it. Why had Penny gone back to her husband? Why? He had refused to get help. He had done nothing to change his life. All he had done was cry and plead and promise he'd never hit Penny again. The same promise he'd made dozens of times before and never kept.

And *still* Penny had gone back to him.

"Elise, I know you're upset, but—"

"Yes, I'm upset! I talked and talked to her, Meg. I told her what was going to happen. Why didn't she listen to me?"

Meg gave her a rueful smile. "For the same reason you didn't listen when people tried to talk to you. You thought things would change. And you were afraid."

"Yes, but I didn't have someone like me as an example. I didn't have a place like the shelter to fall back on. Penny does." Elise ran her hands through her hair. "I keep thinking this is somehow my fault."

"Now stop that! You can't blame yourself. You did everything you could, but the choice was Penny's to make. You know that."

Elise sank back into the chair in wordless defeat. Yes. The choice *was* Penny's to make. But why hadn't she listened?

"I also told you not to get so personally involved, sweet pea," Meg said kindly. "That soft heart of yours has got to be toughened up a little."

"I know, but—"

"Penny reminded you of yourself, didn't she?"

"Yes," Elise whispered. But they all did. And Meg knew they all did.

"How many times have I told you that the work we do here is very like being a nurse or a doctor? You never want to lose your compassion, but you've got to stand back just far enough so that what happens to these women doesn't affect you to the point you can't function. When that happens, you're no good to anyone."

"I know." But Penny. There had been something special about Penny; Elise had felt it the first time she'd met the waiflike young woman with the huge, frightened gray eyes. "I want to go see her."

Meg sighed. "They're not letting anyone but family see her right now. She's on the critical list."

"Family! You don't mean her husband?"

"No, of course not. He's in police custody."

"For a minute there, I was afraid maybe he'd managed to get away with beating up Penny. After all, he's done it before."

"Yes," Meg said, "but not this time. This time the next-door neighbor heard enough to tell the police exactly what happened. And the oldest boy corroborated what she said."

For the rest of the day, Elise thought about Penny and wondered if there had been anything else she could have done to prevent this latest episode. Intellectually she knew she'd done everything possible to help and counsel the other woman. Emotionally was another story.

By the time six o'clock and the end of her shift came, Elise had a pounding headache. She had planned to attend a lecture at the university that evening, and until she'd heard the news about Penny, she'd been anticipating it with pleasure. The campus had been buzzing lately about tonight's lecturer, a Professor Devereaux. He'd arrived in mid-May—right before the summer session, which had begun the first week of June—on a year's grant from the Acadian Society of America. Elise knew that the professor was a noted anthropologist who, while enjoying visiting professor status at USL, would study Cajun culture in Louisiana.

Tonight's lecture on Cajun family life particularly interested her. Although she wasn't an anthropology student, she had a keen interest in her roots and a growing appreciation for the values and moral fiber of the Cajun people.

Oh, shoot, she might as well go. If she went home, she'd just sit and think about Penny, and inevitably, about her own past. Going to the lecture would be a good way to take her mind off her sometimes depressing job and the always-depressing subject of abused women and children. She'd just grab a quick sandwich, take a couple of aspirin to relieve her headache and head for Griffin Hall and the lecture.

At five minutes to seven, Elise gratefully sank into a seat in the last row of the lecture hall—one of the few seats still available. She glanced around. Good. The professor had drawn a nice crowd. Elise was pleased. She was proud of her school and wanted them to make a good showing.

The lecture hall hummed with conversation. Elise settled back in her seat and waited expectantly. She was glad she'd come.

A few minutes later the head of the sociology and anthropology department walked out to the podium. He welcomed everyone, then began reading an introduction of the speaker. "...highly acclaimed for his work...received his doctorate at Columbia University...we feel privileged to have Dr. Devereaux with us this coming year..."

Elise half listened. She wasn't really interested in credentials; she wanted to hear what the man had to say about her heritage.

"Let us please welcome Dr. Sloan Devereaux."

Elise clapped along with everyone else as a tall man dressed in an olive-green jacket, khaki pants and an open-necked yellow shirt walked out and took over the podium. As he adjusted the microphone, Elise studied him. He was nothing like she'd expected. She'd pictured someone older, maybe in his sixties, with gray hair and spectacles. Someone scholarly looking, who perhaps wore a beard and crumpled, nondescript clothing.

This man was nothing like that. He appeared to be in his early forties, and he was tanned and good-looking, with thick brown hair worn a bit longer than the current style and a loose-limbed body that looked as if it belonged on the tennis court or ski slopes. As she watched he put on a pair of wire-rimmed glasses, but rather than detracting from his appeal, they added to her overall impression of a casual sophistication.

He shuffled through his notes, cleared his throat and raised his face to look out at his audience.

Why, I know him! she thought with a jolt of surprise.

He was the man she'd been seeing in the park, she was sure of it. The man with the green eyes, as she had begun to think of him. The man who watched her so intently, yet covertly. The man she had pretended she didn't notice. Flustered, she lost the drift of what he was saying and missed his opening remarks.

Settle down, she told herself. So he's the man from the park. So what?

But she couldn't help feeling a little unhinged by her discovery. And if she were being completely honest with herself, she'd admit that this man, with his dark intensity, had stirred something in her from the first time she'd noticed him.

Gradually, as he talked, she managed to put aside her personal awareness of him and became caught up in what he had to say. He had a pleasant speaking voice, crisp and authoritative, but low-pitched. With a nice flair for drama, he talked about the evolution of the Cajun family in America, covering areas Elise was already familiar with. Since discovering her father, she had done a lot of reading about Cajuns, wanting to understand him and the rest of her family.

Professor Devereaux moved from the early history of Cajuns to their eventual migration to Louisiana. He talked about their work, their traditions, their superstitions and their music. "The *fais dodo* on Saturday night was the brightest spot in the week. Cajun men and women would toil in their homes and their fields all week long, but on Saturday night they would don their finest and head for the community dance hall.

"Many a courtship was conducted at the *fais dodo,* and the rules for courting were strict, especially where the girls were concerned. A girl could accept a boy's attention as long as she was inside the dance hall under the watchful eyes of her mother and father. Under no circumstances was she allowed to leave the dance hall without her mother. If she did, she couldn't come back because her reputation had been tarnished. This rule was strictly enforced." He smiled. "Many Cajuns regret that those old rules no longer apply." Elise smiled, too. She was glad times had changed. Perhaps those old rules sounded romantic, but she liked the freedom of her life today.

The professor continued to talk about the differences between how boys and girls in Cajun families had been treated in the early days. "It was normal and even expected that the boys would sow their wild oats, but the girls were expected to behave with propriety at all times, and from a very early age they were taught how to care for the household and family." His voice took on an amused note. "This was, of course, in addition to their work in the cotton patch."

He continued to describe early Cajun family life. "Although many things have changed over the years, some things have not. Cajuns have an expression *lâche pas la patate,* or *don't let go of the potato.* Figuratively translated, that means 'hang in there,' or 'fight for what you believe in.' And one of the things they strongly believe is worth fighting for is family. In a recent survey of one hundred Cajun families, the Acadian Society found that without exception, all were very close, up to and including third and fourth cousins."

Elise grinned. That was certainly true. She'd discovered so many cousins, she'd never keep them all straight. One of her cousins, Lianna, had now become her best friend. Elise's mind wandered again as she thought about Lianna and how much she treasured their friendship. How Lianna's cheerfulness and independence had been a welcome foil to the misery and helplessness Elise encountered in her work at the shelter.

"...but Cajun families are suffering the pressures of modern-day life just like other American families. The divorce rate is climbing. The family is no longer sacrosanct. The reasons are varied, of course, but there is a commonly held theory that the fabric of family life unravels in direct proportion to the number of women holding jobs outside the home." He raised his eyes from his notes.

"Statistics show the decline of the American family began after World War II, when Rosie the Riveter found she liked playing a man's role in society. That decline was accelerated in the sixties, during the birth of the women's movement. All subsequent studies have indicated that women abandoning their traditional roles and heading into the work force in ever-increasing numbers has been the single most important contributing factor to the destruction of American family life."

Elise frowned. She wasn't sure she liked the turn his talk had taken. Wasn't he kind of veering from his subject?

Dr. Devereaux cleared his throat and hesitated. "I know this won't be a popular viewpoint with the women in the audience, but many theorists believe that until American families—and, of course, that includes Cajun families—are willing to put family welfare ahead of material concerns and until women are willing to once again consider their traditional roles of wife, mother and caretaker as important as they did in earlier decades, all families will be more and more at risk.''

Elise's frown deepened. Didn't the professor realize at least half the women in today's work force worked because they *had* to?

''I'd like to quote directly from an article that appeared in *The Family Journal* several years ago. The article was written by Dr. Johan Freidberg, director of the American Family Council.'' He picked up a piece of paper and began to read. ''As the numbers of women in the work force increase, society will see a corresponding increase in incidents of alcoholism, drug dependency, child abuse, wife battering, depression and an overall breakdown of the family. Statistics show that although many women must work, many work by choice. These women want to have it all. No one can have it all. Something or someone must suffer. Unfortunately it is our children, our families, who are suffering.'' He laid the paper on the podium.

Elise could feel the hairs on her arms rising. What was he saying? That if women didn't work, all those social ills would disappear magically? That it was the fault of women that families had succumbed to the pressures of modern-day living? That women got beaten up because they had somehow failed their husbands? The unfairness of his statements infuriated her. What he had just said was so typical of the obtuseness of the male point of view. She was so tired of this kind of antiquated thinking.

She glared at the professor. Whether what he had read were his views or the views of the author of the article didn't matter. Because of who and what Dr. Devereaux was, more importance would be attached to what he had just read. As far as Elise was concerned he was just as guilty as the unknown Dr. Freidberg.

The more she thought about Dr. Devereaux's remarks, the more angry she became. Elise wasn't the kind of person who enjoyed calling attention to herself—in fact, she rarely did—but at this moment she felt like leaping to her feet and challenging Dr. Devereaux, who made his statements so decisively and with such authority.

She didn't, but only because she knew there would be a question-and-answer period at the end of his lecture. She could wait. For the remainder of the lecture, she fumed silently, hardly hearing the rest of his talk.

Finally the lecture was over.

After the applause died down, he removed his glasses, laying them on the podium. "Are there any questions?"

Elise stood. Before anyone else had a chance to say anything, she said, "Dr. Devereaux, I take exception to the conclusions you presented concerning the theory about why so many families today are dysfunctional."

He raised his eyebrows. "Oh?"

The raised eyebrows acted like a lighted match thrown on dry wood.

"I'm shocked that any educated and thinking person can really believe all of our social ills are the fault of women." She heard the quaver in her voice and fought to keep it steady. She would *not* become emotional.

"Uh . . . I don't believe I said that, Miss . . . ?" He picked up his glasses and put them back on. Even though Elise was seated at the rear of the lecture hall, she could see him frown.

"Miss Cantrelle," she said firmly. "And you *did* say that. I heard you, and I'm sure all the rest of the women in the audience heard you, too."

There was a smattering of applause, which emboldened Elise. "I'm currently working in the area of family counseling, in particular with battered women, and I can tell you unequivocally that not only are you wrong in your conclusions...you're *dead* wrong!" Elise clasped her hands in front of her to keep them from trembling. She was so angry she could feel herself shaking. "Your insinuation that if only these women had been more traditional, they might not have been battered—that it's somehow their own fault they got beat up—is irresponsible and untrue, and I think you owe them—and us—an apology."

She stared at him defiantly and waited.

Chapter Two

He'd been right about one thing, Dev thought. She had a beautiful voice, even when she was furious, as she obviously was now. He was still reeling from the discovery that the angry woman glaring at him was the woman he'd been spinning fantasies about the past couple of weeks. Not normally at a loss for words, he struggled to regain his composure.

"Uh...Miss Cantrelle...I'm sorry if I offended you—" he began.

"You more than offended me, Dr. Devereaux. You made a statement that is untrue, misleading and dangerous. It's not just me you owe an apology. You owe every woman in the audience an apology, and not only that... you owe us a retraction."

Dev sighed. Why was it that women became so emotional when anyone dared to criticize anything they did? Most of the women he'd ever known felt it was perfectly acceptable to male-bash, but the moment anyone said the least thing that could be construed as a criticism, they became irate. Not only irate, but demanding and aggressive.

Choosing his words carefully, he answered quietly. "If anything I said or read offended the other women in the audience, I also apologize to them. However, I think you've misinterpreted my remarks."

"If you didn't agree with the statements contained in the article, why did you read it?"

"Miss Cantrelle, as an anthropologist, it's my duty to explore all theories, all evidence and draw my conclusions based on my discoveries. However, even though I did not personally research and write the quoted article, Dr. Freidberg's statements can be and are backed by verifiable statistics. If you like, you can stay after my lecture, and I'll show you the documentation."

Although she was at least thirty or forty feet away from him, Dev could see that his reasonable answer didn't placate her, an impression she cemented when she answered. "I don't care about your *verifiable statistics,* Doctor. In plain language, facts and figures can be twisted to fit any theory, no matter how asinine. I deal with human beings, and I think they tell a truer story."

She continued to stand there, her stance a clear indication of her intention to wait forever, if necessary, for a retraction.

Dev had to admire her dignity. Even though it was obvious to him and everyone else that she was very angry, she had never raised her voice. He wondered what he should do now. The silence stretched for uncomfortable minutes, and a restless stirring began in the audience. Several women raised their hands.

"Miss Cantrelle," he said quietly, "you are certainly entitled to your opinions. However, contrary to what you've just said, facts and figures rarely lie. Yes, I can see how some people might choose to misrepresent them, but I assure you, I have not done so, and knowing what I know about the integrity of Dr. Freidberg and his staff, I can also assure you he has not done so, either."

Dev took a deep breath. "I also don't believe either I or Dr. Friedberg implied that abused women bring their abuse upon themselves. No reasonable person would ever suggest such a thing, and I'm sorry if that's the impression I gave you. Now, we seem to have some other questions...." Relief washed over him as she sat down.

But he found his gaze straying in her direction throughout the remainder of the question and answer period. Several times, their gazes locked, and Dev wondered what she was thinking. He also wondered if she'd take him up on his offer and stay afterward. He found himself hoping she would.

Finally, when all the questions were over, and the audience filtered out of the lecture hall, Dev scanned the crowd again. Disappointment arrowed through him when he didn't see her dark head or the pale blue of her sweater. Too bad. He would have liked the chance to talk to her close up, one-on-one. Convince her that he had never insinuated that abused women had brought the abuse upon themselves. He might even have invited her to have a cup of coffee with him, he thought with regret.

As several enthusiastic members of the audience milled around him, Dev fielded all their comments, but his heart wasn't in it. Normally he enjoyed the admiration of students and colleagues—the scholarly banter and exchange of ideas. Anthropologists didn't get a whole lot of attention or publicity, and it was nice to know someone appreciated and understood your work. But tonight, after the confrontation with the woman he'd secretly admired for weeks now, Dev felt let down and vaguely depressed.

"Dr. Devereaux, you were wonderful," gushed a pretty blonde. "Don't pay any attention to that girl. She was overreacting."

"Thank you," he murmured, but despite the blonde's assurances, Dev couldn't shake the disappointment and depression—and the inevitable reminders of a past he had tried hard to forget.

The face of his ex-wife, as clear as if she were standing beside him, flashed through his mind. He grimaced. Although the dark-haired, delicately built Cantrelle woman looked nothing like Joelle, who was tall and blond and larger-boned, her challenging stance tonight had sharply reminded him of the dozens of feminist causes Joelle had espoused over the years—causes that had been her number one priority. More times than Dev cared to remember Joelle had been off making speeches and taking part in marches while her husband and small daughter were neglected at home.

Not that he really thought that what the Cantrelle woman had said bore any relation to Joelle's militant beliefs, but still—it had been a shock to discover the sweet-faced woman he'd imagined to be quiet and gentle was a fighter who wasn't afraid to speak her mind in front of hundreds of people.

Finally everyone was gone, and Dev gathered up his papers and walked toward the exit. As he left the hall and walked the four blocks to his rented town home, he told himself that he should forget about the Cantrelle woman. Why did he care what she thought, anyway? What did it matter that she had turned out to be different from the way he'd imagined her?

But her lovely face, with its glowing freshness, and her courage in speaking up for something she believed in impressed Dev, even if she *had* misinterpreted what he'd said.

He didn't want to forget about her.

He wondered if he should try to find out where she lived. Maybe he would call her.

No.

Instinctively he knew calling her wasn't a good idea, even if he could find her number.

Then what? He really *did* want to talk to her. It was important to make her understand he wasn't some kind of Neanderthal who believed all women should be back at the cave tending the children.

Well, he could still talk to her. She'd been coming to the park every other day, and she hadn't come today. So she'd probably come tomorrow.

He could talk to her then.

She'd mentioned working with battered women. He would never have imagined her to be involved in that kind of work. He'd thought she was an artist. He'd pictured her designing delicate, pastel greeting cards or illustrating whimsical children's stories. He laughed softly at his foolishly romantic notion. So much for that.

Wonder if she'd recognized him tonight. If so, she might not show up tomorrow.

Fine. Then your decision will be taken out of your hands. You can just forget about her.

But as Dev walked inside and closed the door behind him, he knew he wouldn't.

Thirty minutes after she'd left the lecture hall, Elise pulled into the driveway of her cousin Lianna's house located in a middle-class Lafayette neighborhood filled with young families. She was still angry over the professor's remarks and the pat on the head he'd given her. She still seethed every time she remembered how he'd practically said, "Yes, little girl, we heard you, but now it's time to sit down and be quiet."

Elise gritted her teeth. Oh, she wished she'd had nerve enough to say more, but what good would it have done? Obviously, even though a few people in the audience had been sympathetic to her views, most were uncomfortable with her challenge of the esteemed Dr. Devereaux. After all, the professor had the credentials, and she was just a lowly counselor who didn't even have a college degree. Of course, they couldn't have known that, but still ... She wondered how many of the people in the audience knew someone like Penny. Unfortunately, even if they did know a woman who was being abused by her husband or boyfriend, they might not be aware of the abuse. Too many women—for exactly the reasons behind the apathy of tonight's audience—never told anyone.

And why? Elise thought angrily. Because too many people assumed that if a woman was being abused, there was probably a good reason for it, that she was partly to blame. It infuriated Elise every time she encountered this ignorance. You'd think that after all the publicity given to the problem of spouse abuse, people would be more sympathetic and understanding.

She sighed. What good would it do to keep going over and over this? She was just upsetting herself, to no good purpose. Determinedly she pushed the lecture out of her mind. It was time for her to forget about tonight and the misguided Dr. Devereaux. It was time to go inside and enjoy her visit with Lianna.

A pleasant anticipation flowed through her as she rang the doorbell of her cousin's house. In the past eighteen months, Lianna Cantrelle Nicholls had become Elise's best friend.

And her fourteen-year-old daughter Charlotte, affectionately called Charlie, had claimed a special spot in Elise's heart.

Like Elise, Lianna was divorced, but unlike Elise, her ex-husband hadn't been physically abusive. Chuck Nicholls's problem had been women. Lots of them. Lianna had finally had enough. That had been five years ago, when Charlie was nine. Now Lianna was struggling to raise her daughter on her own, and Elise thought she was doing a great job of it.

The door opened. A lanky Charlie stood framed in the doorway, her athletic body garbed in skin-tight bicycle shorts and crop top. "Hi, cuz. C'mon in."

Elise grinned, and they hugged briefly. Charlie smelled like soap and peppermint. "Where's your mother?"

"Where else?" Charlie rolled her expressive brown eyes toward the kitchen, and Elise chuckled.

Lianna owned a thriving catering business, which she ran out of her home, so Elise knew Charlie wasn't exaggerating. "Is she getting ready for a job tomorrow?"

"No, but she has two jobs Saturday. A luncheon and a wedding." Charlie made a face. "She's makin' me help. She'll put you to work, too."

"I don't mind." Lianna had once explained that Saturday was a caterer's busiest day. Many times Saturday was the only day in the week she had a job booked. Compounding that was the fact that this was summer, the most popular season for weddings. So Elise wasn't surprised that Lianna had two jobs lined up for Saturday. She knew her cousin couldn't afford to turn anything down that she could humanly manage to fill. Charlie had been pressed into service many times, although she'd confessed to Elise that she didn't much like the work. As with most teenagers,

Charlie would have preferred to get a job where she'd be around kids her own age.

Elise ruffled Charlie's long red hair, dodged a retaliating hand and headed toward the kitchen. "Hi," she said to the back of Lianna's lithe figure, which was almost bent in two as she peered into the bottom shelf of the refrigerator. At Elise's greeting, Lianna straightened and grinned, her hazel eyes full of welcome. She pushed a strand of her chestnut-colored hair back from her face.

"Hi, yourself. How'd your test go yesterday?" she said.

"I think I did real well."

"You *always* do real well," Lianna replied.

Elise grimaced. "Not always. Don't forget that seventy I got on my French test last semester."

Lianna rolled her eyes. "Oh, pardon *me*. How could I forget that seventy? Why, that was just *awful*. I don't know *why* I have anything to do with you. I mean, it's embarrassing to be around someone who got a *seventy!*"

Laughing, Elise took a toothpick out of the holder on the kitchen table and threw it at Lianna. Lianna loved to tease her about her obsessive need to do well at everything. "You don't have to prove anything to anyone, 'Lise," she'd once said. "Uncle Justin isn't going to love you any less if you don't get straight A's in school."

"What smells so good?" Elise said to change the subject.

"Crawfish *étouffée*," said Lianna. "That's what the Junior Forum wanted for their luncheon Saturday. Want some?"

"No. I had a sandwich earlier."

"A sandwich! That's not dinner. Come on, have some. I made extra."

"You twisted my arm."

As Elise ate her *étouffée*, Lianna rolled pastry dough, which she then used to line tart shells.

"Um, this is good," Elise said.

"Thanks. I expected you to drop by earlier." Lianna expertly filled the last shell and crimped the edges.

"I went to a lecture at the college." Elise frowned, remembering again how angry Dr. Devereaux had made her.

Lianna's gaze met hers. "From your tone of voice, I take it you didn't enjoy the lecture."

Elise sighed. "That's putting it mildly." She then told Lianna what had happened. "You know," she said thoughtfully, "I might not have gotten so angry if I hadn't had a particularly bad day at the shelter." She explained about Penny. "And then, to have to listen to him say such stupid things . . . well, it's maddening. The final straw was when he gave me a pat on the head and practically told me to sit down and shut up like a good little girl!"

"I'm sorry about Penny," Lianna said softly, her hazel eyes full of sympathy. "I know how much you like her."

Elise nodded. "The trouble is, I understand her so well. I was like that myself for too many years." A sudden vivid picture flashed through her mind. Derek raising his fist. Her cowering. The fist coming closer . . . She shuddered, forcing the image away. "I'm just thankful I finally came to my senses and got up the courage to leave."

"Well, I don't blame you for getting steamed tonight," Lianna said. "But it sounds like you gave that old geezer something to think about."

"Uh . . . well . . . he's really not . . . an old geezer."

Lianna walked to the sink and began washing her hands. "Oh?" She dried her hands on a paper towel and cocked her head, waiting with an expectant look on her face. "Well, come on! Tell me about him."

"Well, he's . . . uh . . ." Elise could have kicked herself for hesitating.

"I'm waiting," Lianna said softly, a twinkle in her eyes.

"He's about forty, and he's very attractive," Elise said. She took a deep breath. She and Lianna were always honest with each other. "Remember the man I told you about? The good-looking man with the green eyes. The one in the park?"

Lianna's eyes widened. "You don't mean—"

"Yes. I do."

Lianna whistled. "Well, well, well," she drawled. "So what are you going to do now?"

"Nothing."

"Oh, come on, Elise. Things are just getting interesting here. Don't you want to educate the man? Why, you owe it to all women to show him the error of his ways."

"No. I don't think so. Oh, I'll admit I toyed with the idea. But I've decided against it."

"Oh, you're no fun! This is exciting. What are you going to do when you see him in the park again? Pretend he doesn't exist? Pretend you don't recognize him?"

"I'm not going to the park again. I'd rather just forget I ever heard the name of Sloan Devereaux."

She wasn't coming today.

Dev shoved his hands into his pockets and walked to the edge of the lake. He picked up a pebble and skipped it over the water, watching the circles rippling across the surface. He blew air out of his mouth in a gust of frustration. He'd hoped to have a chance to talk to her without having to seek her out. It would have been so easy, so natural, if only she'd come today. He could have acted surprised, smiled and casually spoken to her, said something like, "Hi. It's Miss

Cantrelle, isn't it? I thought I recognized you at the lecture last night."

He might even have joked about their confrontation, treated it as if the words that had been exchanged between them were uttered in the heat of the moment but meant nothing today.

And who knows? Maybe that approach would have worked. Maybe today they could have talked quietly, exchanged ideas without getting emotional. Of course, *he* hadn't been emotional during his speech the night before, but she certainly had been.

Well, she wasn't coming. That was obvious. He might as well head on back to his office. He walked slowly across the Quad, his mind still wrestling with the problem of what to do about the woman who had filled almost all of his thoughts the past eighteen hours. He wondered if she had been thinking about him, too. If their confrontation last night had bothered her as much as it had bothered him.

A group of giggling female students stood just outside the main door to his building, and as Dev walked past, several of them greeted him. They reminded him of brightly colored birds, with their animated talk and gestures. They were all fresh-faced and young. So young. He wondered if he'd ever been that young.

He smiled at them as he passed by. Although he'd only been at USL a couple of weeks, he already felt at home on the campus. He wished the university had a full-fledged anthropology department, because he could imagine himself settling in here after his year was up. He wondered how Daisy would like it if he decided to remain in Lafayette.

Daisy.

For the past nine years, his fourteen-year-old daughter had been his raison d'être. When Joelle had walked out of him—on them—if it hadn't been for Daisy, Dev wasn't sure what he would have done. Joelle's casual defection, without a backward glance, had been a savage blow—to his pride and to his heart. Even though their marriage had been shaky almost from the very beginning, Dev was a traditionalist. He really believed in the vows he'd spoken. He had never imagined he would become one of the statistics, with a broken marriage behind him.

He had never intended to end up like his own parents.

But he had.

It had taken him a long time to stop feeling like a failure. Sometimes he still did.

Elise was mad at herself. She should have gone to the lake today. Why had she allowed that stupid professor to scare her off, prevent her from doing something she enjoyed and looked forward to? If her therapist knew, she'd probably be disgusted with her. Elise smiled fondly as she thought about Thelma Fisher, the psychologist with whom Elise had met twice a week for nearly two years. Thelma had been responsible for so much of Elise's recovery and her new-found confidence and insight into her insecurities and fears. One of the most important things Elise had learned during her counseling was the importance of standing up for herself, of not letting other people control her actions.

What's wrong with you? Elise asked herself now in disgust. Why'd you let a little thing like a difference of opinion with the misinformed professor keep you away from the lake? Now he probably thinks you're afraid to see him again. Lianna was right. You had the perfect opportunity to talk to him again. And who knows? Maybe you *might* teach the man something. Maybe he just needs to hear another side to the story.

Oh, well. It was too late now.

Elise climbed the outside stairs to her second-floor apartment and unlocked the door. She had no sooner walked inside than her telephone rang. She dropped her book bag and purse and dashed into the bedroom.

"Hello?"

"Hi. It's me," Lianna's husky voice greeted her.

Elise plopped onto the bed and kicked off her sandals. "Hi! What's up?"

"Did you know that that professor you were telling me about last night—that Dr. Devereaux—is appearing on Johnny Hagan's show tonight?" Lianna was referring to a popular radio talk show in Lafayette.

Elise sank back on the bed and stretched. "You're kidding. What's *he* going to talk about?"

"His work, I guess."

Elise scowled. "Well, I certainly hope he doesn't start on his women-in-the-workforce-are-at-the-root-of-all-society's-evils theory."

"Why don't you come over here tonight and we'll listen to the show together? I'll feed you dinner."

"Oh, Lianna, you're always feeding me!" Elise protested. "Besides, don't you have a hot date?"

"I'll give you 'hot date.'" She made a sound of disgust, and Elise laughed. The two of them constantly teased each other about their lack of dates or any kind of love life.

"My feeding you is no big deal," Lianna insisted. "What's one more? Especially in my house where there's always more food prepared than I need."

"Well—"

"Good. That's settled. I'll expect you around six-thirty."

"Hi, Dad! Are you nervous about tonight's show?" Daisy asked the minute Dev walked in the door that afternoon. She reached up to give him a hug.

Dev always experienced a rush of pleasure when he saw Daisy after an absence of any kind—even a few hours. She was such a special child, he thought, sweet and beautiful, and she'd never given him a moment's worry. Well, he guessed he should amend that. Daisy had never done anything to *cause* him to worry, but from the day her mother had walked out on them, Dev had done a lot of worrying.

He'd worried that he wouldn't be able to give Daisy all the guidance she needed.

He'd worried that he wasn't a good enough father, that he didn't know enough to raise a daughter on his own.

And the biggest worry of all: that despite everything he did, Daisy would turn out to be like her mother.

Thank God none of those worries had materialized. He'd been acting as mother and father to Daisy for nine years, and his daughter was a happy, well-adjusted, normal fourteen-year-old, and nothing like her mother.

"No, I'm not worried about the show," Dev said. "Not anymore."

"What do you mean, not anymore?"

"Well, when Johnny Hagan first asked me to appear I was worried I might bore the audience to death."

"Why should they be bored?" Daisy asked.

"What I do isn't exactly considered entertaining."

"But it's interesting," his daughter insisted loyally.

"Also controversial, if last night's lecture is any indication."

Daisy nodded. She'd been waiting for Dev when he returned from the lecture, and he'd told her all about the exchange with the Cantrelle woman.

"I've been thinking about what happened," Dev continued, "and I know exactly what I'll do so no one tonight will react like she did last night."

Daisy grinned. "You'll blow 'em away, Dad!"

By now they had walked back to the kitchen, and the smell of spaghetti sauce assailed him. Dev hid his dismay. Daisy meant well, but her cooking skills were limited to three or four dishes. Consequently they ate spaghetti at least once a week. Dev had tried, as diplomatically as he could, to tell Daisy that he didn't mind cooking a few times a week, but she refused to take the hint. At a very young age, she had assumed the role of caretaker in their household, and Dev couldn't bear to hurt her feelings by being more blunt about his likes and dislikes.

They talked while he helped Daisy set the table. As she dished up the spaghetti, Dev watched her. Her glasses kept falling down on her nose as she worked, and twice she pushed them back up absentmindedly.

She was very pretty, he thought, even though she didn't seem to be aware of her attractiveness. The long, silky blond hair she'd inherited from her mother hung straight to her shoulders, framing a small heart-shaped face and large, expressive green eyes that were identical to his. He wondered if boys her age saw past her shyness and bookishness. Actually he hoped they didn't. Time enough for all of that. Dev firmly believed in letting children be children as long as possible. He'd had to grow up too fast, and he still resented his parents for it. At times he felt guilty for doing to Daisy exactly what he'd never meant to do, but he had never forced her to take on the responsibility of their household. She seemed to want to do the things she did, and she would get a hurt look in her eyes if he tried to persuade her not to.

"How'd your day go?" he asked as they sat down to their dinner.

She shrugged. "Okay." The fine curtain of her hair fell forward as she took a bite.

"I'm sorry about you having to work so hard this summer."

Another shrug. "It's okay, Dad, really. I don't mind."

No, Dev thought. She didn't mind. Unlike so many kids her age, Daisy loved school. She'd always excelled at things like history and math. When they'd first discussed Dev's taking the assignment in Lafayette, Dev had investigated the schools and the curriculum thoroughly. When he'd discovered that the private high school he wanted for Daisy required two years of French before admittance, he knew he'd have to do something. Luckily she had studied Spanish and Italian for several years and seemed to have a flair for languages. Together they had decided that she would take first- and second-year French in summer school. So now she was attending classes three hours every morning, five days a week.

"Besides," Daisy said, "what else would I do? I don't know anyone here."

Guilt knifed Dev. "I'm sorry, honey. But you'll make friends in school. Haven't you met some kids you like?"

"Yeah. There are a couple of girls in my class who seem nice, but you know how it is in summer school. Everyone comes from all over the place, and . . . well, it's not like regular school."

No, Dev supposed it wasn't. "What about here? I noticed a couple of girls who look like they're about your age hanging around the pool the other day."

Daisy nodded.

"Have you gone to the pool in the afternoon yet?"

She shook her head.

"Why not?"

"I've been too busy. I've had lots of homework, and you know, cooking and all."

"Daisy, I've told you before. You don't have to spend your days working around the house." Dev sighed and laid down his fork. "Tell you what. Why don't I ask around at the university? Maybe I can find a maid, someone to come in once or twice a week and that'll leave you freer—"

The stricken look on her face stopped him from completing the sentence.

"But, Dad, I *like* doing things for you."

Dev could have kicked himself. He knew she was sensitive on this subject. Why hadn't he been more careful? "And I like having you do them, honey, but you're just a kid. Kids are supposed to have some fun. You're stuck in a stuffy classroom all morning. Wouldn't you rather lie around the pool in the afternoon? Maybe meet some kids?"

"I sunburn when I'm outside too long," Daisy mumbled. She didn't meet his gaze.

Dev wanted to say something else, but he decided not to. Maybe this wasn't the best time to discuss this subject. Daisy was probably nervous about making friends, and pushing her wasn't the way to encourage her.

They finished their meal in silence.

"Do you want to come to the studio with me tonight?" Dev asked as they finished loading the dishwasher.

"No, I'd rather just listen to you on the radio. That way I can tell you how you sounded." Daisy grinned. "I'll pretend to be an impartial listener. I'll give you a critique when you come home."

Dev rolled his eyes. "You're beginning to make me wish I'd never agreed to do this."

"You're gonna be great. All you really have to do is answer questions, isn't that right?"

"That's what the woman said who called and asked me to do the show."

"Well, no problem, then." Daisy laughed. "My dad, a star in the making!" she teased. "Today Johnny Hagan. Tomorrow Oprah!"

Dev ruffled her hair and grinned.

He wondered if the Cantrelle woman would be listening tonight.

Chapter Three

Elise laid down her fork and sighed with satisfaction. "That's the best apple pie I've ever eaten."

Lianna grinned. "You say that about everything I feed you."

"That's because you're a phenomenal cook."

"No, that's because you're such a *terrible* cook." The subject of Elise's lack of culinary skills was one they'd laughed over many times, so Elise ignored her cousin's gibe. Still chuckling, Lianna picked up her plate and Elise's and walked over to the sink where she began rinsing the dishes.

Elise glanced up at the wall clock. "It's nearly seven-thirty."

Lianna opened the dishwasher. "Turn on the radio, then." Five minutes later the table was cleared and the cousins were seated again with fresh cups of coffee in front of them. The introductory music faded out, and the rich Cajun accent of Johnny Hagan's voice replaced it. He made a few wisecracks by way of opening remarks, then said, "We have a real interestin' guest this evenin'—a visitin' Yankee professor of anthropology—come down here to Ragin' Cajun land to study the natives."

Hagan went on in his slightly mocking tone—a trick of innuendo he'd perfected over the years—to list Professor Devereaux's background. Elise had to admit that his credentials were impressive. Even Johnny Hagan couldn't make the professor sound less than credible. Then Hagan said, "And now, let's all welcome Dr. Sloan Devereaux to Hagan's Hot Seat." He made his trademark hissing noise, something his listeners had come to expect every time he said *hot seat*.

After a moment, the now-familiar low-pitched voice of Dr. Devereaux said, "Hello, Johnny. I'm glad to be here. Although I've only lived in Lafayette a few weeks, I'm already a fan of yours."

Hagan laughed softly. "Don't be too hasty, Doc. After you've been on the hot seat for a while, you may not feel that way."

They talked for a few minutes, with Hagan asking fairly innocuous questions about the professor's work. Elise wondered when Hagan would introduce something controversial. That's what he was known for. That's why people liked him. Because he liked to mix it up, as he called it. Finally her question was answered, when Hagan said, "I understand that your presentation last night really stirred up some trouble for you, Doc."

Elise and Lianna exchanged glances. Here it comes, Elise thought.

"I don't know if I'd call it *trouble*," Dr. Devereaux said smoothly. "One of my remarks was misinterpreted by a member of the audience. We had a short debate about it, but that's all that happened."

Misinterpreted. A short debate. Elise gritted her teeth, wondering if the professor really believed that's all that had happened, or if he was simply trying to downplay the situation. Oh, it still made her mad to think about how many people might get the wrong idea because of what he had said.

Johnny Hagan gave a low, sly laugh. "That's not the way I heard it, Doc. In fact, my source tells me you made some really incendiary remarks and that you said that abused women are usually askin' for it. Is that true?"

"Absolutely not. That's not what I said, and it's certainly not what I meant. I quoted from an article written by Dr. Johan Freidberg, director of the American Family Council, wherein he stated that many of society's modern-day ills, including wife abuse, have proliferated since so many women have entered the full-time work force." There was a slight pause, then the professor added, "I never implied that women were responsible for the abuse they've received at the hands of their spouses. All I said was that this problem seems to be magnified because of today's situation, not because of the women themselves. I guess I didn't make myself clear. I just meant that, as a scholar, I understand the situation. I certainly don't *advocate* it."

"I understand, Doc," Hagan said. "But why don't we see what our listeners think? 'Cause I see we've got some calls waiting."

Elise looked at Lianna, who was avidly listening to the exchange.

"Hagan's Hot Seat," Johnny Hagan said. "You're on the air."

"Professor Devereaux," said a female voice. "I was in the audience last night. You really *did* leave the impression that you agreed with that professor's article, you know. I don't blame that woman for getting angry. I was angry myself."

"I'm sorry it appeared that way," Professor Devereaux answered, "I was simply quoting statistical findings based on scholarly research by a colleague. I still don't know enough about the subject to have formed my own opinions. Neither you nor the other woman are looking at this topic objectively. You're letting your emotions rule. Anytime emotions are involved, people overreact and misinterpret."

"It's hard not to overreact when you say things like you said last night," the woman insisted.

Elise grinned at Lianna. "She's right."

Lianna nodded.

"I mean, I wish I didn't have to work. I wish I could just stay home with my two kids. But the fact of the matter is, my husband's salary doesn't cover anything but the essentials. So I *have* to work. And he's the first one to say so!" the woman said, her voice rising angrily.

"I understand that," the professor said. "I can't argue with what I know is true. But I can't discount the statistics, either. Like it or not, the statistics tell a story."

The woman made a sound of disgust. "You know, Professor, like most men, you just can't admit when you're wrong, can you?" There was a click, then a loud buzz.

"Well, Doc," Johnny Hagan said, his voice reflecting amusement, "I guess she told you. Let's listen to what our next caller has to say... Hagan's Hot Seat. You're on the air."

A man's gruff voice filled the room. "I just wanta say I agree with you, Doc. My wife don't listen to a thing I say anymore, not since she got herself a job. Thinks she's hot stuff now! Ask me, we oughta keep 'em all barefoot and pregnant and in the kitchen!" He gave a loud guffaw. "I don't believe in all this wife abuse, anyways. I think most of those women make up this stuff to get even with their men, don't you?''

"What an ignorant jerk!" Lianna exclaimed.

"Uh, I'm afraid *you've* misinterpreted my remarks, too," Dr. Devereaux said, "I—"

"Hey, Doc, that's okay. I know you can't agree with me on the air without half the women in Lafayette comin' down on you. I just wanted you to know I think you're right. Lots of us out here think you're right. Don't pay no attention to that woman who just called. I'll bet if she didn't spend so damn much money she wouldn't *have* to work!"

Elise clenched her teeth. "What an idiot!"

Professor Devereaux sounded slightly discomfited as he answered quickly. "I'm sorry, sir, but I don't agree with you at all, and I certainly don't want anyone out there listening to think I do."

The caller laughed. "I *knew* you'd have to say that, but like I said before, it's okay. We all know how you feel!"

"No, I don't think—" There was a loud buzzing noise.

"He hung up, Doc," Hagan said.

"Listen, Johnny, I've got to set the record straight," the professor answered, sounding distracted.

"*Somebody* should set the record straight," Elise said. She was so angry she felt like spitting. It was because of men like that stupid fool who'd called in that women like Penny were nearly killed every day. Oh, if she weren't a non-violent person herself, she'd like to smack him silly. See how he liked it.

"Why don't you?" Lianna said. "Call in and set him straight. Set them *all* straight!"

"I don't know—"

"Come on, cuz. You work at the shelter. You know what's really going on in the world today. That ignoramus who just called in needs educating, and you're just the one to do it. After all, this is your area of expertise."

"Well..." Elise really didn't want to call attention to herself again, but she knew Lianna was right. She owed it to the women at the shelter, to women everywhere, to at least present the true picture—something Elise wasn't sure the professor was capable of doing. She sighed. "Well, okay."

Several minutes later, after being shuffled through the station's screening process and then waiting for what seemed an interminable amount of time during which she'd almost hung up, Johnny Hagan's voice abruptly sounded in her ear, causing her to jump and her heart to start beating wildly. "Hagan's Hot Seat. You're on the air."

"Yes," Elise said, gathering her courage. "This is Elise Cantrelle. I'm the one who challenged Dr. Devereaux last night at the lecture."

"Well, *hello,* Miss Cantrelle," Hagan said. "Glad to hear from you. What do you think of all that's been said so far tonight?"

"Well, regardless of whether or not women in the work force have changed the way American families function today, it's obvious to me that neither Dr. Devereaux nor your second caller have any real knowledge of the true situation concerning abused women. That's the part of all this that concerns me—that Dr. Devereaux has somehow left the impression that he thinks women who are abused have brought that abuse upon themselves."

Elise paused for a minute, then continued. "That's the issue I'm concerned about. For the past two years I've worked at the St. Jacques Women's Shelter here in Lafayette, and I've seen hundreds of women pass through there. But that is beside the point. No matter what any of these women did, it was impossible for them to bring this abuse on themselves. Not one of them was a troublemaker. Not one of them caused her husband or boyfriend to abuse her. Not one of them is to blame in any way for what's happened to them."

Elise took a deep breath. "They're *victims*, Johnny. *Victims*. Just like children who are abused by their parents. Just like old people who are abused by their children. Just like people who are mugged or raped or murdered. Victims. Saying women 'ask for it,' whether it's abuse or rape or whatever, is ignorant. Worse, it's harmful. Because no matter how many of us out here know that's not true, there are bound to be others who will believe it—simply because someone like Dr. Devereaux said it."

Before Hagan could interrupt her or the professor could say anything, Elise plunged in again. "I'd like to tell you some stories, Johnny. I'd like to tell both you and the professor and all your listeners some stories. *Then* I'd like to see what you have to say!"

"Sounds like a challenge to me, Doc," Hagan said. "Whadda you think?"

"I'd like to hear what Miss Cantrelle has to say," the professor said.

"Well, we sure can fix that," Hagan said. "Miss Cantrelle?"

"Yes?"

"How'd you like to come on to my show Monday night? You and the doc, both? We can have us a real debate. And you can have your say."

Oh, heavens. How had she gotten herself into this? She knew how Hagan operated. He'd probably try to embarrass her or discredit her. Just like he'd done with the professor. All Hagan was interested in was ratings. He couldn't care less about the women at the shelter.

Elise glanced at Lianna. Lianna was mouthing *yes* and shaking her head up and down.

Elise sighed. "All right," she said quietly, swallowing her misgivings. Lianna was right. Elise owed it to the women at the shelter. She owed it to Penny and Meg and herself. Most of all, she owed it to herself. "I'll be there."

So her name was Elise. And he was going to see her again on Monday night. As Dev drove home, he thought about the ramifications of that night's show.

He wasn't sure how he felt about going back on "The Johnny Hagan Show" Monday night. He was glad he'd have the opportunity to see Elise Cantrelle again, but the show—that was a different story. Tonight had been a disaster, and Dev didn't think he'd acquitted himself well at all. He should have known Hagan would try to put him on the spot, but somehow he hadn't expected it. Monday night would probably be no different.

And that jackass who'd called in! God, the man had been a total jerk. Dev hoped none of the listeners had thought he'd agreed with that fool.

What if, on Monday's show, Hagan tried to embarrass Elise Cantrelle the way he'd tried to embarrass him? Tried to make *her* look foolish. Dev's hands tightened on the steering wheel. He would not let that happen. No matter what else happened, he would not let Hagan hurt Elise Cantrelle in any way. She might be too emotional and she might have overreacted to his statements, but she was obviously sincere. She was also a lady. She didn't deserve to be made the object of ridicule or scorn.

So, no, he would not let Hagan intimidate or embarrass her.

No matter *what* he had to do.

* * *

"Elise, *chère,* have some more ham," Lisette Cantrelle said.

Elise smiled at her stepmother. "I couldn't eat another bite. I'm stuffed. But everything was wonderful."

"And what about you, Lianna, would you like more?" Lisette said.

Lianna grinned. "Lord, no, Aunt Lisette. I've already had two helpings."

"Charlie? You want more, don't you?" Lisette's sweet face was wrinkled in concern.

"Aunt Lisette!" Charlie protested. "Between you and my mother, I'm gonna get fat!"

Elise smothered a smile.

"Well, if we're through eatin', it's time for the birthday cake, no?" Justin said, his dark gaze loving as it rested on his wife's face. "And we'll all sing, and then we'll have the presents."

"Oh, Justin, don't make such a fuss," Lisette protested. "It's only a birthday."

"Only a birthday," Justin said, giving Elise a wink. "My wife of forty-three years is seventy years old today, and it's *only a birthday.*" He smiled gently. "Today is a very special day in the life of a very special lady."

"I agree," Elise said, getting up and walking over to Lisette's chair. She put her arms around her stepmother and kissed her soft cheek. The faint scent of roses clung to Lisette's skin. "A *very* special lady."

As Lisette continued to protest, and Justin continued to tease her, Elise wondered how many other women would have been able to accept their husband's illegitimate daughter the way Lisette had accepted her—a child she hadn't known anything about until presented with the shocking fact of her existence. How many other women could accept a total stranger with so much love and no reservations? Her stepmother was a truly good woman, for she had done just that. She had wholeheartedly welcomed Elise into the family, and she had never acted as if she resented her in any way. She had agreed with Justin—in fact, encouraged Justin—when he said he wanted to make Elise his legal heir.

Elise smiled at her stepmother. She owed her so much. She owed both of them so much, for they had helped her over the roughest period of her life. Thinking of that time reminded her that she'd meant to tell her father and stepmother something. "I got a letter from Desiree yesterday," she said now.

Both Justin and Lisette smiled. They, like Elise, would always have a special place in their hearts for Desiree Cantrelle Forrester, the youngest daughter of Justin's brother René, because she was responsible for bringing them all together. She and her husband, Jack Forrester, an investigative journalist with World Press, were the ones who had found Elise after she'd run away from her abusive husband. They were also the ones who discovered she was Justin's illegitimate daughter from a mid-life liaison with his secretary, Elise's mother.

"How is Desiree doing?" Lisette asked, her dark eyes shining.

"She sounds wonderful...and so happy," Elise said. She paused, drawing out the moment she'd been looking forward to. "She's expecting another baby." She grinned. "Actually she's expecting *two* babies. The doctors say she's carrying twins."

"Twins! Oh, how wonderful!" Lisette exclaimed. "But she is certainly going to have her hands full now."

Justin smiled. "How does Jack feel about all this responsibility?"

"Desiree says Jack is thrilled. And he's already asked his boss for a transfer to the States." Desiree and her husband were currently living in London, where Jack was head of the London Bureau. "She thinks he may get the job of heading up the Houston Bureau. Won't it be terrific to have her close to home again?"

They talked about Desiree for a few more minutes, then Justin said, "I don't know about the rest of you, but I'm ready for that cake."

"Okay, okay, I'll go get it," Lisette said.

Thirty minutes later, after they'd all sung "Happy Birthday" to Lisette and she'd made a wish and blown out her candles and opened her presents, Justin turned to Elise and said, "Your stepmama and I, we listened to the Johnny Hagan Show the other night."

His handsome, distinguished face was wrinkled in concern. Before Elise could answer, Lianna chimed in. "She was *wonderful,* wasn't she?"

Justin nodded thoughtfully. "Yes, she was wonderful, but I'm worried about her going on that show."

"I'll be fine, Papa," Elise said quickly. She didn't want her father worrying.

"I don't know, *chère.* That Johnny Hagan, he is notorious for baiting his guests. Even the most intelligent guests sometimes have trouble with him."

"My friends, they've all been calling me," Lisette said. "They're all proud of you." She smiled gently. "*I'm* proud of you, *chère.*"

"Me, too," Charlie said, her brown eyes shining.

"Ditto," Lianna said.

Justin sighed. "Yes, it goes without saying that we're proud of you, *chère,* but, well, I don't want to see you hurt."

"I have to do this, Papa," Elise said. She'd given the subject a lot of thought since Friday night, and she knew she was doing the right thing. "For too many years, I didn't do anything. I let myself be victimized. I let a bully push me around."

"I know," Justin said, his voice taking on the hard edge Elise had come to expect whenever she mentioned her ex-husband.

"Those days are over," she said swiftly to diffuse his anger. "I'm in charge of my life now, and when I see other women going through what I went through, I can't stand by and do nothing."

Lisette leaned over and patted Elise's hand, and a warm feeling squeezed Elise's heart.

"Good for you, cuz," Charlie said.

Justin nodded, his dark gaze meeting Elise's. She smiled reassuringly. "I'll think about you and all my friends listening. I'll be fine."

"You'll be more than fine," Lianna said. "You'll knock 'em dead!"

Elise took a deep breath as she locked her car and walked toward the building housing the radio station. She'd told herself all day that she wasn't nervous, but as she smoothed down the skirt of her peach linen dress, she could feel butterflies skittering around in her stomach.

She glanced at herself in the opaque black glass door as she approached the entrance. Her dress was businesslike and sedate, the hem just above her knees. Her black pumps had sensible heels and matched her black clutch bag. Her hair had been tamed into something resembling order and was held back from her face by silver clips on either side of her head.

You look fine, she told herself. *And you'll do fine. Quit worrying.*

A few more deep breaths, and she was ready. She opened the door.

The receptionist, a young freckled-faced woman, said, "Mr. Hagan asks his guests to wait in the Green Room. I'll take you there, and someone will brief you before the show goes on." She smiled in a friendly way, and Elise smiled back, although her stomach still felt hollow.

When Elise walked into the Green Room, Professor Devereaux was already there. Her stupid heart accelerated as he quickly rose and turned toward her. "Hello, Miss Cantrelle," he said quietly, extending his hand. "I realize we've spoken before, but we were never introduced. I'm Sloan Devereaux."

As she shook his hand, she gazed up into eyes that were a shade of green that reminded her of new leaves—warm with golden overtones. The hollowed-out feeling in her stomach intensified, but her voice, when she answered him, sounded steady. "Hello, again, Dr. Devereaux."

He held her hand for a moment longer; then he smiled a bit uncertainly, as if he weren't sure of the proprieties in a situation like this. The smile, and his obvious discomfort, helped settle Elise's nerves. Just knowing he felt awkward, too, had a calming effect on her. He motioned to one of the chairs, and Elise sat down. He sat across from her. There was silence between them for a few tense seconds.

She cleared her throat. His gaze met hers, and her silly heart went *blip.* What was wrong with her? Just because the man was good-looking and had gorgeous eyes didn't give her any reason to act like a teenybopper who has finally caught the eye of the star football player.

And he *was* good-looking, just the type of man who appealed to Elise. Today he looked particularly attractive. He was wearing tan-colored jeans with a white shirt and a caramel-colored, loosely constructed jacket. His loafers were a soft, shiny brown leather and looked expensive but understated. They also looked just worn enough to be a natural part of him.

Yes, he definitely appealed to her. Too bad their ideas were so far apart.

As these thoughts rushed through her mind, Elise felt suddenly tongue-tied and couldn't think of a thing to say. Finally, after the silence stretched for a long moment, he said, "You didn't come to the park on Friday or today."

Elise's pulse raced as her gaze locked with his. "No, I didn't," she managed to say quietly.

"Was it because of me?"

The question caused her heart to thud, and the air suddenly seemed charged with electricity. She swallowed hard and thought about lying. Meeting his gaze steadily, she said, "Yes, I guess it was."

Something flickered in the depths of his eyes. "I'm sorry. I wish we could turn back the clock. Start over fresh."

"Does that mean you've changed your mind?"

Before he could reply, the inner door opened, and a young woman with inky black hair and thick glasses walked into the room. She was holding a clipboard. She gave the professor a quick smile. "Hello, again, Dr. Devereaux," she said. "Glad to see you back."

"Hi," he said.

The woman looked at Elise. "And you must be..." She referred to her clipboard.

"I'm Elise Cantrelle."

"Of course. I'm M. J. Howard, Johnny's Hagan's assistant. I'm here to brief you on what you can expect."

For the next ten minutes, M.J. explained how the show worked, then she said, "Well, it's time to go into the studio."

Elise's nervousness returned as she walked into the studio and looked around. It was a small room dominated by a kidney-shaped table with several chairs grouped around it. On the right side of the room was a wall of glass behind which she could see another room filled with equipment. M.J. showed her where to sit, Elise's mike was clipped to her dress and then M.J. explained about the red light that would indicate when they were actually on the air.

"It'll go out during commercials and come back on ten seconds before you're live again," M.J. said. "Billy, he's the producer—" she pointed to a man wearing headphones who was seated behind the glass window in the other room "—will count down to one, then give Johnny the signal to talk."

Elise wet her lips and nodded her understanding.

"Don't shout into the mike or anything," M.J. said. "Just talk in your normal voice. And try to relax. Okay, are we ready for a sound check?"

A minute later, Johnny Hagan entered the studio. Elise had seen his picture dozens of times, so she recognized him. He had thick, carroty hair that curled into tight corkscrews and vivid blue eyes. He was slightly built, which Elise hadn't expected. Somehow, because his voice was so deep and rich, she'd thought he would be a big man.

He winked when M.J. introduced him to her. "Too bad this isn't TV," he said. "You're too pretty to waste on the radio." He looked her up and down. "Way too pretty."

Elise shifted uncomfortably. She hated it when men leered the way Hagan was doing now. "Hello, Mr. Hagan."

"Johnny, Johnny," he said. "None of this 'Mr. Hagan' stuff. It's Doc, Elise and Johnny. Nothing formal for my listeners." He turned to the professor. "Hey, Doc, how ya doin'?"

"I'm fine."

Elise turned to look at Professor Devereaux. His voice had sounded curiously cold when he'd answered Hagan. For a fleeting moment, she wondered why. But she didn't wonder long, because the producer—Billy, M.J. had called him—said, "Okay, Johnny. Two minutes."

Johnny Hagan seated himself across the kidney-shaped table from Elise and the professor. He riffled through some papers, then laid them aside.

"One minute," Billy said.

M.J. opened the door and walked into the glass-enclosed room. She sat down next to Billy.

"Thirty seconds."

Elise's heart began to pound. She licked her lips. Why had she ever agreed to do this?

"Fifteen seconds."

A man walked into the glass enclosed room. He sat next to Johnny.

The red light went on.

Billy counted down. "Three...two...one..." Music swelled around them. The newcomer—who Elise now realized was the announcer—read the introductions. Then Johnny Hagan began his opening. All too soon, he said, "Okay, folks. If you listened on Friday night, you know we had an interestin' discussion goin'...." He laughed. "Well, actually it was more of a disagreement...between my two guests...Dr. Sloan Devereaux and Elise Cantrelle. Both Elise and the Doc are here with us tonight. I think I'll just let Elise talk to you first, then we'll let the Doc have his say. Elise, honey, you ready?"

Elise bristled over the patronizing *honey*. Suddenly her nervousness vanished. She looked Johnny Hagan straight in the eye. "Believe me, sugar pie, I'm ready." She waited one heartbeat. "Are you sure *you* are?"

Chapter Four

Dev smothered a grin. He had a feeling Hagan wasn't often speechless but he recovered quickly, smiling and saying, "Hey, Elise, no offense meant."

"None taken," she said coolly, and Dev was filled with admiration. Elise Cantrelle might be quiet and a lady, but she also had a lot of spunk. And if it hadn't been for the betraying flush of color on her cheeks, Dev might have been fooled into thinking Elise hadn't been bothered by Hagan's disparaging way of addressing her. But that faint pink gave her away. She was upset but struggling not to show it, either in her demeanor or in her voice. Dev suddenly wished he had the right to squeeze her shoulder or take her hand—anything to indicate his support. He shook his head, knowing he couldn't.

After all, Elise Cantrelle was a stranger to him. Just because he'd seen her a few times, spun a few fantasies about her, didn't mean he knew her. Still, there was this undeniable sense of connection between them—at least on his part. He wondered if she felt it, too. There'd been a moment there—when they were both sitting in the Green Room— when the air had felt alive with the awareness sizzling between them.

"So, Miss Cantrelle," Hagan said jovially, blue eyes glittering, "You wanted to tell us a little about the St. Jacques Women's Shelter."

Dev settled back in his chair and listened as Elise gave a short history of the shelter, which she said had been in existence seventeen years. She opened a small notebook and read statistics on the amount of money it took to run the shelter as well as the number of women and children who had come there for help during the past three years. Then she began to tell Hagan and the listening audience about specific women and their case histories. "I'm using fictitious names, of course," she said.

Her voice became stronger and more impassioned as she spoke. Dev couldn't help noticing how her lovely dark eyes shone with intensity and how her soft voice became husky with emotion as she related one tale after another.

From the way their chairs were placed around the table, Dev had a good view of her slender body and he admired the way her soft, feminine curves filled out her pretty peach dress. His attention wandered as his gaze rested on the hollow of her throat, visible in the slight V neckline. There was a slender gold chain around her neck, and it glinted as it was captured in the overhead lights.

As he watched, she crossed her legs and leaned forward in her chair. The action caused the hem of her dress to creep upward, revealing the sweet curve of her thigh.

Dev took a deep breath. He could look at her for hours, he decided. She was beautiful. He couldn't remember when he'd been so attracted to a woman. Too bad it had to happen with *this* woman, he thought. If he'd learned nothing else from his failed marriage, he'd learned that if and when he became involved again, it would be with a woman who would reserve her passion for him. He wasn't interested in anyone involved in causes. He had no intention of taking a back seat to anything, no matter how noble or worthwhile the endeavor. Joelle's obsession with women's rights, her determination to make a name for herself while she traveled around the country trying to change the world, had destroyed their marriage and very nearly destroyed him.

Dev sighed and turned his attention back to what Elise was saying.

"...that's the reason I took such exception to Dr. Devereaux's remarks," she said. "Because he made the problem of battered women sound as if it had an easy explanation. And it doesn't. Women are battered for all kinds of reasons, and most of them have nothing to do with logic." She paused for a second, then her voice became harder. "I'm reminded of a young woman who came to our shelter sometime last year. Her husband started beating her up because they were getting phone calls where the caller didn't say anything, just did some heavy breathing, then hung up. This woman—I'll call her Mary—had no idea who was harassing her and her husband, but her husband was convinced she had a boyfriend who wouldn't talk unless *she* answered the phone. So he beat her. And finally, when Mary couldn't stand it any longer, she left him."

Elise glanced at Dev. Her dark gaze pinned his for a long moment. "And Mary was a stay-at-home, bake-cookies-in-the-afternoon wife," she said softly. "She had never wanted anything but to take care of her family."

Dev swallowed uncomfortably.

Johnny Hagan gave him a sly smile. "Well, Doc, got anything you want to say?"

"Yes, Johnny, I do." Elise turned toward him. He met her gaze steadily. "I just want to remind Miss Cantrelle and your listening audience that my original remarks were a quotation from an article and nothing more. I regret that she still seems to feel we're on opposite sides, because we're not." Silently he willed Elise to believe him. Suddenly it was very important that she understand. "I think the stories she told tonight are appalling, and I do not condone that type of behavior. I'm sorry if anything I said made Miss Cantrelle or anyone else think I do."

"Miss Cantrelle?" Johnny said. "Do you want to answer that? Or shall we take our first call?"

"Why don't we take some calls?" she said, her dark eyes thoughtful as she studied Dev.

Hagan punched one of the blinking buttons on his telephone console. "Hagan's Hot Seat. You're on the air."

"Hello, Johnny," said a soft, hesitant female voice. "I just wanted to say 'God bless you' to Miss Cantrelle. My husband used to beat me up at least twice a week. And I was a stay-at-home wife, too. Kenny—that was my husband's name—he didn't want me to work, so I never did. And because I had no skills or education or anything, I was scared to leave him, even when the beatings got worse. But finally I *did* leave him. I stayed at the St. Jacques Women's Shelter for three months, and they helped me find a job. They're wonderful people, and they're doin' wonderful work."

There were five or six more calls, most in the same vein, most from women who had been battered or were being battered, and all supported what Elise had said.

Dev was beginning to wish he'd never brought up the subject. He'd never imagined his innocent remarks would cause such a commotion. That he would be so misunderstood.

"Well, Dr. Devereaux?" Elise said, turning to him when they were finally off the air. "Are you convinced of the error of your ways?"

"The only thing I'm convinced of is that I was totally misunderstood," Dev said.

"Is that a 'yes' or a 'no'?"

Dev could feel a smile beginning at the corners of his mouth. She reminded him of a terrier with a bone. It was amazing that such a delicate-looking woman could be so doggedly determined. "You never give up, do you?" he said.

Now she smiled, the most bewitching smile he'd ever seen. "No. Not when I'm right."

"Miss Cantrelle, wait! I'll walk out with you."

Elise turned and waited for the professor to catch up with her. "I wasn't sure you'd still be speaking to me, Dr. Devereaux."

He shrugged, his eyes glinting with amusement. "I don't hold grudges."

Elise's heart gave a funny little hop as his gaze held hers. "That's good to know. I still haven't convinced you, though, have I?"

"I believe that what you said tonight is accurate."

Elise sighed. "I wish you'd come and visit the shelter, Dr. Devereaux. It would be quite an education for you." She wasn't sure why it was so important to her that he understand, *really* understand, on an emotional level as well as an intellectual level.

He smiled. "And I wish you'd drop that formal address and call me Dev."

He should smile more often, she thought distractedly.

When she hesitated, he added, "After what we've been through together, Dr. Devereaux sounds pretty stiff. Makes me feel old, too." Their gazes met again, and something warm and liquid slid into Elise's stomach at the expression in his—an expression she didn't quite understand.

She looked away, confused by her reaction to him. When they reached the outside door, he pushed it open for her. She couldn't avoid brushing against him as she walked past. She felt almost breathless, which was so silly. Why, she hardly knew this man, and the few times she'd been in his company, all they'd done was disagree.

Darkness had finally fallen, and the humid night air closed around them as they exited the station. The sweet scent of gardenias floated in the air from the dozens of miniature gardenia bushes planted on either side of the wide steps leading into the building.

Elise headed toward her car, parked across the lot a few feet away. Although they didn't speak, and she didn't look at him again, she knew he was right behind her. When she reached her car, she turned. "Well," she said casually, "I guess this is good-night, Dr. Dev—"

"Just Dev," he said. "Please."

"Dev." She liked the feel of his name on her tongue. She had a strong desire to say it again. Instead, she looked up. There wasn't enough light in the parking lot for her to see the expression in his eyes, but somehow she knew it would be filled with that same . . . awareness . . . she'd seen before. For that's exactly what she'd sensed and felt. Sloan Devereaux was just as aware of her as she was of him.

"Do you mind if I call you Elise?"

Elise's heart skittered as if he'd asked if he could kiss her instead of something as innocuous as permission to call her by her first name. "No, I don't mind."

"It's a beautiful name," he said softly.

Elise was sure he could hear her stupid heart, which had now decided to mimic a drummer banging away at a bass drum. "I was named after my mother," she finally managed to say, praying she didn't sound as rattled as she felt.

For a long moment, he said nothing. Elise had a wild impulse to run, to open her car and jump in and take off as fast as she could. A nameless fear flooded her. She felt an impending sense of danger. She didn't like the feelings this man evoked, the uncertainty and bewildering emotions churning inside her. She felt out of control again, and she hated that. It had taken her too long to get control of her life. She would not relinquish that control easily.

There was a long, tension-filled silence between them. Elise was excruciatingly aware of Dev standing beside her. Somewhere close by a cricket sang.

Dev finally spoke, and when he did, Elise sensed that he, too, had pulled back. Now his voice was casual, almost cool. "Be careful driving home."

Conflicting emotions cascaded through her. Regret, relief, disappointment. For a moment there, she'd almost thought he was going to ask if he could see her again. At the very least she'd hoped he would say he wanted to come by and visit the shelter. Why hadn't he? She wondered if he'd sensed her doubts, her reluctance to go forward, if that was why his voice had become cooler and more detached. Maybe he had felt she would reject any advance he made, so he'd retreated.

And that was what you wanted, wasn't it? Yes, of course, she answered herself almost angrily.

So why are you disappointed?

All the way home she remembered the way he'd looked at her. And each time she did, that same warm, unsettled feeling curled into her stomach.

She told herself to forget about tonight.

To forget about him.

She wondered if that would be as simple as it sounded.

* * *

All the way home Dev thought about Elise and the way she'd looked during the radio show. The way he'd felt when he'd watched her. And especially about the way he'd felt later, in the parking lot, when they'd stood so close together, and all the air around them was filled with her light, flowery fragrance.

Forget about her, he told himself. She's not what you thought she was. Don't let yourself be drawn into another relationship with another crusader. As he had earlier, he couldn't help but think of the parallels between Elise's passion for the work she did and his ex-wife's passion for her causes.

He couldn't handle another relationship like that.

He couldn't handle another Joelle.

He vividly remembered the day he'd first set eyes on Joelle Flanders. It was during the last year of his work toward his doctorate at Columbia University and she'd been standing on top of a low concrete wall outside the administration building. She'd been talking and gesturing, punctuating her points by shaking her fist in the air. It was April, and one of those perfect spring days that grace New York City occasionally, with clear blue skies and mild breezes. The sun shone down on her long, straight blond hair, lighting it so that it looked like spun gold. Her blue eyes gleamed with emotion and intensity. Her voice throbbed with conviction, and as she talked, students gathered around, and they cheered her on.

She'd been talking about a recent decision handed down by the Supreme Court—a decision that she felt would negatively affect all women—and her passion enthralled him. She had been so vivid, so bright and so filled with fervor. He stood there and watched her, and when she was finished, and all the other students save for a couple of hangers-on were gone, he walked over and introduced himself, complimenting her on her speech.

From that day on they'd been inseparable. Dev, although not the crusader Joelle was, had been proud of her. He'd been idealistic, too, and he'd encouraged her to speak and work in the women's movement. He had admired her determination and zeal, a zeal she brought to everything, including her lovemaking. In fact, their lovemaking was so good it had blinded him to a lot of other things he might have noticed if his hormones hadn't been in such a constant state of uproar.

God, he'd been crazy about her, so crazy they were married within three months of meeting.

Marry in haste, repent at leisure.

Dev grimaced. Truer words had never been spoken. One day Dev woke up with the grim realization that he and Joelle might not make it. They wanted different things out of life. Their first major disagreement came in the fall of that year, after he'd accepted a teaching post at Columbia. They were living in a minuscule rent-controlled apartment across from Gramercy Park, just northeast of the Village, and he'd made some innocent remark about how he'd hate having to find a bigger place when they started their family.

Joelle had looked at him as if he were crazy. She informed him she had no intention of having children. Children were a burden she could do without. She had better, more important things to do with her life. "I can't imagine where you got the idea I wanted kids, Dev."

He had just stared at her, shocked by her disclosure.

"Don't try to tie me down," she warned, a hard edge creeping into her voice as she stared back at him defiantly.

When, by accident, she became pregnant the following spring, she accused him of betraying her, of planning the pregnancy. He hadn't, but he couldn't hide his pleasure in the *fait accompli*. When Joelle told him she wanted to have an abortion, he'd been coldly furious. He told her he'd fight her, go to the Supreme Court if he had to. Since she had recently applied for a research grant he knew she wouldn't want any negative publicity.

"You can't make me have this baby!" she shouted. "I don't want a baby! A baby will only slow me down! Damn you, Dev. Damn you."

They didn't speak for eleven days. Finally, in a last-ditch attempt to salvage the situation, Dev decided to try another approach with her. He told her he'd take on full parental responsibility if she'd compromise and have the baby. He promised he'd take care of the baby and allow Joelle complete freedom to continue her work. Reluctantly Joelle agreed.

Thank God she'd had an easy pregnancy. Dev had always wondered what would have happened if she'd been sick. Would she have kept her word?

So three days before Christmas, in the middle of one of the worst snowstorms in years, Daisy was born. Daisy, the light of his life, the best Christmas present Dev had ever had. He'd kept his word. He'd done everything—gotten up in the middle of the night to feed her, changed her diapers, nursed her when she was sick. He was the one who found a woman to care for Daisy while he was at work. He was the one who shopped for her, read her stories and put her to bed.

He'd never minded. Even though juggling everything— his job, the responsibilities of Daisy and their household— had sometimes seemed overwhelming, he'd managed. He'd fulfilled a mother's as well as a father's role in her life and he'd never resented a moment of it. Even when he was exhausted and frustrated and lonely, he'd never resented Daisy.

Once in a while Joelle had shown an interest in Daisy. But Dev, who had become cynical where Joelle was concerned, noticed that that interest seemed to manifest itself whenever a reporter wanted an interview or a photographer wanted to do a photo spread.

By the time Daisy was two, Joelle had written her second controversial bestseller. She was famous and in great demand as a speaker. She spent more time on the road than at home.

Still, Dev was more or less content. He resigned himself to his life, to only seeing Joelle occasionally. His life centered around his beautiful, bright little daughter and his satisfying, burgeoning career at Columbia. And when Joelle *did* come home, he tried to make the time together as pleasant as possible.

Then he discovered Joelle was having an affair. When he'd confronted her with his knowledge, she hadn't even bothered to deny it. She hadn't cared enough about him or Daisy to pretend Dev was mistaken.

"So what?" she'd said. "I don't expect you to live like a monk when I'm gone, and I didn't think you expected me to, either."

Her flippant disregard for their marriage vows, for everything that Dev believed in, sickened him. He wasn't even shocked when she informed him that if he wanted a divorce, that was fine, but he didn't have to think he was going to fob off Daisy on her.

Even now, after nearly twelve years, Dev still remembered how cold he'd felt. How hollowed-out and empty. How desolate knowing what a sham his marriage had been.

Yes, he'd certainly learned his lesson. He had a good life now—a full life. He didn't need or want that kind of emotional turmoil again.

So there would be no more impassioned crusaders for Dev. Elise Cantrelle, no matter how lovely, no matter how gentle-spirited and feminine, no matter how different she seemed from Joelle—was not for him.

"Dad, is that you?" Daisy called from the living room as he let himself in the front door.

He grinned. "No, it's the boogeyman."

Daisy stood up from the couch as he entered the living room. She walked over and hugged him. He hugged her back. She walked back to the couch and plopped down, and he sat in the big easy chair, kicked off his shoes and wriggled his toes. "Ah, that feels good." He looked at Daisy. "Did you listen to the show tonight?" he asked.

"Uh-huh."

"Well? What did you think?"

"I thought you did good."

"Come on. Be honest."

Daisy grimaced. "Well, I thought that woman made some important points . . . uh, don't you think so?"

Dev nodded. He and Daisy rarely disagreed on anything, probably because so far in her young life, Daisy had seemed to think he could do no wrong. "You don't have to be afraid to say it. Yes, she did say some important things. But even so, I still think she overreacted to my original comments."

"Yeah, I guess you're right." In an abrupt change of mood, she jumped up, a bright smile on her face. "Hey, are you hungry? I saved some supper for you."

Dev shook his head. "I had a sandwich before the show. I'd like something to drink, though."

"I'll go get you some iced tea." Daisy started for the kitchen.

"I'll just go up and change first," Dev said, rising and picking up his shoes. He headed for the stairs.

When he came back downstairs he was wearing his favorite at-home outfit, shorts and a faded T-shirt. His feet were bare, and he enjoyed the feel of the cool tile under his feet. He walked back toward the kitchen where Daisy was already seated Indian fashion on one of the kitchen chairs. A tall glass of iced tea stood on the table across from her. Dev sank into a chair and picked up the frosty glass, taking a long swallow. He smiled at his daughter, who had a pensive expression on her face.

"Dad..."

"What?" He stretched his legs out in front of him.

"Some of the stories Miss Cantrelle told tonight were really awful."

"Yes, they were."

Daisy's forehead knitted, and her green eyes were troubled. "Why do men do those things?"

Dev sighed. "I wish I could explain why, honey, but I can't. I guess it's because sometimes people can't deal with their lives, and they take out their frustration and anger on others."

Daisy nodded. "That's sad, isn't it?"

"Yes, it is."

She sighed, twisting a strand of her flaxen hair around her index finger. "I really liked that woman."

Dev frowned. "Who? Elise Cantrelle?"

"Yeah. I...I think the work she's doing...well, it's great, you know?" Daisy's gaze met his, and in her clear green eyes, Dev saw hero worship.

Suddenly uneasy, Dev chose his words carefully. "I agree that the work she does is admirable, Daisy, but Miss Cantrelle is studying to be a family counselor, so it's really a part of her job."

"It sounded like more than a job to me," Daisy insisted stubbornly. "It sounded as if she really believes in what she's doing. I . . . I wish I could be like her."

"You're fine just the way you are." Dev's uneasiness grew. He didn't like the turn the conversation had taken.

"But Miss Cantrelle, she's helping change the world. I'm not doing anything but going to school," she said, disgust in her voice.

"You're doing what you're supposed to be doing right now. Getting an education and being a kid."

"Dad, I'm fourteen years old." Daisy's voice trembled slightly. "I'm not a kid anymore. I want to be involved in something meaningful. Something that will help other people. Something like what Miss Cantrelle is doing."

Dev's uneasiness segued into alarm. "You know, Daisy," he said firmly, "there are a lot of people out there who spend all of their time trying to change the world while they neglect their own families, when, if they turned that energy toward their own lives and the lives of their families, we'd all be better off." He finished off the last of his iced tea and set it down harder than he'd meant to.

Daisy stared at him. "You know, Dad, you sound just like that woman said you did. You sound narrow-minded and opinionated."

"Opinionated! Daisy, I'm your father. I have a right to tell you what I think."

"Well, I have a right to tell you what *I* think."

"I never said you didn't, honey. I just—"

"The trouble is, you think I'm a baby! You don't realize what's going on in the world. You know, girls my age are . . . are . . . having sex. They're having babies!"

"For God's sake, Daisy! Don't tell me you want to have a baby!"

She sighed wearily, giving him one of her rare why-can't-you-understand-me looks. "Don't get all upset. I didn't say that. I just meant . . . well, I'm tired of being treated like a child."

Hurt in spite of himself, Dev said, "I don't think I treat you like a child." Maybe that was the problem, he thought. Maybe he'd let her assume too much responsibility too fast. Maybe he *should* have been treating her like a child.

"Maybe you don't think so, but sometimes you do."

"Well, I'm sorry, honey, but you *are* still a child."

"Dad! You're doing it again!"

Dev started to reply, then lapsed into silence. It seemed to him that no matter what he said tonight, it was going to be misunderstood. God, women! Young or old, he wasn't sure he'd *ever* understand them. Finally, when the silence became oppressive to him, he tried once more. "Look, Daisy. I'm sorry. I didn't mean to belittle your feelings, but...well, you know how I feel about do-gooders. I just don't want you to romanticize what Elise Cantrelle is doing."

Daisy leaned forward, an earnest look on her face. "Dad, I'm not romanticizing. I just think the work she's doing is wonderful. In fact, I was thinking tonight as I was listening to her, I want to do something like that when I'm older."

"Don't be ridiculous!" Dev said before he could stop himself.

Daisy flushed and stuck her chin up in the air. "I don't think I'm being ridiculous. Maybe they'd even let me work at the shelter now if I went over there and asked them."

He pounded the table with his fist. Daisy jumped. "I forbid you to do anything of the sort!" he said.

She stared at him. Then her bottom lip trembled, and she ducked her head, but not before Dev caught the sheen of tears in her eyes. "I...I think I'm going to bed," she mumbled.

"Daisy, I—"

She stood. "Good night, Dad."

"Daisy..."

But he left his sentence unfinished as Daisy walked quickly out of the kitchen.

Dev slumped back into his chair. Weariness permeated his entire body. He sat there for a long time, staring into space, thoughts churning in his mind. He'd blown it tonight. Damn. Why hadn't he handled things with Daisy better? Now he'd hurt her feelings, made her feel he didn't respect her opinions, and he'd made light of something that obviously meant a lot to her.

But he couldn't, he *wouldn't* let her work someplace such as a shelter for battered women. It was fine for an adult like Elise Cantrelle to work there, but a *child?* He shuddered at the thought. He didn't want Daisy exposed to that kind of ugliness and violence. Besides, who knew when some irate husband might turn up and threaten the workers? Visions of some crazy fool brandishing a gun flashed through his mind.

And danger aside—there was another aspect to this idea of Daisy's that bothered him as well. He had no intention of letting Daisy turn out like her mother. Daisy was too young to understand, but sometimes people allowed their good instincts to turn into obsessions—obsessions that could ruin their lives.

Sighing, he stood. He rinsed out his tea glass and put it into the dishwasher, then checked the back door to make sure it was locked. He turned out the kitchen lights and slowly walked out into the hallway. As he climbed the stairs to the second level, he wondered if he should knock on Daisy's door. Try once again to apologize and make things right between them.

No, he thought. Better to leave well enough alone. By tomorrow she'd be over this. And in a couple of days she'd have forgotten all about her foolish idea of working at the women's shelter. This was just a case of hero worship because Daisy didn't have a female role model.

Actually, he thought, if Elise Cantrelle weren't so involved in her volunteer work, she would probably be a wonderful role model for Daisy.

But she was involved.

He needed to remember that.

Chapter Five

Daisy lay facedown across her bed and listened to her father's footsteps as he climbed the stairs. She held her breath as she heard him pause outside her doorway. *Go away. I don't want to talk to you anymore tonight.* As if God had heard her unspoken plea, her dad walked past and went on down the hall to his own room.

A relieved sigh escaped her lips as she heard his bedroom door close. "You *are* a child," he'd said. Why couldn't he understand that she wasn't a little girl anymore? He couldn't just tell her not to do something for no good reason. Especially when there was nothing wrong with what she'd suggested.

She closed her eyes, unhappiness rushing through her like water rushing over a dam. Rolling onto her back, she flung her arm across her eyes, blotting out the light. She bit her bottom lip and swallowed against the lump in her throat. For the thousandth time she wished they'd never moved to

Louisiana. Longingly, she thought of their apartment in New York, of her best friend Maura Finnegan and how, after school, they'd ride the bus home to their Washington Square area apartments together. She thought of their long conversations, of how they'd talk for hours about everything.

She thought of Miss Alessandro, her Spanish teacher, whom she'd so admired. She thought of the little bookstore on Christopher Street and the many happy hours she'd spent there, digging through the treasure trove of old books—books like *Heidi* and *Black Beauty* and *David at West Point*.

She thought of Samantha—Mrs. Zuckerman's cat—and how, the minute Mrs. Zuckerman put her out in the morning, she'd come meowing around Daisy's door, looking for a handout and some attention.

She thought of Salome, the artist who lived on the first floor of their building, and how she always blew Daisy a kiss when she saw her. And of Jason, the dancer who lived down the hall from Maura's apartment, and of how he'd tweak their noses and call them "gorgeous."

She thought of Mr. Brindizzi, the funny old man who owned the corner market where Daisy shopped for food. Mr. Brindizzi had never learned to speak English properly, and his speech was salted with Italian words and phrases that Daisy loved to hear.

She'd felt comfortable in their old neighborhood. She knew everyone, and they knew her. She hadn't felt like an outsider, someone who didn't know how to dress or how to talk or how to behave. In her New York neighborhood, it wasn't unusual to be unusual.

Here in Lafayette, Daisy stood out like a sore thumb. The kids here looked at her as if she'd come from Mars. The minute she opened her mouth, everyone knew she was different—her New York accent in glaring contrast to their soft drawls. The girls here in Lafayette seemed to know something she didn't.

Hot tears trickled from behind Daisy's arm.

She'd lied to her father the other day. She was miserable here. Sure, she'd have liked to go to the pool, meet some kids, maybe make a friend. But the one time she'd walked over by the pool in the afternoon, the two girls and the boy that were already there started to giggle and whisper behind their hands. They shot covert looks her way, as if she couldn't see them. Daisy had swallowed hard, stuck her chin up in the air and marched off. She could feel them looking at her back, feel their eyes boring through her, feel their whispers sliding around her.

I wish Maura was here. I wish I had a mother to talk to.

The second thought, forbidden, one she'd pushed away many times, wormed its way into her head. Immediately she felt guilty. She felt disloyal to her dad. She knew how he felt about her mother. He hated her. Daisy shivered. Her mother hadn't wanted to be with them. She'd left them.

Why? Hadn't her mother loved her at all? What was wrong with her? But her dad loved her. Her dad tried so hard to be a good father. She knew he did. She saw the proof of that every day. He'd always been there for her. So why was she angry with him? Why did she wish she could talk to her mother?

Because there were some things she couldn't talk to her father about, no matter how hard he tried to understand.

In New York, she'd kind of shared Mrs. Finnegan, Maura's mother. Mrs. Finnegan had sparkly blue eyes and a friendly smile, and she'd always listened. She always had time for Maura and Daisy, no matter how busy she was. And she *was* busy. She worked for a major bank as a loan officer. But she'd set aside whatever it was she was doing, and she'd listen. She gave good advice, too, always seeming to understand even when Daisy had a hard time explaining how she felt. Daisy would be forever thankful to Mrs. Finnegan for helping her when she'd first started getting her period. Things like that were impossible to talk to your father about.

Daisy sighed, brushing away her tears. Mrs. Finnegan and Maura were thousands of miles away. Quietly she got up and tiptoed to her chest of drawers. Almost stealthily, she slid the bottom drawer open, and from under a neatly folded stack of underwear, pulled out the frayed newspaper photograph, the one her father had thrown into the trash.

She stared at the face of the blond-haired woman who was her mother. She stared for a long time.

Her mother's intense blue gaze seemed to stare right back. It seemed to say, *Who are you?*

After a long time, Daisy carefully put the picture back in its hiding place.

Who *was* she?

Daisy wasn't sure. The only thing she *was* sure of was that she was changing; the old Daisy, the little-girl Daisy who accepted every word her father said as gospel truth, had just about disappeared.

As Daisy slowly undressed and pulled on her nightshirt, and during the time she brushed her teeth and washed her face, and then, after she'd climbed into bed and squeezed her eyes shut, the same question reverberated in her mind.

Who was she?

"Who's that?" Elise asked Frieda, a fellow worker at the shelter.

"Who?" Frieda's broad face creased into a nearsighted frown. She straightened from her task of transferring books from a large carton to one of the shelves of the bookcase in the library alcove of the community room.

Elise inclined her head toward the far doorway where a pretty blond teenager wearing large round glasses stood talking to Judy, Meg Bodine's assistant. "The little blonde," she murmured.

Frieda shrugged. "Dunno. I've never seen her before."

A few seconds later Judy walked over to where Elise and Frieda were working. "I want to introduce you two to someone new," she said. She turned to the teenager, who stood just off to the side, a shy smile on her small, heart-shaped face. "This is Marguerite, a new volunteer. She's going to be helping us out two afternoons a week."

Elise smiled and held out her hand. "Welcome, Marguerite," she said as they shook hands. "I'm Elise." The girl's glasses slid down her nose, and she pushed them up, her eyes meeting Elise's. *Pretty eyes,* Elise thought. *They're the same shade of green as Dev's* . . . The thought jolted her, and she hastily thrust it from her mind.

"And I'm Frieda." Frieda stepped forward, extending her hand.

"You know we only use first names here at the shelter," Judy explained.

"Yes," Marguerite said.

"And you know why, don't you?" Judy persisted in her patient, teacher's tone of voice that always tickled Elise.

The pretty teenager nodded. "To protect the identity of the women and children who are sheltered here," she said.

Elise smiled. Judy had done her work well. "We're very glad to have you here, Marguerite. We need all the help we can get." Once more, their gazes met, and for the second time Elise was struck with the beauty of the girl's eyes, which even her glasses couldn't disguise. And they *were* that same warm, golden-green as the attractive professor's. The attractive professor that Elise had not been able to stop thinking of since Monday night.

Three days. By now she should have managed to put him out of her thoughts forever. Instead, his face had lurked at the back of her mind, popping into the forefront of her consciousness at odd moments throughout her days.

And her nights.

"I . . . I heard you on the Johnny Hagan show," the girl said shyly, steering Elise's thoughts away from their dangerous bent. "I thought you were wonderful."

"Thanks," Elise said.

"We're all proud of her," Judy said.

"She certainly told that professor a thing or two, didn't she?" Frieda said. "Men! They're all a pain, aren't they?"

The girl shifted uncomfortably. Elise gave her a reassuring smile. Frieda, with her booming voice, could be a bit overwhelming.

"Well," Judy inserted smoothly, "we'd better get going, Marguerite. I've still got a lot to show you."

"Bye," the girl said. "It was nice to meet you." Her eyes were shining as her gaze met Elise's. Elise smiled again.

"Nice meeting you, too," Elise and Frieda said in unison.

"Cute kid," Frieda said when Judy and her young charge had walked away. "Looks scared, though."

"Oh, they're all a little scared when they first come here. She'll get over it." Elise remembered her own first day and how nervous and unsure she was. Some days she still was, especially when faced with an especially difficult situation.

"Well, if she doesn't, she'll be gone in no time."

Elise nodded. That was true. Volunteers fell into two camps: those who only lasted a day or so, and those who stayed for years. Elise hoped the teenager stayed, though. There was something very appealing about her. Elise thought the children at the shelter would probably like Marguerite very much—her shyness would be an asset with them. Sometimes, when children first arrived, the more capable and confident volunteers overwhelmed them. They related best to the quieter, less domineering women.

Marguerite, with her sweet expression and beautiful eyes, would be a hit. Elise just knew it.

Funny about her eyes. That shade of green certainly wasn't common, and it was strange to have seen it twice in just a few days.

Thinking about the teenager's eyes brought Dev back to Elise's mind, and for the rest of the afternoon, as she worked alongside Frieda, and then later, as she led a therapy group, thoughts of him kept intruding.

She wondered if she'd ever see him again.

Gosh, Elise Cantrelle was even nicer in person than she'd sounded on the radio. Daisy carefully inched her bicycle into traffic and began pedaling toward home. The shelter was exactly 5.4 miles from their town house; she'd measured it on Tuesday, her first day there. Her thoughts wandered back to her meeting with Elise. She was so pretty, Daisy thought. And so smart. And she was doing such great work, helping so many women.

She's just the kind of person I'd like to be when I'm grown-up.

Guiltily Daisy wondered what Elise would think if she had any idea who she really was. If she knew who Daisy's *father* was. *Maybe I should have told her.*

But what if she did tell her? And then Elise didn't like her because of her father? Oh, gosh, that'd be awful. Daisy couldn't chance that happening. She admired Elise too much, and she wanted Elise to like her. Daisy smiled. She was glad she'd decided to go to the shelter and volunteer, even though she was disobeying her father by doing so. But he'd been wrong to tell her she couldn't. And when someone was wrong, you didn't have to obey them, did you? After all, sooner or later, whether her dad liked it or not, she had to start making her own decisions.

Monday night, when she couldn't fall asleep, she'd thought and thought about everything. Finally she realized that if she were going to be happy living in Lafayette, she had to do some things to change her life. And the first thing she wanted to do was go to the shelter the next day and volunteer her time. She knew her father would be furious if he knew, but she'd already decided his objections were unreasonable. She hated deceiving him, but he'd left her no choice. She was old enough to decide on her own if she wanted to work at the shelter, and she had. As long as it didn't interfere with her schoolwork or her responsibilities at home—he had no right to object. She was doing something good, something to benefit others. Her dad should be proud of her, not forbid her to do this. She'd made the right decision.

And she'd made the right decision about her name, too. She'd decided to go by her real name of Marguerite. Daisy was a nickname, and it sounded babyish. Marguerite sounded more grown-up.

As Daisy whizzed around the corner onto her street, she decided she was not going to feel guilty about anything she'd done. Because she wasn't doing anything wrong.

Dev was tired. It had been a long day. He was looking forward to a cold beer and some pizza. He had told Daisy not to cook anything tonight, and she had agreed. She hadn't seemed to hold a grudge over their disagreement on Monday night, either, for which Dev was grateful. Tuesday morning she'd been a little cool, but by Tuesday night, she'd been her old cheerful self. Dev had been a bit surprised.

He'd expected her to introduce the subject of the shelter again. It wasn't like Daisy to back down easily. She could be very tenacious, a trait she'd inherited legitimately, for both he and Joelle were doggedly determined people when they had set a course.

So he'd been surprised, pleasantly so, when she seemed to have forgotten all about the shelter and Elise Cantrelle.

He wished he could put Elise out of his mind as easily. He hadn't been able to stop thinking about her since they'd parted Monday night. It was no wonder, though, because everywhere he'd gone the past couple of days, people had mentioned her and the Johnny Hagan Show. It wasn't just the things she'd said, though, it was the woman herself.

Face it, he told himself, you've been drawn to her from the first moment you laid eyes on her.

Dev grimaced. Despite all the reasons why he knew he shouldn't, he wanted to see her again. What harm would there be in asking her out on a date? It wasn't as if he intended to get seriously involved or anything. So why not indulge himself—at least once. If he spent an evening with Elise Cantrelle, maybe he'd stop thinking about her so much. Maybe she'd turn out to be not so great after all.

As he climbed the three concrete steps leading to the front door of his town house, he wondered what she'd say if he simply picked up the phone and asked her to go out with him tomorrow night.

Thursday night Elise settled down to watch "Cheers." With a grateful sigh of relief, she propped her tired feet up on one arm of the comfortable old love seat, which her father and stepmother had given her, while she leaned back against the other arm. She pulled her bowl of buttered popcorn closer and switched on the TV.

The telephone rang.

"Oh, darn," she complained, wishing for the jillionth time that she had an answering machine. It was probably somebody selling something. She had half a mind to just let the phone ring.

But something about a ringing phone always drew her. It could be something important. She simply couldn't ignore it. Sighing, she got up.

"Hello?" she said as she grabbed the receiver in the middle of the fifth ring.

"Elise? This is Sloan Devereaux," said the voice that she hadn't been able to forget, no matter how much she'd tried.

Her heart lurched. "Oh . . . hello."

"I've had a difficult week, thanks to you," he said.

"Have you?" She still felt stunned. "Why is that?"

He chuckled, the sound warm and resonant. She could picture the twinkle in his eyes, and she shivered.

"Well, everywhere I've gone, people have reminded me that you bested me the other night." He sounded amused.

"Does that bother you?" She was proud of herself. She didn't sound rattled at all. In fact, she sounded cool and sophisticated, something she'd never been.

"Not really. How has your week been?"

"Pretty good, actually." What did he *want?* Had he just called to make small talk?

"I was wondering . . ."

"Yes?"

"Would you like to go out to dinner with me tomorrow night?"

For a minute, she was speechless. "Dinner?" she finally said. Now where had her newfound coolness gone?

"Yes, I . . . I'd really like to talk to you about your work at the shelter. You've gotten me interested in the problems of battered women. I'd like to know more."

How could she refuse? Here was her opportunity, just as Lianna had said, to educate him, and through him, maybe hundreds of other people.

He continued to talk. "A couple of people at the university have recommended Don's, and I thought—"

"Oh, Don's *is* good," Elise said, finally finding her tongue.

"So you'll go?"

"I . . . yes, I'd love to go."

A few minutes later, after they'd made arrangements for him to call for her at seven the following evening, they hung up. Elise stood there for a few seconds, wondering what to make of his call. She really hadn't expected to hear from him again. He had given her no indication that he'd wanted to see her again, either. On the contrary, he'd seemed cool and distant as they said their goodbyes the other night.

And he'd also given no indication that he was interested in her work. What was behind this invitation?

As she settled herself back down in the front of the TV and absently ate her popcorn, she couldn't help smiling to herself. *Admit it. Whatever his reasons, you're pleased that he called you. You wanted to see him again.*

And not just because this is a great opportunity to educate him, either.

No, she was pleased about seeing Dev because he excited her.

Because she was attracted to him.

Because when she was with him, he made her feel like a woman.

* * *

Dev dressed carefully for his date with Elise. Charcoal-gray slacks. Pale blue shirt. Gray tweed sport coat. Black loafers. Red-and-navy striped tie. He looked at himself in the mirror, smoothing his hair back one last time. He looked okay.

When he walked into the living room to say good-night to Daisy, she whistled. "You look really nice, Dad. Where're you going?"

"I told you. I have a date."

"You mean a *real* date? Like you asked some woman to go out with you?"

Dev laughed. "Yes, a real date."

Curiosity gave Daisy's eyes a lively sparkle. "That's great. I thought you meant you had an appointment or something. Who's your date with? One of the teachers?"

Dev hesitated only a fraction of a second before answering. "No, not a teacher. I'm...taking Elise Cantrelle to dinner."

Daisy's mouth dropped open. "Really?"

Dev studied the play of emotions across his daughter's expressive face. He knew he'd surprised her, but if he wasn't mistaken, he'd also alarmed her, although the emotion, if it *was* alarm, was quickly replaced by a delighted grin.

Later, though, as he drove toward the address Elise had given him, Dev wondered about that momentary flash of alarm in Daisy's eyes. What had caused it? Was there something about Elise that Daisy didn't like?

Dev frowned.

He'd thought Daisy liked Elise from what she'd said about her after the Johnny Hagan show. In fact, Daisy had given him the impression that she had a beginning case of hero worship.

As he pulled up in front of Elise's apartment complex, he decided to forget about Daisy's mixed reaction to his announcement. Tomorrow he would question his daughter about her feelings. Tonight he would just enjoy himself.

Smiling, he walked up the steps to apartment two-seventeen.

Chapter Six

When Elise's doorbell rang, at exactly seven o'clock, a flutter of nerves attacked her stomach, and she had a moment of panic. It had been a long time since she'd had a date. In fact, this was her first date since her divorce three years earlier. She took a couple of long, deep breaths to steady herself, hoping she still remembered how to act. She guessed she'd be okay if she stuck to her resolve to talk about the shelter. Yes, that was it. If she kept their date away from anything too personal, she'd be fine.

She took another deep breath, tugged down the skirt of her pastel print dress and opened the door. "Hi," she said. "You're right on time." Dev smiled back, and his eyes crinkled agreeably at the corners. "Don't you know that anthropologists are all Type A personalities and compulsively prompt?"

She was grateful to him for his light, teasing comment. It helped put her more at ease. But, heavens, he certainly did have a killer smile. She wondered if he had any idea how attractive he was, especially when he smiled. Silently she laughed at herself. Of course he did. Given the shortage of available men in the world today, she was sure women chased him in droves.

And why not? He was successful. Educated.

And sexy. Don't forget sexy.

The thought slid through her mind as she took in his appearance. She loved the way he looked in his well-tailored gray slacks and sport coat—sophisticated, yet completely natural. She admired the way the material of his coat hugged his broad shoulders and the way the pale blue of his shirt deepened his tan.

As he walked past her into her apartment, she caught a whiff of his after-shave—something lemony and crisp— which, combined with the healthy smell of male, caused her flutters to return. Maybe she'd been kidding herself. Maybe it wouldn't be so easy to keep their date on a safe, impersonal level. Not if he was going to have this effect on her.

"Nice apartment." He glanced around her living room.

Elise shrugged. "Oh, it's just an apartment. Nothing special."

"But you've made it look special."

She followed his gaze as he took in the dozens of plants she had placed all over the room, the fresh flowers Lisette had thrust on her when she'd stopped by yesterday after work, the needlepoint pillows that had been, and still were, her therapy when life became too stressful, the overflowing bookshelf, the easel containing her sketch pad and charcoals, and the Yamaha guitar propped in the corner.

"Do you play?" he asked, walking over and lifting the guitar. He strummed the open strings.

"A little."

"I've always had a secret desire to play the guitar," he admitted. "But I'm not very musically inclined." He carefully placed the instrument back into its niche. He laughed. "Actually I wanted to be a rock musician."

She laughed, too. "Somehow I can't picture you in a rock band."

"No, you're right. As a kid I was more the nerd type. You know, brainy instead of cool." He smiled, but there was an element of wistfulness to this smile, and for some reason it tugged at her heart. She knew without him saying so that the abilities that were such an asset as an adult had caused him pain as a child. Well, she could relate to that. She'd never been any good at sports, and she still remembered how much it had hurt when she was the last one chosen for the softball team or the dodgeball game. All children wanted to be part of the crowd. No child wanted to be different.

"Would you like something to drink before we go?" she said to change the subject.

"Not unless you do." The wistful look disappeared, and he was once more the confident man of the lecture hall.

"No, I'm ready."

"Why don't we go then?"

Ten minutes later she was strapped in beside him in a dark blue Mercedes. The car had been a real surprise. She'd had some idea that an anthropologist was probably paid on a par with a social worker. Obviously she'd been wrong. "This is a beautiful car," she said as he expertly maneuvered into traffic on Pinhook Road.

"It is, isn't it? I'm leasing it for a year." He glanced toward her, smiling at her puzzled look. "Remember, I'm from New York City. I don't really need a car there."

"Oh, of course."

"There are times I'd like to have one, though. It's a pain to have to rent a car when you want to go out to the country for the weekend. But it's too expensive to keep a car in the city. There's no place to park it."

"I've read about that," Elise offered. She wondered what it was like to live somewhere like New York. "What about garages? I thought most people parked their cars in garages."

"Most *rich* people," he said with a laugh. "I don't happen to be rich."

"Tell me about New York," she said, completely forgetting her vow to steer away from personal topics. "Were you born there?"

"Me? No, I was born in Louisiana."

"You *were?*"

"Why are you so surprised?"

"I don't know. I guess ... you don't have an accent or anything." That wasn't all, and she knew it. He just didn't act like a Southerner, but she wasn't sure he'd like it if she said that.

"I imagine I used to have an accent, but I haven't lived in Louisiana since I was a boy."

"Are you from Lafayette, then?"

"No. New Orleans."

"Really? I grew up in New Orleans, too."

He turned and smiled at her, and her heart did another of its little flips, unnerving her. "I knew we had a lot in common," he said softly.

Elise swallowed. That smile, the expression in his eyes, the tone of his voice: he was flirting with her. She wasn't quite sure how she felt about that. It was getting harder and harder by the minute to keep pretending they were only going out so that she could tell him more about battered women.

"My parents moved to New York City when I was twelve," he continued as he braked for a red light.

"Do they still live there?"

"My father does." His jaw tightened. "My mother lives in Fort Lauderdale. With her third husband."

"I see." Elise saw that the subject was a painful one. She wished she could think of something to say that would make him relax again. She decided it was safest to stick to the topic of the city. "So tell me what it's like to live in New York."

The light turned green, and the car moved forward. "I like it. Although lately..."

"Lately, what?"

"Well, lately I've been thinking it might be nice to live somewhere where the pace is slower. Where there's less crime and less to worry about. Somewhere more like Lafayette, for example." His face took on a pensive expression. "But I'm not sure how my daughter would like that. I don't think she was overjoyed about moving here."

"You have a daughter?"

"Yes. Daisy's fourteen. She's a terrific kid." His voice had softened. He obviously cared a lot for his daughter.

"Fourteen." Elise thought of Charlie, who was also fourteen. "Wh—" She hesitated, then plunged ahead. "What about her mother? You're not still married, are you?" The thought had just occurred to her, startling and unwelcome.

He laughed harshly. "No. I've been divorced twelve years."

His tone was curt, even dismissive, and Elise knew that he, too, had a past he preferred to forget. She understood that, and she respected it. She wondered what had happened, though. It was unusual for a man to gain custody of a daughter. Of any child, for that matter. And from what he'd said, his daughter lived with him.

By now they'd reached Don's, the popular Cajun sea-food restaurant, and they didn't talk again until they were seated in the bar while they waited for their table. Dev placed their drink order—a strawberry daiquiri for Elise and a beer for himself. The bar was crowded and noisy, filled with an exuberant Friday night crowd. "Would you like some oysters on the half shell, too?" he asked.

"No, thanks."

"So what about you?" he said, turning on his bar stool to face her. "How did you end up in Lafayette?" His green-gold gaze settled on her face.

Something inside Elise tumbled over as her gaze met his. What was it about this man that affected her so? All he had to do was look at her, and her body betrayed her in ways it hadn't betrayed her for years. There was definitely a pow-erful connection between them. She wondered about it. It seemed stronger than a pure physical attraction, but maybe she just wanted to think that. Maybe it really was some-thing as basic as chemistry, or hormones. Whatever it was, the feelings were unsettling, and Elise wasn't sure she liked them. "Well, as I said, I grew up in New Orleans, but, well . . . after my mother died, I moved to Houston."

"Why? Didn't you like New Orleans?"

"It wasn't that. The job situation was better in Houston. Besides, I don't know, after Mom died, I needed a change. New Orleans reminded me too much of her." Even now, after eleven years, Elise felt a lump forming in her throat. She had loved her mother so much. She still missed her ter-ribly.

She took a shaky breath, then a sip of her drink. Once her emotions were under control again, she continued. "I lived in Houston until I left my husband, then I came back to Louisiana. That was three and a half years ago. I've been in Lafayette for the past three years."

"So you *have* been married."

The way he said it, she knew he'd wondered. Well, she'd wondered, too. At first if there was a Mrs. Devereaux, and now, what had happened between him and his ex-wife that he'd ended up with custody of his daughter. "Yes." Elise met his thoughtful gaze. "I'm sure you've already guessed I was an abused wife. That's the reason I got so involved with battered women."

His eyes darkened, and the muscles in his jaw tightened. "I'm sorry. I had no idea."

Just then their table was called, and Elise felt a gush of relief. She didn't want to talk about her marriage. She didn't want Dev to feel sorry for her. She didn't want to see that look on his face, that look that said, *How could you have let some man beat you up? What's wrong with you?*

They were led to a table tucked into a corner, and once they were settled with menus in front of them, Dev said, "You've eaten here before, haven't you?"

"Many times. It's one of my father's favorite restaurants." Every time she said the word *father* she felt a stirring of pride.

"What do you recommend?"

"The stuffed shrimp is wonderful. That's what I usually get. But everything's good."

He smiled. "The stuffed shrimp it is, then."

Their waiter, a young fresh-faced student type, filled their water glasses and took their orders. When he'd left, Dev said, "So what are you studying at the university?"

"I'm working toward a degree in counseling. They've promised me a full-time job at the shelter when I graduate."

"Which will be?"

"I have one more semester until I receive my bachelor's degree."

"And what about your master's? Do you plan to continue?" He finished off his beer.

Elise ran her index finger over the condensation on her water glass. "I've decided to give myself at least one semester off while I decide." She looked up, meeting his gaze again. His eyes fascinated her. They were a kaleidoscope of color: green, gold, amber. She guessed people would call them hazel, but the green was dominant. "I probably *should* go on, get my master's. It's difficult to progress in the field of social work without an advanced degree, but I don't want to have to make a decision right now."

He nodded as if he understood. Elise wasn't sure he could understand. After all, he was a man. Most men were used to being in charge, to being in control. He might not be able to relate to someone like her, someone who had allowed other people to make her decisions all of her life, someone who had even allowed herself to be bullied. How *could* he understand that even the conscious decision *not* to make a decision was a huge step forward for her?

"So tell me about your work at the shelter," he said. "How did you get involved in it?"

"When I left my own abusive relationship, I came to Lafayette to live with my father. We'd been separated. Actually I'd never known him, because he and my mother weren't married." Elise met Dev's gaze squarely. She was leaving a lot unsaid.

There was something in his eyes, an empathy and quiet understanding she hadn't expected. Suddenly Elise knew Dev had experienced a similar loneliness and pain. If they hadn't been in such a public place, surrounded by other people, she might have told him everything.

But they were. So she couldn't. Instead she began to tell him about her decision to help other battered women who might not be as fortunate as she was—women who didn't have supportive, caring families to help them.

She described her first uncertain days at the shelter. As their food came, and as they ate, she told him about Meg and Frieda and Judy and Kim. She described the many services offered by the shelter and how many volunteers and paid workers it took to keep it staffed. She told him about the various women she'd met—the strong ones working at the shelter, and the not-so-strong ones who were learning to rebuild their lives. She told him about the group therapy sessions she led and what she hoped they accomplished and the great sense of satisfaction her work gave her.

He remained quiet and attentive throughout her long explanation, nodding or encouraging her to continue with an intelligent question or two—questions that showed a great deal of sensitivity. He was easy to talk to, she realized, and the best part of all—he really listened. She almost forgot that the reason she was here with him tonight was because of his remarks during his lecture.

"The people at the shelter believe that the way to end violence is through education and information. Women need to know they have other options, that they don't have to stay in an abusive relationship." She took a forkful of coleslaw, chewed and swallowed. "Recently the shelter received a $125,000 grant from International Oil. That's going to make such a difference. Now we'll be able to hire a full-time, paid Hot-line Director, something we desperately need."

At his questioning look, she said, "Last year we handled two thousand eight hundred domestic violence calls. This year alone we've received nearly that many, and it's only July. That means by the end of the year, if this pace keeps up, we'll have handled six thousand calls."

He whistled softly. "I had no idea."

"Most people don't. That's why it's so important that people like you, people who have the public's eyes and ears, a respected member of the academic community, is informed. We need your help."

"I don't know what I could do."

"You could do a lot, Dev, if you wanted to. Domestic violence is such a serious problem, affecting so many people. Progress is so darned slow." She sighed. "But things are getting better." She wiped her mouth with her napkin and leaned back in her chair. "Last April was Sexual Assault Awareness and Child Abuse Prevention Month. All the shelters in the city pooled their resources and blitzed the media with public service announcements about violence against women and children." She drank some of her water. "It was a well-planned campaign, and we think we did a lot of good."

Their waiter walked up to their table. "Would you like some coffee? Dessert?"

They refused dessert, but both said yes to coffee. For the remainder of their time at the restaurant, Elise steered the conversation to Dev's work. She'd talked about herself long enough.

Before she knew it, it was time to go. She was amazed when she looked at her watch and saw it was nearly nine-thirty. The time had gone so fast. She'd been so comfortable in Dev's company, she hadn't even realized how long they'd been at the restaurant.

They didn't talk during the drive home. Dev inserted a cassette into the tape player and they listened to Vivaldi's Four Seasons concerto. Elise laid her head back against the headrest and let the delicacy of the music take hold. She felt pleasantly full of good food and completely relaxed. She was very glad she'd accepted Dev's invitation tonight. She felt as if she'd accomplished what she'd set out to do—and in the process gotten to know a really nice man.

All too soon they pulled up in front of her apartment. He turned off the ignition and opened his door, walking around to her side to open hers. He took her hand to help her out, and the touch of his smooth, warm palm sent a pleasant tingle up Elise's arm. They walked slowly up the walk to her stairway.

It was another warm, humid night, and sounds of the city surrounded them: the chirp of crickets, two cats calling to each other somewhere in the distance, the hum of tires against concrete from the road beyond, a muted burst of music from one of the nearby apartments.

Elise turned to face Dev. "I had such a nice time tonight. Thank you."

He gently touched her shoulders. She looked up. The parking lot was well lit, and the strong planes of his face were clearly delineated. "I enjoyed it, too," he said. "I hate for it to end." At his words, her pulse soared.

"Would you like to come up for another cup of coffee?" As soon as the words were out of her mouth, she knew the invitation was a mistake. This man made her feel too many things. She wasn't ready for a relationship. There were still too many areas of her life that she wanted to work out before she got involved with a man again. But she hadn't been able to help herself. The invitation had popped out, without conscious thought, something that she'd been unable to resist.

"I'd love to."

Five minutes later Dev was seated on her slightly shabby love seat, and coffee was dripping through the filter into the pot, its fragrant aroma already filling the apartment. Elise opened the freezer. "How about some coffee cake?" she asked, looking back over her shoulder. Her kitchen and living room were only separated by a bar, so she could see Dev.

"Sounds good."

She popped the coffee cake into the microwave and set the timer. While she waited for it to heat, she busied herself arranging cups, spoons, cream, sugar, plates, napkins and forks on a tray. When everything was ready she carried it all into the living area and set the tray on her coffee table. Dev had gotten up from the love seat and was looking at a partially finished sketch on her easel. He turned. "You're a talented artist."

"Thanks. I'm totally untrained, but I like to draw." She'd like to draw him, she thought.

"Do you mind if I take this sport coat off?" he said.

"Of course not."

He removed his coat and tie, unbuttoning the top button of his shirt. "Ahh, that feels good. I hate ties."

"Most men seem to." She remembered how Derek, her ex-husband, had always chafed against wearing a tie, but as a salesman, he'd had to wear one all the time.

Elise poured their coffee and served the cake. He sat on the love seat again, and she sat across from him in a pale blue wing chair, one of her few pieces of new furniture. They ate in companionable silence for a few minutes, then Dev said, "I was hesitant about calling you, you know."

"Were you?" Well, she'd been hesitant about seeing him again, so they were even.

"I wasn't sure what your reaction would be."

"I couldn't pass up the chance to educate you," she said with a soft laugh.

"You've certainly done that."

"Have I? I'm not convinced that you believe me."

"Of course I believe you."

"Oh, I think you believe the facts I've given you. But I'm afraid you haven't abandoned your original theory—your Dr. Freidberg's theory—that if only women went back to staying at home and filling traditional roles, these problems would disappear." When he didn't immediately answer, she said, "Dev, believe me, if you'd visit the shelter, talk to some of these women yourself, you'd see that almost all of the women at the shelter were very traditional wives—the kind who try in every way to please their husbands—and they still got knocked around. In fact, the harder they tried to please, the more abusive their husbands were."

He frowned, his gaze locking with hers.

Elise knew she was saying too much. She knew he was probably sick of the subject. She knew she should just drop it and make pleasant conversation until he left. But she couldn't. She cared too passionately. It suddenly seemed to be the most important thing in the world that he understand. "I should know, Dev. I was the most traditional wife you'd ever want to see. And all it ever got me were black eyes and broken bones and a miserable life." She heard the quaver in her voice and it made her angry. She hated this weakness of hers. She hated not being able to talk about what had happened to her without getting all emotional.

"Would you like to tell me about it?"

The soft question was nearly her undoing. She bit her bottom lip to still the sudden trembling and carefully laid her cup and saucer down on the coffee table.

Dev watched her face as she poured out her story.

"At first the beatings were isolated incidents, and I made excuses for him," she said. "I told myself that I'd asked for them because I'd disobeyed him, or nagged him, or done something to make him angry." She shook her head, gave a contemptuous laugh. "It's incredible, isn't it? He was beating me up, and I was taking the blame for it."

Dev clenched his teeth as he thought about anyone raising a hand to the delicate, gentle woman sitting across from him. He couldn't imagine what kind of man could do something like that. There had been times, in his marriage to Joelle, when she'd made him furious, so furious he felt like strangling her. But he'd never touched her. He'd walked away until his emotions were under control, no matter how much she taunted or pushed him.

"Anyway, the beatings got more vicious and occurred more often as time went on. It got so the least little thing would set him off. It became almost routine for him to blacken my eyes. There were days at a time when I never left our house because I didn't want anyone to see me."

"Was there no one who could help you?"

She sighed. "It's so hard to explain, Dev. I was too ashamed for anyone to know. I tried to hide what was happening. I thought I was to blame."

"But what about your job? Didn't your co-workers notice anything?"

"Derek didn't want me to work. He insisted my job was to take care of him and our home."

Now her gaze met his again, and the expression in her soft brown eyes caused a knot to form in Dev's chest. He wished he had the faceless Derek here so he could give him a taste of his own medicine. "So go on. What happened next?"

"Well, when we'd been married about four years, I finally got up the nerve to do something I'd always wanted to do. I signed up as a set designer with a little theater group in Houston. I didn't tell Derek, of course. He would've had a fit. But he was a traveling salesman, so he was away a lot of the time. I figured he'd never know. Anyway, I used my father's name at the theater instead of my married name. Derek didn't know about my father.''

That simple statement told Dev more about her relationship with her ex-husband than anything else. If she hadn't trusted him enough to tell him about her background, their marriage was a farce.

''Anyway, I met a woman at the theater group who became a good friend. I confided in her, told her about Derek and how he'd threatened to kill me if I ever tried to leave him, but she said she'd help me. About two years after I met her—her name is Jenny—Derek left on a week-long selling trip. The night before he left he beat me worse than he'd ever beaten me before. I guess he wanted to be sure I wouldn't leave the house while he was gone. Well, that beating snapped something in me. I knew I had to get away from him, right then. I called Jenny, but she was on vacation, so I had to figure out how to do it all on my own.''

Elise went on to explain how she'd taken the money she'd hoarded for two years, bought herself a bus ticket and gone to her great-aunt Marie who was in a nursing home in Evangeline. ''I never dreamed that Jenny would be so worried or I'd have written and let her know where I was. I knew she'd never tell Derek.''

''Wouldn't you have been worried if your situations had been reversed?'' Dev asked.

''Yes, but I wasn't thinking straight.''

''So what happened after you got to the nursing home?''

''My aunt arranged for me to live with a friend of hers in Abbeville, and I started seeing a counselor. Gradually I began to understand what had happened to me and why. I was even able to understand Derek and why he was the way he was. That was an important part of my recovery.''

Dev started to say something, but she launched into the rest of her story, cutting him off. ''In the meantime, unknown to me, Jenny had asked her brother Jack Forrester, who's an investigative journalist with World Press, to try to find out what had happened to me. She was afraid Derek had killed me, you see."

Dev listened quietly as Elise told him how Jack had traced her to New Orleans because of the fact that she'd used the name Cantrelle with the little theater group.

"It was funny how everything worked out," she said. "Jack found a woman he was positive was me because we looked enough alike to be twins, and she turned out to be my cousin, Desiree. Of course, I didn't know her, or any of my father's family at the time. But Desiree and Jack eventually found me, and in the process, lured Derek to New Orleans where he tried to kill Jack. Anyway, Derek ended up in jail—he's *still* in jail, by the way—and I ended up finding my father." She smiled, all traces of her earlier tears gone. "And a huge, wonderful family to go along with him."

"I'm glad everything worked out well for you, but—"

"But you can't understand why I stayed with him so long, can you?"

"No, I guess I can't."

"The thing is, Dev, abused women feel helpless, hopeless. See, the more abused you are, the more worthless you feel."

"Okay, that I understand. But you almost sound as if you've forgiven your ex-husband. That's what I find incredible."

"No, I haven't forgiven or forgotten. But I learned through therapy that until I could let go of my anger, I wouldn't be able to heal myself. Perhaps my anger never will be gone. But at least I've rid myself of the bitterness."

Dev couldn't help voicing his immediate reaction to her statement. "Men are trained to hold on to their anger—and they don't forget. That's the difference between men and women."

"But Dev, a person can't be emotionally whole if he or she carries around a load of bitterness and hate. You have to put the past behind you if you hope to go forward."

He shrugged. Some things needed to be remembered. So people didn't make the same mistakes twice. "You're a better person than I am, then. Because I couldn't do it."

She started to say something, then stopped. There was a troubled expression in her eyes. Suddenly Dev felt acutely uncomfortable. She was looking at him as if she felt sorry for him. Hell, he should be feeling sorry for her, not the other way around. Abruptly he stood.

"It's late," he said. "I'd better be going."

She nodded. Damn her. Why was she looking at him like that? As if he'd hurt her feelings, or something.

"Thank you for the lovely dinner," she said as he put on his sport coat.

"It was my pleasure," he said, hating himself. What had happened that their easy camaraderie had disappeared? Why did he somehow feel as if he had done something wrong?

"Good night," she said, opening the front door.

He hesitated a fraction of a second, but she looked down, and he didn't know what to say. The evening had been ruined, and he wasn't even sure why.

He walked out, and the door shut behind him with a decisive click.

Chapter Seven

The following day, when Elise walked into the shelter, Kim beckoned to her. She placed her hand over the mouthpiece of the telephone and mouthed, "Meg wants to see you."

Elise nodded and headed for Meg's office.

"Good news, kiddo," Meg said. "Penny's gonna make it, and she's asking to see you."

A great surge of relief, followed by a flood of happiness, washed over Elise. She knew her smile reflected both. "That's wonderful. I'll go when my shift is finished."

"You can go now, if you want."

As eager as Elise was to see Penny, she still decided to wait until that evening. She had a lot of work to do at the shelter; she didn't want to get even more behind. Besides, she had no plans for the evening. All she'd do would be sit and think about Dev and what had gone wrong between them last night.

She wasn't going to see him again. She knew it. He wouldn't visit the shelter, and he wouldn't call her. She sighed. Obviously something had happened last night, and since she wasn't sure what it was, she couldn't very well do anything about it.

For the rest of the day, she forced herself to put Dev out of her mind. When her shift was over, she climbed into her car and headed straight for the hospital.

Thirty minutes later she was seated next to Penny's bed, holding Penny's hand and smiling into the pale gray-eyed gaze of the diminutive woman.

"I look awful, don't I?" Penny said.

She *did* look awful. Her face was a riot of colors: black, purple, blue and a sickly looking green. She'd had to have several stitches through her right eyebrow, and two of her front teeth were broken. Her upper lip was still swollen, and her right cheek had a long, nasty gash across it.

But those weren't the worst of her injuries. As the nurse had explained to Elise before she came into Penny's room, her most serious injuries were internal. Evidently Bert, her husband, had pummeled her abdomen, and in the process, ruptured her spleen. She also had several cracked ribs and a punctured lung. "You'll look better soon," Elise finally said, forcing herself to answer without giving away her helpless anger.

Penny smiled, then grimaced. "It hurts to smile." She squeezed Elise's hand a little tighter. "Thanks for lying about the way I look. You're a good friend."

"I try to be."

"I...I'm sorry I disappointed you," Penny said.

"Oh, Penny..."

"I wouldn't have blamed you if you never wanted to see me again."

"You know I'd never feel that way. I know, better than just about anyone, exactly where you're coming from."

Penny nodded. "You'd think I'd've learned my lesson by now, wouldn't you?" Her face twisted, and a tear slid down her cheek. "What's wrong with me, Elise? Why'm I so stupid? Bert's right, you know. I *am* stupid. It's my own damned fault this has happened again. I should've never gone back."

Elise wanted to cry, to scream, to vent some of her rage. Instead she fought against her impotent fury. Getting angry, shouting, wouldn't help Penny. Wouldn't help anything. She tightened her hold on Penny's hand. "Listen to me," she said calmly. "And don't interrupt."

Penny's eyes widened, and she fastened her gaze onto Elise's face.

"You...are not to blame." Elise bit each word off, emphasizing its importance. "You were never to blame. The worst thing you did was believing that Bert would change. That all you had to do was forgive him, and go back, and try harder, and somehow, things would be different."

Penny wet her lips, but her gaze never wavered.

"Do you understand me, Penny?"

Penny nodded.

"Bert is the sick person. You're the victim of his sickness."

Penny swallowed, and her gaze slid away.

"Penny..." Elise waited patiently until Penny looked at her again. "Penny, promise me you won't go back. Promise me that when you get out of the hospital, you'll come back to the shelter, let us help you find a job, get an apartment and get on your feet."

"Yes," Penny whispered.

"I mean it. Promise me."

"I promise."

They talked for over an hour, and when Elise finally picked up her purse and bent over to kiss Penny's cheek lightly, she felt optimistic. She hoped Penny meant what she'd said. She hoped everything would work out all right for her. For all the women who had sought and would seek refuge at the shelter. And for all those who wouldn't come because they were too afraid. Or because they didn't know help was available. That someone cared. All the way home Elise carried on a two-sided conversation, acting out what she'd say to Dev if she had him there with her.

"See, Dev? Do you see? It's so important that you understand!"

Finally she ran out of steam. A few blocks from her apartment, she decided she couldn't face an evening alone, either. She turned around and headed for Lianna's house.

"Boy, am I glad to see you," Lianna said, opening the door wide. "I tried to call you. Last night, then again this afternoon. Where've you been?"

"Last night I had a date, and—"

"A date!" Lianna's eyes sparkled with curiosity. She shoved her shoulder-length hair back from her face and inclined her head toward the kitchen. "C'mon back. Have you eaten? I want to hear everything." The words tumbled out. "Charlie's out, thank God."

Elise followed her cousin toward the kitchen. Lianna, as usual, looked great. It didn't seem to matter what she wore, she always looked good. Of course, it helped that she was tall and slender, that she had the kind of figure every woman wished for: long legs, flat stomach and just the right amount of curves. She wore clothes well. Today she had selected a loose cotton sundress in fire-engine red, big red earrings in the shape of a triangle, and flat sandals. An outfit like that would have overpowered Elise, and she knew it. She looked down at her own mint-green skirt and matching sleeveless sweater. So bland. So...boring. She envied Lianna her casual grace and her sense of style. She could throw anything on, and it would look good. Elise sighed. Oh, well. No sense wishing for things she couldn't have.

Over something Lianna called Chicken Spectacular, a combination of chicken, tortillas, cheese, and all kinds of spicy, delicious vegetables and condiments, Elise told her about the date with Dev.

"What do you think set him off? Obviously something you said bothered him for him to leave like that." Lianna smiled. "'Cause it's obvious to me that the guy's *very* attracted to you."

Elise shrugged. "I thought so, too. But now...I don't know. The only thing I said was that if we can't let go of our anger against the people who wrong us, we're scarred ourselves. Do you think *that* could've upset him?"

Lianna pursed her lips, then said dramatically, "Hmm... maybe the sexy professor has a deep, dark secret in his past, and you reminded him of that. Maybe he's harbored hate in his heart. Maybe he's planning a terrible revenge."

"Oh, come on...be serious!"

"I *am* serious!"

Elise sighed. "What does it really matter, anyway? I wasn't planning to get involved with him, or anything. I mean, he just asked me out to talk about the shelter, and we *did* that. I might as well quit wasting my energy thinking about him."

"Listen, cuz, if you think that man asked you out just to talk about the shelter, you're even more innocent and naive than I thought you were."

Elise wished Lianna was right. She wished...oh, shoot, she wasn't sure what she wished. She had no business thinking about Sloan Devereaux. She had no time, no energy, for a romantic relationship. She simply wasn't ready for a man in her life. Not now. And there was no use having regrets about it, either. Sometimes people met people at the wrong time, and things didn't have a prayer of working out between them. She might as well accept that. She and Dev had met at the wrong time. They had absolutely no future together.

So why did she still harbor a sneaky little hope that she'd see him again?

To take Lianna's mind—and her own—off Dev, Elise said, "Why were you trying to call me?"

Lianna grimaced. "Oh, yeah. Don't remind me."

"Remind you of what?"

Lianna sighed wearily. "You know, sometimes I wonder why I ever wanted to have a child."

"Oh, come on! Charlie's a great kid. You wouldn't give her up for anything."

"I know, I know, but sometimes even the greatest kids can be a real worry, you know?"

"What happened?" Elise wiped her mouth with her napkin and laid it down. She patted her stomach. "That was delicious."

"Thanks. What happened is, last night Charlie asked me if I would allow her to get a prescription for birth control pills."

"What!"

"Yeah," Lianna said, frowning, "that was my reaction, too."

Elise sat back in her chair, stunned. Charlie. Charlie was just a kid. She was only fourteen, for heaven's sake. She was fresh and young and innocent and untouched. Just the way she should be. Even the thought of Charlie having . . . sex . . . with some groping, pimply-faced teenager, or worse, with some experienced, knowing, *older* boy made Elise feel sick to her stomach. "Wh-what did you say?" she finally said.

"I said I'd allow her to have birth control pills when hell froze over. That if she so much as *thought* about having sex now or anytime soon, I'd throttle her."

"And what did Charlie say?"

Lianna chuckled. "She said, and I quote, 'Well, Mom, I just thought I'd *ask!*'"

Elise laughed, too. But then, when their laughter subsided, she said, "But, Li, if she asked, there was a reason."

"Oh, I know. She and I talked for a long time. She told me that Becka—you know Becka Chiasson, don't you?— has been having sex with her boyfriend for almost a year now."

"Oh, God..." Elise breathed. Becka Chiasson had turned fifteen just the previous month because Elise remembered Charlie going to Becka's birthday party and sighing about not turning fifteen herself until September. "Do Becka's parents know? Is she on the Pill?"

"From what Charlie said, her mother is the one who suggested she get a prescription."

Elise shook her head. "Why would she do that? Make it easy for Becka? Actually encourage her?"

"Well, don't judge her too harshly, because I don't know what I'd do if I thought Charlie was likely to have sex despite what we talked about. I mean, I wouldn't want her to take any chances."

"Yes, but with AIDS and everything, wouldn't it be better to try to get these kids to use condoms? I mean, if they're going to have sex, why not get them to protect themselves on all counts?"

Lianna nodded. "You're right, of course. Charlie and I talked about that, too. Oh, God, 'Lise, I just pray she grows up without messing up her life. I hope that I've taught her something, that she'll be sensible and make good decisions for herself.''

"I hope so, too. But if she doesn't, if she makes a bad choice along the way, just knowing that you'll be here for her is important," Elise said, reaching across and taking Lianna's hand.

They smiled at each other.

"I love you," Lianna said. "I'm so glad we found each other."

"I love you, too."

Dev almost didn't go to the lake on Monday. He was halfway there, and he almost turned around and went back to his office. It was hot, he told himself. Too hot to sit and eat lunch outdoors.

Oh, hell, who was he kidding? He just didn't want to take a chance on running into Elise. The minute he admitted that to himself, he settled down. He *would* go to the lake. No woman, no matter how attractive or how desirable or how appealing, was going to scare him away, cause him to change his life. It was no big deal. He'd go to the lake the way he always did. Eat his lunch. Commune with nature. And if Elise showed up, so what? They were both adults, weren't they? He wasn't afraid of her, was he?

Within minutes he was seated on his usual bench. He unwrapped the egg salad sandwich Daisy had packed for him and began to eat it. He watched several canoe loads of students pass by. They were shouting and laughing, carefree and young.

And then he saw her.

She was walking toward him. His heart caught in his throat as he watched her. She looked beautiful. She was wearing a sundress in a shade of blue so deep it almost looked like purple. Her hair bounced around her shoulders with each step she took. As she came closer, he saw that her tanned legs were bare, and she had tan espadrilles on her narrow feet. Silver earrings dangled from her ears, catching the sun as it filtered its way through the cypress trees.

She stopped a few feet away from his bench.

His gaze met hers. Why did she have to look so beautiful?

"Hello, Dev," she said softly. Her mouth looked soft and warm as it curved into a gentle smile. Her lips were full and pink and inviting.

"Hi." His heart was beating too fast. He had an almost irresistible urge to stand up, gather her in his arms and kiss her. See if that mouth tasted as sweet as it looked.

"Do you mind if I sit down?" She glanced at his bench.

"No, no, of course not." He moved over, making room for her.

She sat only inches away. She smelled like wildflowers and soap and sunshine. Her hair glistened in the dappled sunlight, as sleek as ebony. She turned, her eyes dark and mysterious as she studied him gravely. "I almost didn't come today," she finally said.

He wanted to touch her. He wanted to touch her more than almost anything he'd wanted in a long time. Her nose looked sunburned, and there were several freckles high on her cheeks. There was also a fine sheen of perspiration across the top of her lip, and he wanted to take his forefinger and touch the tiny drops. He could hear his heart beating, feel his blood rushing through his veins, and an ache started deep in his belly.

He wanted this woman.

She scared the hell out of him with her passion and her honesty and her courage.

Still he wanted her.

He had sworn he would never again get involved with a woman who would put him second—to anything.

Still he wanted her.

"Dev?"

He took her hand and felt its warmth. Her fingers curled around his. He smiled. "I'm very glad you did come. I wanted to see you."

On Wednesday, Elise shared Dev's bench at Cypress Lake again. On Thursday they had breakfast together. On Friday they met at the lake again. Each time they were together, she felt closer to him. The connection between them and the mutual attraction intensified with each meeting.

She had kind of expected him to invite her out for another evening, but he didn't. He seemed to be waiting, for what she wasn't sure. But she wasn't really disappointed. In fact, she was relieved. She still wasn't sure she could handle a relationship right now, and Dev... well, she didn't know what his reservations were. During their conversations at the lake and during their breakfast together, they didn't talk about anything very personal. The only personal topic he brought up was his increasing worry over his daughter, who seemed to be changing and growing away from him. He told Elise he wasn't quite sure what to do about that.

She told him about Lianna and Charlie and the issue of the birth control pills. He laughed mirthlessly and told her that his daughter had mentioned that kids her age were having sex... as well as babies.

"It's a terrible worry, because I can't watch her all the time. I have to trust her."

"If you've been open with her, talked with her, that's all you can do, Dev," Elise said.

"I don't know. Sometimes I think I'll never be able fulfill all her needs. How can I? I'm a man, and she's growing into a young woman."

Elise wanted to ask about his ex-wife, but she didn't dare. Without being told, she knew Dev would close up. She wondered if he ever talked about his ex-wife, to anyone.

On Friday he asked her if she'd like to see a movie with him that evening. "My daughter has finally made a friend at our town house complex," he said, "and she's been invited to go to a concert with her and her parents."

"I'd love to go to a movie," Elise said, pushing aside her lingering doubts. There was no better way to find out if she wanted to continue seeing Dev than to go out with him, she rationalized.

He took her to see a popular comedy. He bought her popcorn, and they laughed aloud at the zany antics of the actors, and every once in a while he'd glance at her, and she'd feel his gaze, and when she turned his way, they'd share a smile and her heart would flutter.

Afterward, as they walked out of the theater, he casually took her hand. "That was fun," he said. "I haven't seen a movie since I moved to Lafayette."

"It *was* fun," Elise said, trying not to notice how good his hand felt holding hers.

"Are you hungry? Would you like to get a hamburger or something?"

"Thanks, but I'm not hungry."

They had reached his car, and he had to let go of her hand to unlock it. But then he touched her again when he helped her into the passenger side, and even this light touch sent a warm shiver of awareness down her spine.

I should have pretended to be hungry, she thought as, too soon, they pulled into the parking lot of her apartment complex. She really didn't want the evening to end.

As if he'd read her mind, as he cut the ignition, he said, "I hate for the evening to end." He turned to her, moonlight silvering his hair. "I had a really nice time."

"Me, too."

"You're very easy to be with." With his index finger, he brushed her cheek.

Her breath caught. Her stomach had that hollowed-out feeling again. "Thank you. So are you." *Well, except for what you do to my stomach...*

His finger lingered, then traced a path to her chin, lifting it slightly. Slowly he leaned toward her.

Elise's heart went crazy as his lips descended.

The kiss was light, feathery, whisper-soft. It only lasted a second or two, but that was long enough to tell her she wanted more. Much more. She felt an aching sense of loss when he pulled back.

"We'd better get you inside," he said.

His voice sounded strange—a little rough—or was that her imagination? *More like wishful thinking.*

She waited for him to come around and open her door. She placed her hand in his, and he helped her out. He didn't let go of her hand, though. After a moment, she looked up. Their gazes met. "Elise," he said softly. His grip on her hand tightened.

She swallowed. She knew she should withdraw her hand, say good-night and walk toward the stairway leading to her apartment. That's what she *should* do, but it wasn't what she wanted to do.

"What are you doing tomorrow night?"

"I...I don't have any plans."

"Would you like to have dinner with me?"

She knew if she had any sense, she'd say no. "Yes."

He smiled. "Why don't you think about where you'd like to go, and I'll call you tomorrow?"

"Better yet," she suggested—thinking, *Oh, shoot, I might as well go for broke as long as I'm not using good sense, anyway*— "why don't you come here, to my apartment, and let me feed you? After all, I owe you a dinner."

Then she got panicky. What was she doing? Hadn't she decided it wouldn't be wise to get involved with him? She'd made so many bad choices in her life. She hated to make another one. If she were really smart, she'd stop seeing him. She was very afraid her initial assessment of their situation had been right: this was the wrong time for them.

Yet she wanted to keep seeing him.

Even after he'd gone, and she went over everything that had happened that evening, and all her reasons for nipping this relationship in the bud, for pushing him away before she lost the will to push him away, she didn't change her mind.

It might be foolish, but there was something about Dev that drew her. Something that cried out to the nurturing woman in her. Something she wanted, needed, to explore further.

On Saturday she asked Meg if she could leave the shelter early, and Meg said okay.

Now it was Saturday night and almost time for Dev to arrive. Elise put the finishing touches to her table, arranging flowers in a cut-glass vase and stepping back to admire her handiwork.

The table looked nice. It was covered with a mauve cloth and matching lace-trimmed napkins. Elise knew men didn't care about things such as lace-trimmed napkins, but *she* did. Mauve candles, crystal candle holders and flowers from Lisette's garden combined to make an elegant setting.

Everything was ready. She had taken a lot of time with dinner, coached every step of the way by Lianna. "It's best if you make something simple," Lianna said. "My recipe for Shrimp Creole is fail-safe. Anyone can make it, even you.''

"I hope you're right," Elise said.

"Trust me."

She followed Lianna's instructions to the letter, and she had to admit, the Creole *did* turn out well. Even her rice didn't stick to the bottom of the pan, the way it usually did. And anyone could make a salad and buy a loaf of French bread, although she'd gone out of her way to buy the bread at Poupart's because she wanted the best.

Elise looked at the clock. Ten minutes until Dev would arrive. She hurried back to her bedroom and surveyed herself in the full-length mirror on the outside of her closet door. She picked up her hairbrush and brushed her hair again. Always curly, it had gone haywire because she'd been rushing around and had gotten hot.

She looked nice, she thought. Not long and sophisticated like Lianna, but nice in her own way. She was wearing her favorite dress—a teal cotton with a gently flaring skirt and square neck. And she'd splurged on soft leather flats the same color.

Satisfied that she looked as good as she was going to, she walked back to the living room to wait for Dev.

"That was a wonderful dinner," Dev said.

Elise smiled happily. "Thanks." Everything had gone so well. The food had tasted delicious, and Dev was so attentive. More than attentive, admit it, she told herself as she stood and reached for his empty plate.

He stood, too.

"No, you sit. I'll do it."

"I insist upon helping." He smiled down at her, and the tempo of her pulse rate accelerated. That smile of his would be her undoing, she knew it.

She walked around and into the kitchen with her load of dishes. He was right behind her. She set her dishes down on the counter, then turned, and just as she did, he leaned around to set his dishes on the counter, too.

They collided.

Startled, Elise looked up, expecting Dev to back up and move away.

He didn't.

Instead, his green-gold gaze held hers for a long moment, then he carefully and slowly set the plates down. His gaze traveled down, fastening on her mouth.

Elise's heart thudded up into her throat.

He was going to kiss her.

The knowledge sizzled between them until the very air crackled with it.

He touched her bare shoulders, and a shudder raced down her spine.

It was so quiet in the kitchen she could hear her own heart beating. His head dipped, and Elise closed her eyes. When his lips settled against hers, something warm and wonderful and delicious twisted through her. She sighed against his mouth and lifted her arms to twine them around his neck.

He tugged her closer, fitting her body against his so that she could feel all its hard lines. She could also feel how much he wanted her, and an answering want fired her belly as his tongue gently invaded her mouth.

Desire spiraled through her as the kiss deepened and the seconds ticked away. His hands roamed her back, finding each curve and dip. They settled against her bottom, cupping her and holding her against his heat.

Elise stopped thinking. All she could do was feel. Long dormant fires kindled inside her until she was burning everywhere, full of needs and wants she hadn't even known she'd possessed.

"Elise," Dev groaned against her mouth as he finally broke the kiss. "I want you."

His words jolted Elise out of the haze of desire that had nearly overwhelmed her. Her reaction to Dev's kiss shocked her. What was wrong with her? It wasn't as if she'd never been kissed before. Why, she'd practically climbed all over him. Embarrassed, she pushed him away.

"Elise..." His voice sounded ragged.

Elise closed her eyes and took a deep breath. Then she looked up. Oh, God, she thought. I want him, too. Badly. But going to bed with Sloan Devereaux is a very bad idea. "Please, Dev, let's stop this right now, okay?"

He backed up, seemed almost to shake himself. "You're right. I came on too strong."

"No, it's not your fault. I don't want you to think that. It's just that if I've learned anything, I've learned that actions carry consequences, and if you're not sure you can live with the consequences, you'd better not act. I...I think we should wait."

He nodded, but he didn't meet her gaze.

Oh, dear. She was afraid she'd hurt his feelings. She touched his arm. "Dev—"

"Look, it's okay. I misinterpreted the signals, that's all." He smiled ruefully.

"Dev, please. I feel I should explain." She tugged at his arm. "Let's go sit down in the living room."

Elise chose her words carefully. A man's ego could be fragile, she knew that. Heck, her own ego was fragile. Anyone's would be if they thought they were being rejected. "Dev, I'm going to be as honest as I can be. I...it's hard for me to say some things, but I'm going to try." She twisted her hands in her lap, nervous and unsure.

"You didn't misinterpret any signals," she continued softly. "I did want you. I do want you. But Dev, going to bed together would be wrong for me. I . . . I'm not the sort of woman who can indulge in casual sex. I wish I were sometimes, but I'm not. For me, there has to be a total sharing. Not just a physical bonding, but a real connection." She shrugged helplessly. "I know it sounds corny, but I'm looking for something deeper than a sexual relationship. Although it's flattering to be desired, I need more. I need commitment and understanding. I need to be needed . . . and loved."

Something flickered in his eyes.

Encouraged, Elise said, "You're not ready to share yourself with me, Dev. Why, you haven't told me anything about yourself. The closest we've gotten to talking about your personal life is the little bit you've told me about Daisy. I've told you everything about my past, my feelings, my hopes, my plans. I don't know anything important about you." Sad now, realizing how right she was, she finished by saying, "I'm sorry, Dev. I'm sorry if I led you on or gave you the wrong idea. But I just can't do this."

Chapter Eight

Daisy was worried about her dad. Actually she guessed he'd been acting weird since Saturday night.

Since his date with Elise Cantrelle.

"Hmm," she said aloud, frowning. She was on her way to the shelter and running late, so she pedaled her bike faster. Even though it was really hot today, and she felt all sticky, she hurried because she didn't want to be late for her shift. She was supposed to be there at one o'clock, and it was almost one now. She concentrated on the traffic as she made the final crossing that brought the shelter into view.

She sped down the street and into the parking lot, braked, then hopped off. Walking to the bike rack, she bent down and wound her lock through the spokes of her bike, then attached it to the rack, clicking it shut.

Her mind was still full of thoughts about her father and his bewildering behavior as she walked up the steps and into the building. Had something happened on his date with

Elise Cantrelle that had caused him to be acting so funny? She hoped not. When he'd first told her he was taking Elise out, she'd been a little scared because her first thought was, what if he found out Daisy was working at the shelter? But she quickly realized that was silly; he wouldn't find out unless she told him, and she *would* tell him one of these days. So then she was really happy about him dating Elise, had even started thinking how great it would be if they really liked each other. So what was wrong with her father?

That's why his weird behavior was bothering Daisy so much. It wasn't like her dad to be so preoccupied. Several times, over the past couple of days, when Daisy had asked him a question or tried to talk to him, he'd hardly heard her. Something was definitely wrong. She wished she knew what it was.

Daisy worried her bottom lip; she hoped *she* hadn't done anything to upset her dad. No. That was silly. He would say something if she had anything to do with his behavior. Sighing, she walked through the shelter, waving to people as she went, but her mind was still absorbed with thoughts of her father. But when she reached the nursery where she'd been assigned to work with the preschool-aged children, she convinced herself she'd have to try to forget about her dad, at least for now. She'd think about this problem again later.

"Well, hi, Marguerite," said Theresa, the supervisor of the nursery. "You look hot."

Daisy wiped her forehead with the back of her hand. "Yeah, it feels like it's one hundred out there."

"I think it's pretty close," Theresa said, grinning.

Daisy looked around, smiling at the kids in the room, all of whom looked up at her. Right now they only had seven children under six at the shelter, and only five of them were in the nursery this afternoon. She walked around, touching heads and hands. "Hi, guys." Just as she finished greeting the kids, a tall girl who looked to be about Daisy's age walked into the room from the opposite end. She was awfully pretty, Daisy thought, with her long, red hair and great figure. She was wearing white shorts and a bright green T-shirt. Daisy had always wished she were tall with long legs like this girl. The girl eyed Daisy curiously.

"Marguerite, this is Charlie, a new volunteer," Theresa said, getting up from the floor where she'd been helping a three-year-old fashion a house of blocks.

Charlie. What a great name. "Hi," Daisy said, feeling suddenly shy as she remembered how the kids at her town house complex had treated her.

"Hi," Charlie said. Then she smiled, revealing a mouth full of braces.

Daisy's shyness evaporated in the face of the friendly grin and the braces. Charlie wasn't perfect, either.

"I was counting on you showing Charlie the ropes," Theresa said.

"Oh, okay." This was the first time Daisy had been asked to teach anyone else, and it was a nice feeling to know Theresa trusted her enough to do it right.

For the next hour or so, Daisy showed Charlie where everything was kept and how they did things. She introduced her to all the little kids and helped her when she wasn't sure what to do when Kevin, a chubby little two-year-old, wet his pants. By three o'clock, Daisy felt as if she'd known Charlie forever. They'd already discussed school, boys, makeup, sex—in whispers, of course—and their parents. The two of them talked as they helped Kevin and the other children make things out of clay.

"So what made you come here and volunteer?" Daisy asked.

Charlie smiled. "My cousin works here, and she talked my mom into letting me help out."

"Really? Which one's your cousin?"

"Her name's Elise. Have you met her?"

Elise! Daisy could hardly believe it. "Yeah, I've met her."

"You seem surprised," Charlie said.

"Yeah, I am."

"Why?"

"I don't know. I guess because Elise is my favorite person here. She's so nice."

"She *is* pretty neat, isn't she?" Charlie agreed. "Actually, even though she's closer to my mom's age than mine, Elise and I can talk about anything. I really like her."

Daisy nodded, still stunned by the revelation that her new friend was Elise's cousin. For a moment, she was tempted to tell Charlie about her dad and Elise, but then she thought better of it. Even though it would be great to confide in someone, it might be a good idea to wait awhile. After all, she didn't know anything about Charlie. She might be a blabbermouth.

"Elise and my mom are best friends, too, so we see her a lot," Charlie continued breezily. "She's always comin' over for dinner, and she and my mom take me to the movies and stuff."

Daisy already knew that Charlie's mom and dad were divorced, like hers, and that Charlie lived with her mom, who ran a catering business. Unlike Daisy, though, Charlie visited her dad often. From the way Charlie talked, Daisy could see she really loved both her parents, even though she'd admitted that her dad had "been a real skunk" to her mother.

Daisy wondered what it would be like to be like Charlie: tall, really thin, really pretty and with a mother to talk to as well as a father. And on top of all that, a cousin like Elise. Boy, some girls were so lucky. Not that Daisy didn't love her dad. She did. But still . . . she thought wistfully.

For the rest of the afternoon, even while she talked to Charlie, Daisy daydreamed about being a part of Charlie's family. She hoped her dad and Elise hadn't had another argument Saturday night, because she couldn't think of anything more wonderful than him and Elise getting together. Imagine. They could be like a real family. Plus, she'd be Charlie's cousin, too. Then when Elise and Charlie's mom went to the movies, she and Charlie would go with them.

She grinned just thinking about it.

"What are you grinning about?" Dev said. He had just come home from school, and Daisy, a happy smile on her face, was sitting at the kitchen table, staring out the window, and doodling on her notebook.

She jumped. "Oh, Dad! I didn't hear you come in."

"Doesn't surprise me. You looked as if you were off in another world somewhere."

Big sigh. "Yeah, I was just thinking about...things." Her small face still held a rapt expression, which she made an obvious effort to shake off as she turned to him expectantly.

Dev smothered a grin. He was glad Daisy still acted like a kid sometimes, despite her recent bid for independence. Guilt pricked him, though, as he realized he hadn't been paying much attention to her for the past week. He'd been so preoccupied by what had happened between him and Elise on Saturday night, he hadn't been able to think about much else. "Do you want to talk about any of those 'things'?" he said lightly. He'd learned lately that putting pressure on his daughter no longer worked—not like it had when she was little.

Daisy looked up, her clear gaze fastening on his. "Yeah, I . . . I've been wanting to ask you something."

"Well, ask away." Dev pulled out one of the kitchen chairs and straddled it. He smiled encouragingly.

She hesitated momentarily, then blurted out, "You and Elise Cantrelle didn't have a fight or anything on Saturday night, did you?"

Her question took him completely off guard. He didn't know what he'd been expecting, but it wasn't this. For a moment, he was at a loss, but he quickly recaptured his equilibrium. "Why would you think a thing like that?"

Daisy shrugged, but her gaze never left his. "You've been acting weird ever since, so I thought something must have happened."

"I've had a lot on my mind lately. I guess I didn't realize I was acting weird."

"Is something wrong at work?"

Dev squirmed a little under that clear-eyed look. He wasn't quite sure what to say. He and Daisy had always been honest with each other. But there were some things a man simply didn't want to discuss with his child. Shouldn't *have* to discuss with his child. He silently apologized to Daisy and told himself that when she reached adulthood, she would understand. "Nothing's really wrong, but this assignment is more complicated than I thought it would be. I guess I've been thinking about it a lot."

"Oh, good," Daisy said, a sudden smile lighting her face. "I was afraid... well, it doesn't matter." She stood up, reached for her notebook and pen. Once more, her gaze met his. "I *really* like...liked Elise Cantrelle." Pink stained her cheeks, and she ducked her head, then mumbled, "I...I've got homework to do. I think I'll do it in my room, okay?"

Dev sat at the table for a long time after she'd gone upstairs. Daisy was changing right before his eyes. He wasn't sure he'd ever understand her thought processes. Why had she seemed so embarrassed after saying she liked Elise

Cantrelle? She'd already told him that a couple of weeks ago.

As they had dozens of times in the past few days, his thoughts drifted to Elise. He admired her for her traditional values. He *had* come on too strong Saturday night. But that wasn't his problem. His problem was, she could become too important to him, and she'd made it very, very clear that nothing was going to come of their relationship unless certain criteria were met.

Criteria he wasn't sure he'd ever be able to meet.

Wasn't even sure he wanted to *try* to meet.

Dev leaned his head down on his folded arms. He closed his eyes wearily. He wasn't sure of anything anymore.

He laughed softly. That wasn't quite true. He was sure of one thing.

He was sure that if he decided it was best not to pursue a relationship with Elise, wiping her out of his mind would be one of the hardest things he'd ever have to do.

Elise had avoided the lake the entire week. She told herself she was giving Dev some space, some time to think about their fledgling relationship, some time to decide if he wanted to go forward or forget about it entirely. But she knew those weren't the only reasons she'd been avoiding him.

She'd been avoiding him because she was scared.

Scared she wouldn't be able to keep resisting him if she saw him.

Scared she'd get herself involved in something she couldn't control.

Scared she'd end up falling in love with him and getting hurt.

Badly.

She had come a long way in the past few years, but Elise knew she was still too vulnerable in too many areas—especially those areas concerning relationships with men.

She sighed as she loaded clothes into the washer early Saturday morning. Down in her gut, she knew Dev was wrong for her. After all, what did she really know about him?

She knew he'd been married but nothing else about that past relationship. No name. No history. Nothing. He'd made it clear he didn't intend to talk about his past. He'd also made it clear he still felt bitter and resentful, even though he'd obviously been divorced a long time.

She knew he had a fourteen-year-old daughter named Daisy and that he worried about being a good parent. That was commendable, but she had no idea how he'd come to be sole custodian of his teenage daughter or anything else about their life together.

She knew he'd been born in Louisiana, moved to New York with his parents when he was twelve. She also knew he harbored bitter feelings toward his mother from his one cynical comment about her and her third marriage.

She knew he now understood and even empathized with her on the subject of abused women, but his understanding and empathy only went so far; he still hadn't taken her up on her invitation to visit the shelter. It was as if he thought it was all right to understand the issue on an intellectual level, but refused to let it involve him on an emotional level.

She also knew he wanted her.

She twisted the knob to start the wash cycle, then opened the dryer and began folding clothes.

She really knew very little about Dev. The things she knew were superficial things. Even after all the time they'd spent together so far and all the talking they'd done—talks in which she'd bared her soul, she thought ruefully—Dev was still an enigma, a stranger to her in all the important ways.

Her hands stilled.

Dev had shared nothing important with her. No matter how much she might wish things were different, there was an enormous barrier between them—one she didn't know if they'd ever be able to cross.

Sighing deeply once more, she continued with her task.

She'd made the right decision.

Until Dev could share himself completely—not just his body, but his mind and heart and soul—Elise could share no more.

"It's your move," Gerald Eggleston said.

Dev frowned, reached for the knight, then hesitated. He and Gerald, a professor in the English Department at USL, had fallen into the habit of playing chess on Sunday nights. Normally Dev enjoyed this chance to exchange ideas and challenge his brain cells, but tonight, like every day this past week, he was unable to concentrate. Sighing, knowing it wasn't his best move, he picked up the knight and advanced it.

Gerald grinned, made a move, grinned more widely and said, "Checkmate." He looked enormously satisfied with himself. "You weren't on your game tonight, old man. Something wrong?"

Dev leaned back in his chair and rubbed his forehead. "No. Not really."

"Not really? That's an evasive answer if I ever heard one." Gerald's gray eyes became thoughtful, and the grin slid off his face. "Want to talk about it?"

Dev wished he *could* talk about it, but he'd never been one to share his deepest feelings. There was something too uncomfortable about spilling your guts out; it left you too open, too vulnerable, like an army in the middle of the desert—totally exposed to the enemy. He shook his head, pushed back from the table and stood up. "No. I think I'm just gonna call it a night. I'm tired, and I've got a long day tomorrow."

Gerald nodded. "If you change your mind, I'm always willing to listen."

"Thanks. I appreciate that."

But Dev knew he wouldn't change his mind. This was a decision he had to make himself. And he'd better hurry up and make it, because all this thinking was driving him nuts.

Monday night Elise decided that it was time to get back to her normal routine, Dev or no Dev. Whether or not she heard from him by Wednesday afternoon, she was going to Cypress Lake again. It was really silly to keep avoiding him. If she were no longer a coward she'd better stop acting like one. That decision made, she immediately felt better. It was always better to be doing something positive. Besides, she knew it was up to her to set the tone of their future relationship. If all they were going to be was casual friends who saw each other at the lake occasionally, so be it. She could handle that, couldn't she?

Still thinking about her decision, she walked into the bathroom and snapped on the light. She had just squeezed toothpaste on her toothbrush when the phone rang.

"Oh, shoot," she said, putting down the brush. "Who's calling this late? It must be Lianna." She sprinted to the phone, snatching it up on the third ring. "Hello?" she said breathlessly.

"Hello, Elise."

Her heart began to pound. *Bam. Bam. Bam.* "Hello, Dev." Gosh, she sounded normal. Her voice didn't waver or anything.

"How have you been?"

"Fine. How have you been?"

"Okay. Listen, I . . . uh . . . I'd like to see you."

Elise swallowed. Hope flared like the sudden flickering of a candle that had almost sputtered out. "Would you?"

"Yes, very much."

Elise was afraid to let the hope expand and take over. She'd had too many hopes crushed not to be cautious, especially where her emotions were concerned. And her emotions were definitely concerned when it came to Dev. In that moment, she realized just how important he had become. Just how much she'd been hoping he would call. Just how much she wanted to continue seeing him. "I . . . nothing has changed, Dev." Gathering strength, she went on. "What I mean is, I still feel the same way."

"Yes, I was sure you did."

His quiet answer allowed the hope to flare brighter.

"I still want to see you, Elise," he added softly.

"All right. When?"

"How about tomorrow night?"

"All right," she said again. She felt absurdly close to tears, and she wasn't sure why. "I work until six tomorrow night, though."

"How about if I pick you up at eight? We'll go to dinner and we'll talk."

After they'd hung up, Elise stood by the phone for a long time. Her reaction to Dev's call told her something—something she really hadn't understood before.

She was more than halfway in love with him.

At three o'clock Tuesday afternoon Elise had just finished teaching a group of women how to balance a checkbook. She walked upstairs to the small lounge where the volunteers who worked at the shelter went for their breaks.

She walked into the room and smiled. Charlie and Marguerite, giggling and whispering, sat together on the couch. Both looked up as she entered.

"Hi, cuz," said Charlie, grinning.

"Hi, Elise," said Marguerite, her smile just as welcoming.

"Well, hi, you two. What're you doing? Talking about boys?"

The girls laughed and nodded. "How'd you guess?" Charlie asked.

"Hey, I was fourteen once, too. Not that any boys noticed!"

Marguerite frowned. "Really? You mean, you didn't have a boyfriend, either?"

Elise shook her head. "Nope."

"But why not? I mean...you're so pretty and everything," Marguerite said.

"Yeah, cuz," Charlie drawled, "why not?"

Elise shrugged and walked over to the soft drink machine. She inserted her money and punched the button for a diet soda. The can hit the tray with a thunk, and she reached for it. "I was really shy. I never knew what to say to boys, so they didn't hang around me much." She popped the top and took a long swallow of the frosty beverage.

"I can't believe you were shy," Charlie said.

"I can," Marguerite said. She ducked her head. "I'm shy around boys, too."

Elise smiled and sat down in the chair closest to Marguerite. She really liked the teenager. There was something especially appealing about her. "Don't worry too much about it," she said. "The trick is to ask them a question about themselves. All boys love to talk about themselves."

Charlie nodded sagely. "Mom says that, too."

"Well," Elise answered, "your mom's right."

"Mom also says you're dating that professor, the one you had that disagreement with."

"I've only gone out with him once," Elise said hurriedly. "And that was because he wanted to know more about the shelter." She pushed down the flash of guilt. She wasn't really lying. The second time they'd seen each other was at her apartment, so technically she'd told them the truth.

"Did he try to kiss you good-night?" Charlie asked innocently.

"Charlie! What a question!"

Charlie grinned, poking Marguerite, who seemed avidly interested in whatever Elise might be about to say. Elise wished the conversation hadn't taken this turn. She had no intention of discussing what Dev did or did not do on their date, but she also didn't want to make a big thing out of it. Knowing kids, they'd just think the worst.

"Well? Did he?" Charlie's eyes twinkled.

"It's really none of your business, you know."

Charlie laughed. "That means he must have, or you would have said 'No.'"

"Charlotte Ann Nicholls, you're being a real brat, you know that?" Elise said, half teasing, half serious. "Why do you want to know such a thing, anyway?"

"Because we were just talking about whether it was right to let a boy kiss you on the first date or not. That's why." She grinned again. "So we need to know what you think."

"What did your mother say?" Elise countered.

"She said a first date was too soon for kissing." Charlie's smile had turned sheepish.

"Oh, you stinker! You're trying to put me on the spot with your mother, aren't you?" Elise glanced at Marguerite. "What did *your* mother say?"

The teenager flushed. "I . . . I don't have a mother."

"Oh, I'm sorry, honey. I didn't know." Oh, darn. She wished she'd known. Sighing, she stood up. "Listen, kids, I've got to get back downstairs."

As she turned to walk out of the room, Charlie said, "Is he a good kisser?"

"Charlie!"

Charlie and Marguerite doubled over laughing. "That must mean he is," Charlie sputtered.

For the rest of the afternoon, every time Elise thought about the girls and Charlie's outrageous question, she couldn't help but laugh.

And relive that really spectacular kiss.

And wonder if there'd ever be another one.

Chapter Nine

Elise paced around her apartment. As usual, she was ready much earlier than she'd needed to be. She was always afraid she might be late, so she usually overcompensated on the time needed to get ready. She'd intended to put her feet up and relax while she waited for Dev to arrive.

She smiled ruefully. Relax. That was actually funny. She was so on edge, she couldn't even sit still, let alone relax.

She walked to the front window, the one that overlooked the parking lot and entrance to her apartment complex. Parting the slats of the miniblinds, she peered out. Her attention was caught by movement in the parking lot below. Several of her neighbors stood in a group, talking. One of them, an athletic-looking young woman, held a beautiful golden retriever on a leash and periodically bent down to pet the dog's head. Elise smiled. She had always wanted a dog. Someday, when she had a house of her own—a house with a yard—she would get a dog, too.

She glanced down at her watch: 7:55. Not much longer to wait before Dev arrived. How would he act? What would he say?

The young woman with the dog waved goodbye to the group and walked off. Elise watched her until she and the dog turned the corner and were no longer in sight. When she finally looked back, she caught a flash of dark blue through the branches of the large persimmon tree that stood sentinel near her unit.

Dev's Mercedes coasted into view.

Elise's heart skittered as she watched him park the car, then climb out. It began to pound harder as her gaze followed him across the lot to the stairs leading up to her apartment.

He looked so handsome, dressed in light-colored jeans and a dark blue open-necked shirt with the sleeves rolled up. The afternoon sun glinted off his dark glasses and fired his brown hair with auburn lights. Elise tried to calm herself by taking deep breaths and adjusting the straps of her yellow-and-white striped sundress. She could hear his footsteps as he climbed the stairs. *Calm down. You don't want him to know how nervous you are, do you?* She smoothed down her skirt, took a last peek at herself in the mirror over the mantel and walked slowly toward the front door.

The doorbell rang.

Elise's heart pounded so hard she was sure Dev could hear it through the door. Her hand trembled as she reached for the lock and twisted it open.

She pulled the door wide and let her gaze meet his. He didn't smile. She wanted to but couldn't. Neither one moved. Neither one looked away. Afterward, she was never sure how long they stood there like that, gazes locked. She wondered if her emotions, so chaotic, so uncertain, showed in her eyes.

Finally Dev broke the silence. "Elise," he said. Then again, "Elise." His voice sounded strange: husky and tender.

Elise reached out her hand to draw him inside. When their fingers touched and their gazes met, it was as if some invisible gate had been opened, and a flood of feeling had been unleashed. He walked inside and kicked the door shut behind him. Then he reached for her, pulling her tightly up against him.

"Elise," he said again, roughly, caressing her cheek, pushing his right hand up into her hair and bringing her head up to meet his. There was no finesse, no delicacy or tenderness in the kiss. His mouth clamped down over hers: hard, hot, demanding, full of unspoken desire and unfulfilled passion.

A lassitude—heavy and erotic—crept through her as she clung to him. The kiss robbed her of any resistance, sweeping away her doubts and fears. She felt the same way she did when she went to the dentist and they gave her gas—as if she were floating away in a sea of sensation. She absorbed the taste of him, the smell of him, the feel of him, as his hands molded her body and his mouth devoured hers.

He touched her everywhere, and she let him, welcomed him. She had no desire to stop him. Her body wanted this, needed this. It had been too long since she'd wanted a man, too long since she'd known this deep fire that was like no other.

Her breasts tingled with an almost unbearable yearning. Her belly ached with an emptiness that cried out to be filled. Her heart thundered in her ears as he plundered her mouth and branded her body, changing it irrevocably.

Finally he tore his mouth away. Voice ragged and thick, he whispered against her ear, "God, I've missed you. All I've done for days is think about you. About kissing you.

And touching you." Elise closed her eyes. His lips—warm and moist—grazed her ear, and a deep shudder raced through her body. With his tongue, he traced the curve of her ear and slid his hands slowly around to cup her breasts on either side. When his thumbs rubbed across their hard nubs her head fell back, and his lips moved to the hollow of her throat, then lower, nuzzling down to the swell of her breasts. She knew that if someone were to set a match to her she would just blaze into the atmosphere and disintegrate into a million tiny points of light. She stopped thinking and absorbed the sensations rocketing through her body.

The only sounds in the room were their soft groans, their rapid breathing, and the loud ticking of her kitchen clock. His hands slipped lower, pulling her body close once more, and she felt the urgency and heat of him against her. She twisted her arms around his neck, and he kissed her again and again—deep, drugging kisses—kisses that were filled with the promise of danger and secret delights. After a long time, he muttered against her mouth, "I want you more than I've ever wanted any woman in my entire life."

The words hit her like a blast of cold water against her skin and effectively doused the flames raging within.

Want.

Not need.

Not love.

Want.

Trembling from the aftershock of Dev's overwhelming kisses and from the harsh dose of reality that had just made its presence known, Elise drew back, pushing his hands away. Trying to regain some semblance of dignity and control, she ducked her head, unwilling and unable to meet his gaze.

"Elise," he protested, reaching for her again.

"No, Dev." She drew a deep breath, willed herself to look up, to meet those smoldering green-gold eyes. She touched her mouth, sore and swollen from his kisses, while his gaze followed the path of her fingers. When he would have gathered her close again, she put her hands up in warning. "No. No more. We have to talk first."

He seemed about to say something else, then stopped. He nodded. "Fair enough."

She managed a shaky smile. "I think I'll just go repair my makeup, okay?"

He rewarded her with a crooked, self-deprecating smile of his own, and his eyes grew soft again, the heat of desire banked for now. "Good idea." The smile expanded, reaching his eyes, and Elise's heart turned over. She loved his smile. She loved— She quickly broke off the thought. "Otherwise, everyone who sees you will know you're a woman who's just been thoroughly kissed."

His voice was full of amusement and more—a tenderness that was almost her undoing.

A tenderness that made her want to launch herself back into his arms, to forget all her worries and live for the moment.

A tenderness that told her that maybe, just maybe, there really was hope for them.

Dev couldn't take his eyes off Elise the entire evening. He'd told himself, before he went to pick her up, that tonight would probably disappoint him. That no one could live up to the expectations he'd built up in his mind. Not even Elise.

But she had.

She'd more than met them. She'd exceeded them.

All he could think about as he watched her eat and drink was how she'd felt in his arms: the sweetness of her mouth;

the firm, soft skin of her arms and back; the enticing roundness of her breasts in his hands; and the way she smelled of flowers and soap and sunshine and warm woman.

He couldn't stop looking at her mouth. He knew he would never be able to get enough of her mouth. He had a feeling that the more he kissed her, the more he would want to kiss her. He couldn't even imagine what it would be like to unbutton that sundress and slip it down. To remove her lacy undergarments—he knew they were lacy without even seeing them—and expose her creamy skin.

His groin ached as desire raged through him, and it was all he could do to keep from standing up and whisking her out of the restaurant and into his car.

He laughed under his breath. He hadn't tried to make out in a car since he was a gawky teenager, but he sure felt like doing it tonight.

"Why are you laughing?" Elise asked, her dark eyes shining in the candlelight. They were sitting at a corner table in a cozy new restaurant near the outskirts of town that Gerald had recommended.

"Are you sure you want to know the answer to that question?"

She smiled a bit uncertainly.

Tenderness washed over him. She was so sweet, just the way a woman should be. He loved her vulnerability, the aura of shyness and uncertainty that came over her at times. "I'm just teasing you," he said. He reached for her hand, covering it with his own. "Actually I was laughing at the picture I'd conjured in my mind." His gaze met hers. "Of the two of us in the back seat of my car, making out like the kids do."

She ducked her head, and he knew she was blushing, even though the candlelight hid the betraying pink.

"Does the thought of that appeal to you at all?" he added softly.

Her head rose slowly. She met his gaze squarely, then murmured, "You know it does."

Dev's heart gave a great lurch. All the amusement drained from him, and he squeezed her hand tighter. "Then let's finish our dinner and get out of here."

She shook her head. "Don't get the wrong idea, Dev. Just because I said the idea held appeal doesn't mean we're going to do it. Remember, we have to talk first," she insisted, withdrawing her hand from his.

Dev sighed. For a minute there, he'd hoped she would let him off the hook. But shy or not, vulnerable or not, Elise had the strength of her convictions—whether they had to do with her work at the shelter or her personal life. She wasn't going to let up. She wouldn't be willing to go a step further until he bared his soul. He wondered if she had any idea what she was asking of him. Opening up, talking about his failures, sharing his fears, had never been his style. He would sooner face a firing squad than put his innermost secrets out there for the world to trample on.

"Dev," she continued softly after a few seconds, "I thought when you called me and said you wanted to see me tonight that you'd already thought about this. That you were saying you understood and were ready to talk to me." Her clear gaze held his. "Was I wrong?"

"No. You weren't wrong."

"Then I'm not sure I understand...."

He smiled ruefully. "It's not complicated. I'm..." *Oh, hell, say it.* "I'm scared, that's all," he blurted.

"Oh, Dev..."

If she didn't quit looking at him like that, he wasn't sure what he'd do. Abruptly, he laid down his fork. "Let's go, okay?'' If he *had* to face the firing squad, he might as well get it over with.

She nodded.

Dev beckoned to their waiter. Five minutes later they were in the car. He started the engine and turned toward Elise. She snapped on her seat belt and met his gaze. He could smell the light, flowery scent of her perfume. ''It's your call,'' he said. ''Do you want to go for a drive, or should we head back to your place?''

''I don't care. Whatever you want to do.''

''Let's go back to your apartment, then.''

They didn't talk during the twenty-minute drive. Dev inserted a tape into the tape player and thought about what he would say to Elise. He wondered what she'd think when he told her who his ex-wife was. He was sure she would recognize Joelle's name. Hell, Elise might even admire Joelle. After all, the work she did, the causes she espoused, were all worthwhile causes. He wondered if Elise would understand how he felt, or if her feelings toward him would change.

As he turned the car into the entrance to her apartment complex, he cut a look at her. Her profile, illuminated by the lights surrounding the entrance, was pure. Pure and clean and beautiful. Just like Elise herself. Something knotted in his gut. He wanted this woman. She was everything he'd ever looked for and despaired of finding; it no longer mattered that she was involved in a cause. Elise was no Joelle. There was a warmth and compassion about her that extended toward all humans and had nothing to do with her passion for her work.

He tightened his grip on the steering wheel. He would have to make Elise understand. Because he didn't intend to let her walk out of his life. He intended to have her.

No matter what it took.

* * *

"Should I put on a pot of coffee?" Elise asked.

"Coffee sounds good." Dev stood by the mantel, one arm propped against it. He looked as if he belonged there. Or was that just wishful thinking on her part? His pose was casual and relaxed, although his eyes looked troubled and there were telltale signs of strain around his mouth. She knew she'd forced him into a corner, but she wasn't sorry. Because there had been so many secrets in her relationship with Derek, and because of the counseling she'd had, she knew that to build a healthy relationship with anyone, an honest sharing of feelings was necessary.

"I even have some brandy..." she offered, wishing he'd smile, wishing the clouds in his eyes would clear, wishing she could make all this easier for him.

"Maybe later."

"Okay." She busied herself in the kitchen alcove, every once in a while glancing up to see what he was doing. He left the mantel and walked around her living room, touching things aimlessly.

Something painful tugged at Elise's heart as his hand lingered over—almost caressed—the piece of needlepoint she was currently working on. What an enigma he was: strong and confident and all male sometimes, uncertain and troubled and vulnerable at other times. At that moment she wanted nothing more than to stop what she was doing, walk over to him, put her arms around him and hold him close. She wanted to tell him everything really would be okay, that he could trust her. In a flash of insight she knew the reason he was frightened was that he was afraid if he revealed all those things about himself that Elise needed to know and understand, she might think less of him.

Suddenly Elise knew she was going to make love with Dev tonight. Actually, she'd known it the instant he'd admitted he was scared. For she'd been scared almost all of her life, and she knew how lonely that fear could make a person. She also knew Dev needed her, even if he hadn't been able to admit it yet. He might not love her—not yet—but he did need her. And for right now, that would be enough.

"Where do you want me to start?" Dev asked, putting down his coffee cup.

Elise drained the last of her coffee. "I want you to start wherever you feel comfortable." She gestured toward the coffeepot. "But first, do you want more?"

"No, thanks. Some of that brandy you mentioned might be welcome, though." A sardonic smile tipped the corners of his mouth. "Using the word comfortable in reference to me talking about myself and my past is oxymoronic, you know."

Elise chuckled softly. At least he hadn't completely lost his sense of humor. She stood and impulsively bent down and kissed his cheek. He clasped her hand, bringing the palm to his mouth and kissed it softly. Elise's breath caught, and she slowly withdrew her hand.

A few minutes later, over snifters of brandy, he began to talk. "You're going to have to be patient. I'm not used to doing this kind of thing."

Elise, who was seated in her favorite blue chair, tucked her legs up under her. "I'm not going anywhere."

Dev, who was seated on the love seat to her left and was close enough to touch, sat forward, leaning his arms on his thighs. He stared into space. "Okay, I guess I should start with my mother."

Elise took a sip of her brandy, welcoming the fiery warmth that crept through her as she watched his face.

"My mother has always been a dreamer, according to my father. When she was young she wanted to be a poet, and she spent so much time daydreaming, she was never able to hold down a job.

"She also liked her whiskey and her men." A bitter smile twisted his mouth. "She liked both things far too much to be a good wife or mother or to remain faithful to my father." He laughed, the sound sharp and cynical. "Of course, my father's no prize, either. He also liked the women." Dev's intense gaze met hers. "My parents had what people euphemistically call 'an open marriage.' I call what they did sleeping around."

Elise winced at the harsh words.

He looked away again, twisting his hands together. "Anyway, I always felt ashamed, as if I were somehow to blame for the kind of people they were. Before I was twelve years old, I knew they were different from most of the parents of my friends. When we moved to New York, it was better... what I mean is, I didn't feel quite so different, because New Yorkers are more tolerant of all kinds of behavior, I guess. I don't know. Maybe it's just that I had lost my innocence, and it no longer seemed so important that my mother and father be like the Cleavers, who everybody knows are just storybook parents, anyway." He shrugged. "Whatever the reason, I just didn't care that much anymore."

Elise knew that wasn't true. He still cared, even if he couldn't admit it. Otherwise, he wouldn't be so embittered. She made an understanding sound, knowing that she really didn't need to contribute much to the conversation.

"There's not much more to tell," he said. "My mother left my father when I was fifteen. She'd met another guy and wanted to marry him. They were planning to move to California. I told her I didn't want to go with her, not that she asked, of course." His bitter laugh tore at Elise's heart.

Another devastating rejection, she thought, swallowing against a lump in her throat. And no matter what he said, how he denied it, that rejection had hurt him terribly. Memories of her own childhood flooded her. Even though she hadn't had a father, she'd always known her mother loved her intensely. Her mother had proven it again and again. She had sacrificed and worked to give Elise a good life, and they had shared everything until the day she died. The knowledge that she was the most important person in her mother's life had meant a lot to Elise. It still did. And Dev hadn't had that. He hadn't felt important to anyone. No wonder the boy Dev had been felt he was somehow at fault in his parents' failings.

"So she left and married her drummer." He made a sound like a snort, and his green gaze met hers again. "Oh, yeah, did I tell you that? She fell in love with a drummer in a rock band. Real upstanding citizens, my parents."

"Oh, Dev..." She reached out impulsively to touch his hand.

He jerked it away. "Listen," he said, his face closing up, "you asked me to tell you about all this. I'm not looking for pity." His jaw hardened. "I'm fine."

Elise knew he wasn't fine. She knew he was hurting. She'd asked him to relive a painful period in his life, one she knew he hadn't yet come to terms with. She couldn't really blame him for withdrawing from her. "I don't feel sorry for you. There's a difference between empathy and pity."

He nodded, but his eyes remained bleak. For a minute she wondered if he would continue. If he would think what they might have together was important enough to keep going. She held her breath. What if he got up and walked out? What if he said to hell with her and her amateur psychology and the demands she'd imposed on him? *Please, Dev, give us a chance,* she prayed.

She slowly relaxed, her fear subsiding as he continued in an almost-monotone. "The marriage didn't last, of course. A few years later, good old Mom was divorced again, and off with a new man. She did have sense enough not to marry this one. *He* was an artist who lived in Sarasota." Dev shook his head. "That relationship lasted exactly six months." He sighed. "A few years later she met this new guy, who she ended up marrying. This marriage seemed to take. Anyway, they live in Fort Lauderdale—he used to sell boats, of all things, but now he's retired—and my mother actually seems to have settled down and become a part of mainstream America. Now she's Mrs. Upstanding Citizen, according to my father, who actually still keeps in touch with her." Another short laugh. "Of course, the fact that she's nearly seventy years old might have a little something to do with it!"

This time Elise didn't make the mistake of saying anything that might be construed as pity. "So have you seen her at all since she left your father?"

"No. I've never had any desire to see her again. And obviously she feels the same way."

Elise cringed inside but forced herself not to let Dev see how really awful she thought that was. And the little she knew about his own failed marriage must have only reinforced all those feelings of rejection that any child would have who had undergone such an experience.

"What about Daisy?" she asked softly. "Has she ever seen her grandmother?"

"No." He stared at his hands.

The silence between them lengthened, throbbing with the tension of so many unsaid things. Abruptly he drained his brandy glass in one swallow and set it on the coffee table in front of him. After long seconds, he looked at her. His expression was enigmatic. "Sure you want to hear more?"

"Yes. I'm sure."

He shrugged. "Okay. You see before you a stupid man. Not only did I have a worthless mother, but I had a worthless wife."

Elise gasped. "Dev..."

He raised his eyebrows. "You think that's terrible, don't you? Hell, it *is* terrible. It happens to be true, though. Of course, I'm as much to blame about the mess my marriage became as Joelle. I mean, I put up with her behavior which meant I condoned it. What's the term? I *enabled* her. That's what the pop psychology books say. We had a *codependent* relationship."

Now the words poured out of his mouth. "My wife's name was—still is—Joelle Flanders."

Joelle Flanders! Shock jolted Elise. Joelle Flanders was famous, almost as famous as Gloria Steinem or Susan Faludi. Why, Elise had even read both Joelle Flanders's books.

"You're shocked, aren't you? I'll bet you think Joelle is some kind of folk hero, don't you?"

Elise bit her bottom lip. She *did* admire his ex-wife's work, even if some of her views were pretty radical. Elise believed in moderation in most things. In fact, the only thing she'd ever been really passionate about was her work with abused women and children. She cared about other issues but was almost always able to see both sides. "Tell me about it," she finally said.

Dev stood up. He walked to the window and looked out. Elise could see by the set of his shoulders that it was taking a lot out of him to talk about all of this. She also knew if he didn't they could never go forward. She might still make love with him later, because she wanted to so very much, but they would never be able to build a solid relationship.

He turned around, shoved his hands into his pockets and met her gaze. "I'm going to make this brief," he said. "I met Joelle at Columbia. She was finishing up her master's, I was finishing my doctorate. I fell head over heels for her. It was a passionate and stormy relationship from the very beginning. If I hadn't been thinking with my lower body parts instead of my brain matter, I would never have married her. I would have known there was no future for us. But I did marry her, and once I did, I was committed to making the marriage work. However, it didn't take me long to realize that Joelle didn't share that same commitment. She and I wanted different things out of life."

He paced over to the mantel, faced her again. "I wanted a traditional kind of life, complete with home, hearth and children. Joelle wanted excitement, speeches, impassioned marches, fame and fortune. She wanted challenges and changes. She wanted other men."

Oh, God. How had he endured this second blow? Elise wondered.

"She also didn't want children. When she got pregnant with Daisy, she wanted to have an abortion—would have had one if I hadn't blackmailed her. I'm the one who mothered Daisy, from the very beginning."

Elise listened as he told her about the first two years of Daisy's life, understanding more and more everything that had shaped Dev into the person he was now. She knew he didn't want her to feel sorry for him; she sensed that an unspoken fear was that she would think less of him because of his past and the failures he believed himself guilty of. If he only knew, if she could only tell him, that instead of pity, what she felt was an overwhelming admiration for the way he'd been able to pick up the pieces, to go on, to raise his daughter and build a good life. Despite all of the pain and the buried feelings of resentment, he had survived. Just as she had survived. They had a lot in common.

Elise knew Dev wasn't perfect. But he had great determination and guts. And courage, for it was certainly taking a lot of courage to spill those guts tonight.

"Daisy and my work have been the two most satisfying things in my life," he said reflectively. "Both have given me a sense of order, a sense that..." He hesitated, then met her gaze squarely. "I'm not used to talking like this, to analyzing my feelings, but, well, what I wanted to say is that both have given me a purpose in life, and a sense of my place in the universe. I know what I'm saying isn't really logical..."

"I think it's very logical."

He smiled crookedly. "Do you?"

"Yes. You like to control your environment. So do I. So does everyone. Sometimes, of course, that's not possible. Especially in terms of dealing with other people."

"Yeah, well, maybe..."

He didn't sound convinced. But Elise felt a spark of hope. He had made a giant step tonight.

"So now you know everything," he said. His eyes blazed a challenge. He grinned, but it wasn't a real smile at all. There was a stiffness in his stance, a wariness in his eyes that betrayed his tension. "What's the verdict, now that you know what a flawed human being I am?"

Elise stood, slowly walking to the mantel. His gaze never left hers as she approached. Her heart was beating hard as she reached for his hands. "I'm a flawed human being, too, Dev. Everyone is, don't you know that?"

He swallowed, and his hands tightened around hers. "So where do we go from here?"

Elise took a deep breath. She looked into his eyes, and what she saw there told her she was making the right choice. She stood on tiptoe, touching his mouth gently with her lips. "We go into my bedroom," she whispered. "And we love each other."

Chapter Ten

We love each other.

Elise's words reverberated in Dev's mind as she led him through the living room, down a short hallway and into a bedroom on the right. His emotions were chaotic as she let go of his hand and, without hesitation, walked to the double bed that dominated the small room. She pulled the flowered comforter down, folding it neatly at the foot of the bed. Then she turned down the top sheet.

Dev stood silently and watched her: the gracefulness of her movements as she bent to her task, the way her dark hair shone in the muted lamplight, the tempting curve of her neck.

How had he been lucky enough to find her?

His pulse raced as she turned to face him, walking slowly back to stand before him. Gently he touched her shoulders, marveling at the silky feel of her warm skin. He rubbed her shoulders slowly, giving her time to change her mind if she wanted to. Finally he asked, "Are you sure? It's not too late to say no." He didn't want her to have regrets later.

"I'm very sure." Her eyes were luminous. "Although—"

"Although what?" If she changed her mind now, he didn't know if he could stand it. He wanted her almost more than he wanted to draw his next breath. He wanted her with an intensity that shocked him.

"I'm afraid it's my turn to be scared." Her voice wasn't quite as steady as it had been before.

He squeezed her shoulders, once, in reassurance. Then he tipped her chin up, kissed the tip of her nose, then lightly touched her full, soft lips. "Don't be," he whispered. "I'd never hurt you."

"I know you'd never hurt me. I…I just don't have much experience."

His heart swelled. He gathered her close, smoothed her shining, thick hair, loving its richness and texture and its clean, light scent.

"I…I just don't want to disappoint you," she murmured against his throat, her breath warm and moist.

"You could never disappoint me." He smiled against her hair. "Don't you know that it makes me happy to know you're *not* very experienced? I love that about you, maybe more than anything else." He realized anew how true those words were. How much he valued her innocence, her lack of artifice, her aura of virtue—an old-fashioned quality Dev hadn't seen much of in his life. "I think you're perfect," he added. "And I'm not sure I deserve you."

"Oh, Dev…" She pulled back to look at him. "Don't put me up on a pedestal, please. I…I'm not perfect. No one is."

"You seem that way to me."

"That kind of thinking scares me, too. I can't live up to it. I'm sure to let you down."

With his hands on either side of her face, he bent down and kissed her again, this time with more intensity. He deepened the kiss, sliding his hands around to bring her closer, relishing the feel of her pliant body aligned with his. His heart thundered in his chest as desire built. He finally released her mouth long enough to say, "Quit talking foolishness."

Without giving her a chance to answer, he captured her mouth again and let himself drown in the sweetness she offered.

No matter what Dev had said, no matter how many reassurances he had given her, Elise couldn't banish her fear. Now, as she lay next to him in her bed, she prayed she would be able to make him happy, be everything he needed her to be.

After her confession of fear, he had slowly removed her sundress, and she had unbuttoned his shirt. Then, while he removed the rest of his clothing, stripping down to his briefs, she had kicked off her sandals. Once they were clad only in their undergarments, he had lifted her up and placed her on the bed, then lain down beside her.

He propped himself up beside her, and she looked up. Her heart raced as he traced the curve of her collarbone with his index finger.

"Beautiful," he murmured. "Beautiful."

He was beautiful, too, she thought, allowing herself to look at him. Hesitantly she touched his chest, feeling the springy curls that matted the center. She heard his quick intake of breath as she traced the outline of his muscles, then trailed her fingers lightly over his abdomen. She loved the feel of him, reveled in the smooth hardness of his body. She had always wanted to do this with Derek, and he would never let her.

Her hands stilled as Dev's touches became more insistent and thorough. She even forgot her fears as she began to lose herself in the emotions swirling through her, in the glorious feeling of abandonment that his lovemaking elicited. He was so different from Derek, she realized, in this as well as in everything else. Dev's touch was gentle but assured, and he paid minute attention to her body, seeming to know instinctively just where and how to touch her and what would please her most.

First he kissed her. Over and over again. Soft, moist, nipping kisses that built a slow urgency in her body. He kissed her mouth, her nose, her eyes. He whispered endearments and compliments. He told her she was so beautiful, so sweet, so enticing and sexy and desirable. His words excited her almost as much as his kisses.

He kissed her throat, then, slowly, oh, so very slowly, unhooked her bra and almost reverently kissed her breasts. First one. Then the other. He held them in his hands and touched his tongue to their hardening peaks, swirling its wet heat around the tingling nubs, until she cried out with the sheer agony of it.

He continued his journey down her body, each kiss leaving a fiery trail in its wake, a tingling awareness, and an unquenchable desire for more.

She reached for him, filling her palm and closing her eyes. But he pushed her hand away. "No," he said roughly. "Not yet. Let me do this first."

She didn't protest. What he was doing felt too good. She didn't want him to stop. She had never experienced such exquisite pleasure before. It was agony, but it was also ecstasy. Heat spiraled through her as Dev worshiped her body, fulfilling every fantasy she'd ever had, showing her, for the first time in her life, what it really meant to be a woman.

He did things she'd only dreamed about, and she didn't feel ashamed. And when he withdrew something from under the pillow—something he'd placed there earlier, he told her—she wasn't ashamed of that, either. Because his planning ahead, his safeguarding of her told her, more than anything else, that he cared for her. That he was a careful, thoughtful man who would never endanger her.

A little later, when under his thorough lovemaking, she began to feel as if there were a coil inside her that was tightening—tightening to the breaking point—she tried to push his mouth away. "No, Dev, wait, I—"

"Don't fight it," he said gruffly. "Let yourself go. Let me do this for you."

So Elise didn't fight it. And when Dev turned his attention to that spot where all her pent-up yearning was centered, she didn't fight that, either. She gasped and could feel the coil ready to spring apart. Within moments wave after wave of excruciating pleasure pummeled her while Dev held her fast. The sensations tore through her body, and Dev kept them coming as he drew the pleasure out for her. Only when she was reduced to a quivering mass did he stop and guide her hand back to him.

She touched him, his heat and his strength, closing her hand around him—feeling the life force pulsing within. She stroked him, smiling as he groaned. Slowly she raised her hips, and he entered her, pushing steadily as she guided him. The feel of him deep inside rocked her even as it gave her a sense of power and more—a wonderful sense of completeness. She felt exalted and proud.

She watched Dev's face as he strained against her and she matched her movements to his. Her heart pounded as their efforts became more urgent, their movements faster. With one great thrust, Dev cried out and a shudder cascaded through his body. She held him tight and felt a renewal of her own pleasure. This time it was different, deeper, more centered within, not as mindless and shattering. Instead it left her with a glowing happiness. She felt smug, glorying in the pleasure she'd given him, knowing that what they'd just shared was the greatest and most wonderful experience a man and a woman could share.

When he would have rolled off her, she tightened her arms, keeping him close. She loved the feeling of oneness. She had never felt so safe.

Or so wanted.

Or so needed.

Or so loved.

Much later, as Elise lay thinking in the circle of Dev's arms, Dev, who had fallen asleep, stirred. He tightened his arms around her, turning her so that they were now lying in the spoon position.

"God, you feel good," he murmured against her hair. One hand cupped her breast, the other lay against her abdomen. "I could lie here forever, just like this." His fingers made lazy movements against her body, and Elise moaned softly. His warm breath feathered her ear. "I wish we could make love again and again," he whispered.

Elise closed her eyes. She'd like that, too.

"I love touching you."

She gasped as his fingers delved into her.

"Do you like that?" His voice was rough.

"Yes, oh yes..." Her own voice sounded strange, too.

"How much?"

"Dev..." She felt wanton as she arched against his probing fingers, urging him on.

"Tell me how much," he whispered, "or I'll stop." His hand became motionless. She could feel his heart beating, echoing the tempo of her own.

"More than anything."

"Anything?" Amusement tinged the question. "Are you sure?"

She nodded, trying to turn in his arms.

He wouldn't let her.

"More than this?" He stroked her body slowly, from neck to thighs, making slow circles over her belly and a teasing foray into the throbbing core of her.

"Ohhhh...you're teasing me. I can't stand it."

He laughed softly. "Sure you can. This is half the fun...stringing out the pleasure."

Elise wasn't sure she could stand much more pleasure, but, of course, she did. The second time was even better than the first, because she got bolder, and she ended up on top, which she loved. She couldn't believe this was really her: shy, quiet, reserved Elise. Why, if anyone who knew her saw her now, they wouldn't believe it. This time, when Dev cried out, she collapsed on top of him, and he wound his arms around her and held her for a long time.

Finally, though, he gently rolled her over onto the bed. "Elise, as much as I wish I didn't have to, I've got to get up, get dressed and go home. I don't want Daisy to wake up and find me gone."

Elise sat up with a jerk. She stared at Dev, who seemed startled. "Oh, my gosh, Dev. I forgot all about your daughter. Of course, you'd better get home." She glanced over at her dresser. The digital clock glowed: 3:12.

He touched her arm. "There's no need to get upset. I told her I might be pretty late. She's fourteen, old enough to be alone for a while. I'm sure she's sound asleep. It's just that I want to get home before daybreak." He hesitated. "I hope you don't mind. I gave her your number in case she needed to reach me."

Elise shook her head, but she wasn't sure how she felt about Dev's daughter knowing—especially if she *should* wake up—that Dev was here so late. What would the girl think? Elise closed her eyes. Oh, dear. This situation might be even more complicated than she'd thought it would be. What if Dev's daughter didn't like her?

"Elise..." Dev pulled her back against him, burying his face in her neck. He kissed her, and she shivered. "Don't worry. It's going to be all right. Daisy will love you. She's already said she admires you."

"She did? How does she know me?"

"From the radio show."

"Oh...of course." Maybe it would all be okay. Maybe she was worrying for nothing. "What did she say?"

"She said she thought you were great. That you were doing wonderful work."

Elise felt a glow of satisfaction. The unknown Daisy must be a pretty smart girl. "I'd love to meet her," she suggested softly.

"And I want you to. In fact, I'm hoping you'll be able to give me some advice. Daisy's been worrying me a bit lately. She's changing. Sometimes it's really frustrating the way she seems to be pulling away from me. I'm not sure I like it."

"It's natural for girls her age to test their wings, Dev. It doesn't mean she doesn't love you anymore."

His arms tightened around her. "It's just that she's growing up so fast. It's scary."

"I know." Elise pulled away and sat up, tucking the sheet around her. She still felt too shy in the newness of their relationship to talk comfortably while naked.

He sat up, too, but his nudity didn't seem to bother him, for he leaned back against the headboard of her bed and didn't bother covering himself. "You can't really know," he said. "Not until you're a parent yourself can you understand."

Elise tried not to feel hurt. And she didn't, not really. After all, he was right. She wasn't a parent. The thought crossed her mind that if she and Dev were to marry, she would be Daisy's stepmother. She swallowed. Dev hadn't even said he loved her, let alone that he wanted to marry her. "That's true," she said, keeping her voice level. "I'm not. But I'm a female, and I know that girls need some space. They need to feel they can make their own decisions. They need to know that their parents trust them."

"I know you're right, but, well, Daisy's different."

Elise smiled. "Oh, Dev, all parents think that."

"No," he insisted stubbornly. "She really *is* different."

"How? In what way?"

He frowned and looked at her. "I told you. I told you what her grandmother's like, what her mother's like."

"So?" What was he driving at?

"So I don't want Daisy to turn out like that. I have to watch her carefully."

"Oh, Dev! That's a terrible thing to say."

His jaw tightened. "Maybe it is, but I'm just being realistic."

"I don't know how you can say that, let alone think it. Don't you think that the way you've raised your daughter might have some bearing on her behavior?"

"She looks just like her mother," he insisted stubbornly. "Well, she's got my eyes, but that's all. Otherwise, she's the spitting image of Joelle."

"So what? It's what's inside that counts. I hope you haven't let Daisy know what you're thinking. You know, with kids, if you expect the worst, sometimes they'll live up to those expectations. It's important that you let her know you trust her and believe in her."

He stiffened. ''I know you mean well, Elise. But you don't know anything about my relationship with Daisy.''

Elise opened her mouth, then shut it. She wondered if she and Dev would ever be able to really communicate, if he would ever be willing to allow her into his life in any meaningful way. She wondered if she'd been kidding herself earlier tonight when she'd told herself that he needed her.

Weariness engulfed her. Until Dev could let go of his anger, and his pain, he would never be a whole man. And if he wasn't a whole man, how could they build a solid, whole relationship?

Had she made a horrible mistake? Had she been naive to think she could make a difference? That she could actually help Dev come to terms with his past?

Fear, thick and cloying, mingled with the weariness.

Only time would tell.

Elise prayed that in the process of finding out if she and Dev had any kind of future together, she would not get her heart irreparably broken.

Chapter Eleven

When Dev left Saturday night, he promised Elise he'd call her Sunday afternoon. As she had every Sunday morning for the past three years, she went to Mass with her father and stepmother, then the three of them had brunch at The Landing on the river—another tradition. But throughout the morning, even though normally she loved being with Justin and Lisette, she just couldn't seem to keep her mind from wandering and reliving every moment of the previous evening with Dev.

"Is something wrong, *chère?*" her father said midway through their meal. "You seem so distracted."

"Yes," Lisette echoed, concern clouding her dark eyes. "I have noticed this, as well."

"Oh, no...I'm sorry. Nothing's wrong."

"You are sure?" Lisette insisted. "You are feeling well and everything?"

Elise finally persuaded them everything was fine. For the rest of their time together, she forced herself to pay attention to the conversation. She was relieved when they finally said their goodbyes, and she was able to escape her father's shrewd eyes. As soon as her father's car was out of sight, she raced into her apartment. She didn't want to miss Dev's call.

For the next couple of hours she was unable to settle down to anything, even though she had homework to do. So the time wouldn't be a total loss, she changed into old clothes and cleaned her bathroom. But soon even her household tasks were done, and he still hadn't called.

Finally, in exasperation, she said aloud, "Okay, Dev. I'm giving you another half hour. If you don't call by then, I'm going out!"

Fifteen minutes later he called.

"Hi," he said.

Her heart leaped somewhere up in the vicinity of her throat, but she managed to say, "Hi."

"I'm glad I caught you in," he said. "I tried calling earlier, but there wasn't any answer."

"Earlier? You mean this morning?"

"Yeah, about eleven o'clock."

"I was at church this morning, then I went out for brunch with my parents. Anyway, you said you'd call me this afternoon."

He laughed softly, the sound a bit sheepish. "I couldn't wait."

Happiness wrapped itself around her like his arms had only hours before. She cradled the phone closer, wishing it were him she was touching instead of a plastic receiver.

"Say something," he said.

"Like what?"

"Like you couldn't wait for me to call, either...."

She closed her eyes. "I couldn't wait for you to call, either," she murmured.

His voice dropped even lower, becoming a husky whisper. "I wish I were there right now."

"Me, too."

There was a long silence. Then Dev said, "Last night was incredible."

Elise swallowed. She wanted to say she thought it was incredible, too, but she couldn't.

"Elise?" he said softly. "Is something wrong? Did I say something wrong?"

"No, you didn't say anything wrong. I...I'm just not very experienced at this. I...I feel kind of awkward." *I wish you were here, where I could see your eyes. Then maybe I wouldn't feel so tongue-tied.* "I'll try to do better."

"Don't worry. You're doing fine."

"W-was it okay when you got home last night? With your daughter, I mean?"

"Yes. She was sound asleep when I got home."

Elise sighed. "That's good." *Oh, Dev. When will I see you again? I need to see you again.*

Almost as if he'd heard her unspoken plea, he said urgently, "I wish I could see you tonight. I've been thinking about you ever since I left you."

"Oh, I have, too." *Oh, you ninny. That sounds stupid.* "Been thinking of you, that is," she explained hurriedly.

He chuckled. "I knew what you meant."

His voice felt like a soft caress, and she shivered.

"But I feel as if I should stay home with Daisy tonight," he continued. "I've even canceled my Sunday night chess game with Gerald Eggleston."

"Oh...you know Professor Eggleston...he's awfully nice, I think."

"How do *you* know him?"

Elise laughed. She couldn't help it. Was that possessiveness she heard in his voice? Suddenly, her self-confidence returned. "What do you mean, *how do I know him?* It almost sounds as if you're jealous, Dev."

"Of course, I'm not jealous," he said quickly, too quickly.

"Well, if you were, there's no need to be. I know Professor Eggleston because I took a course in Shakespearean drama last year. He was the prof."

"What's a psych major doing taking Shakespearean drama?"

"I happen to *like* Shakespearean drama. Besides, it was an elective."

"Well, okay. . ." Then he laughed, too. "All right, I admit it. I *was* jealous there for a minute." He dropped his voice again. "I don't want to share you with anyone."

Elise was absurdly pleased by his admission. He *did* need her. She was important to him. Everything would work out. Last night she'd worried for nothing.

For the rest of the day she continued to hug the knowledge to her. Dev had been jealous of an innocent remark. He'd told her he'd been thinking about her all day. He had admitted that he cared.

Oh, she couldn't wait to see him again.

On Monday she saw him at Cypress Lake. When she arrived, he was already there, seated on a bench. She could tell, by the way he watched the entrance, that he was waiting for her. Both her heart and her feet picked up speed.

"Hi," she said, feeling almost shy as her gaze met his. His eyes looked like the colors of the forest today, dark and mysterious, and matched the olive-green T-shirt he wore with khaki pants. A matching khaki jacket was slung over the back of the bench.

"Hi." He smiled, and her heart turned over. His gaze devoured her as it swept her from head to toe, then rested on her face. "God, you look gorgeous."

Her heart swelled. She had dressed especially carefully today, wanting to look her very best. She knew the apricot cotton sundress she wore enhanced her coloring and flattered her figure.

"Sit next to me," he said softly, patting the bench.

For the next half hour, they sat close to each other, caressing each other with their eyes. They held hands, and with his thumb he rubbed slow circles in her palm. His touch, and the expression in his eyes, filled her with an almost unbearable happiness. She wanted to sing and dance and shout. She wanted to tell the world, *Look, this man thinks I'm gorgeous! Isn't that wonderful? Isn't that unbelievable?* Instead she sat quietly, luxuriating in his nearness and the way he made her feel.

When it was time for her to leave, he said, "Don't go."

She sighed. "I wish I didn't have to, but my class starts in fifteen minutes."

"Skip it. Let's go for a drive."

"Oh, Dev, I shouldn't . . ."

"Come on. I brought my car today." He squeezed her hand tighter. "I want to kiss you," he murmured, "and I can't do it here."

Her heart beat wildly as his gaze fastened on her mouth. She wet her lips.

"Say yes," he insisted, "or I might do something foolish, like kiss you right here."

Oh, it was tempting. So tempting. "All right."

So they walked off together and drove until Dev found a secluded spot near the banks of Bayou Vermilion. Smiling at her, he pulled in and turned off the ignition. Then he pulled her close, and they kissed greedily, urgently, as if they were kids who couldn't get enough of each other. After a while, Dev said, "Let's go to your place. I want to make love with you."

Weakly Elise nodded. She wanted to make love with him, too. All the way back into town, her body trembled with anticipation. She watched his strong profile and thought how wonderful he was. It seemed hard to believe that only a few short weeks ago, she hadn't even known Dev. Now he was the most important person in her life.

Afterward, Elise knew she'd never forget their lovemaking that afternoon. Years later, she knew she'd remember exactly how Dev's body had looked dappled by the filtered sunlight that found its way through the closed slats of her miniblinds. Exactly how it felt to lie in the cocoon of his arms and have him kiss her and touch her and bring her to that radiant peak.

It was a magical afternoon, full of beauty and brilliance, a celebration of the senses and a gift of the best each one had to give.

She stored each word, each touch, each emotion, each sensation—carefully in her memory—to take out and savor again and again.

When he teased her, saying, "For someone with very little experience, you certainly are wanton, making love in the afternoon," she stored that, too, even as she laughed and slapped at his hands, which were gently tickling her ribs.

"I'm discovering all kinds of new things about myself," she admitted.

He stroked her back, bent down and kissed her shoulder. "I'm discovering all kinds of new things about you, too." He bent lower, nibbled at her breast, cupping it in his hands. "Have you ever made love in the daytime before?"

Elise shook her head, unable to speak for the exquisite sensations he was producing with his careful attention to her breast.

"Nice, isn't it?"

Yes, she thought, it was nice. It was wonderful. It was perfect. She wished she could stay here forever.

Later, when he was dressed again and ready to leave, he held her in his arms, stroked her hair, then kissed her gently. "One of these days soon, we're gonna have to talk."

She touched his mouth with her fingertips. "Why?" she whispered.

"Because I think I'm falling in love with you."

For some reason, this admission made her feel like crying, because everything was happening so fast, and it was almost *too* perfect.

That frightened her.

She remembered what her mother had always said about tempting fate. "It's best not to be too happy, *chère*," she would say, "because then the gods might decide to take something away."

Please, God, she prayed after Dev was gone, *don't take him away. Let me have this. If you do, I promise never to take it for granted.*

Monday night, Elise visited Lianna and Charlie.

"So, where've you been? We haven't seen you for a few days," Lianna said when Elise was settled in the kitchen with a tall glass of iced tea in front of her.

Elise smiled, meeting Lianna's gaze.

Lianna's expressive eyes widened. "What?"

Elise couldn't help it; her grin just got wider.

"Tell me!" Lianna sank into a chair opposite her and leaned forward. "It's that hunk—that Professor Devereaux—isn't it?"

Elise nodded.

"Darn you, 'Lise, you'd better tell me, or I'm gonna come around the table and yank it out of you!"

So Elise told her. Everything. Well, almost everything. Some things should never be shared with anyone.

"Oh, God! I'm green! I'm positively green," Lianna said dramatically. "Did he *really* say he thought he was falling in love with you?"

"Yes."

"Ahhhhh!" Lianna screamed. "I can't stand it. I'm so jealous!" She jumped up, came around to Elise's side of the table and hugged her hard. "But I'm happy for you, too, sweetie, because you deserve it."

Tears misted Elise's eyes.

"Hey, don't get so emotional," Lianna teased, but her eyes looked suspiciously bright, too. They both laughed and hugged again.

A few minutes later Charlie bounced into the room, dressed in her usual outfit of shorts and T-shirt, long legs tanned and beautiful. "Hi, cuz," she said breezily, grinning. "What's new?"

"Elise has a boyfriend," Lianna announced.

"Lianna!" Elise protested.

"Well, you *do*."

"Who?" Charlie said, dropping into the chair next to Elise. "Is it that professor? The good-looking one?"

"Yes. Isn't that great?" Lianna said.

Elise rolled her eyes. Oh, great. Soon the entire world would know. "Listen," she urged, "do not, I repeat, do not say one word to my father or Lisette."

"We won't," Charlie said.

"Promise," Elise said, looking at Lianna.

Lianna raised her right hand. "I promise."

"Because I *do not* want them asking me questions. Not yet, anyway."

Charlie grinned and grabbed a Granny Smith apple from the bowl on the table. She polished it on her shorts, then took a noisy bite. "Yeah, I know what you mean. Remember when Mom was dating that guy from the supermarket? That Rambo something—"

"His name was *not* Rambo!" Lianna said, throwing a dish towel at her daughter. "His name was Jim." Then she burst into giggles. "Well . . . they . . . *did* call him Jimbo!"

Then all three of them laughed so hard, tears ran down Elise's face. "Oh, I do remember him," she finally gasped. "He was weird, Lianna."

"Yeah, Mom," Charlie said, "he was really weird. And remember how Aunt Lisette kept saying, 'so, are things serious between you two?'"

"How could I forget?" Lianna said dryly. "She asked me that every time she saw me."

"Remember that, will you?" Elise said. "And don't slip up and say *anything* to her. I . . . I'll tell her about Dev myself."

"So," Charlie said in a perfect imitation of Lisette's voice, "are things serious between you two?"

Now it was Elise's turn to throw the dish towel at Charlie.

Lianna said, "What am I going to do with her? She's getting mouthier every day!"

When Elise was ready to leave, Charlie said, "I'll walk out with you, okay?"

Lianna, who was busily icing a cake for a birthday party she was catering the following evening, waved goodbye. "Call me every day and keep me up-to-date on this romance, you hear?"

"Okay, okay, I hear," Elise said.

She and Charlie walked out into the navy night. When they reached Elise's car, Charlie said, "I . . . there's something I wanted to talk to you about."

"I thought so."

Charlie smiled, her braces gleaming in the moonlight. She kicked at a pebble in the driveway. "I . . . I have a new boyfriend, too," she finally said, her words muffled.

"Oh?" Lianna hadn't mentioned this. "Does your mother know?"

"Nuh-uh."

"Why not?"

Charlie shrugged. "You know how she is. She'd worry. I mean . . . it's no big deal yet. I . . . I just like him a lot, you know. . . ."

Yes, Elise thought, she *did* know. "So who is he?" she asked softly.

Charlie kicked at another pebble. "Well, his name's Rick, and he's the new lifeguard at the pool." She sighed. "Oh, gosh, Elise, he's . . . he's so . . . unbelievable!"

"How old is this *unbelievable* specimen?"

Charlie ducked her head. "Seventeen," she murmured.

"Seventeen!"

Charlie's gaze finally met hers. "I know what you're thinking. You're thinking he's too old for me, but Elise, I'll be fifteen in September! And he just turned seventeen last week."

"I see. Well, what's he like?"

"Oh, Elise," Charlie said, sighing, "he's so great. He's a terrific swimmer. In fact, he hopes to swim in the Olympics eventually. He's won all kinds of ribbons, and everything."

Elise felt relieved. The unknown Rick had goals. He had a future planned. Her relief quickly turned to alarm as Charlie continued.

"His dad's an engineer, or something. He works for some big firm, and his mom's a travel agent. He has two little sisters, and you should see their house!"

"When did *you* see their house?"

"Uh . . . well . . ."

"Charlie . . ."

Charlie couldn't meet her eyes. "I was there this afternoon," she mumbled.

"Were his parents home?"

The teenager shook her head.

"Oh, Charlie . . . you shouldn't be going to a boy's house when his parents aren't there. You know that . . ."

"We didn't *do* anything. We . . . we just kissed, that's all."

Oh, God. Elise reached out, turning Charlie to face her. "Charlie, honey, please, don't do anything stupid. I know how you feel. Believe me, I do. But . . ." Elise took a deep breath. "But don't be in a hurry. Having sex should be something you think about long and hard before you do it. It should never be an impulsive act." *Listen to me. Didn't I do exactly what I'm warning her against?*

"I know that! I'm not planning to have sex with Rick!"

"But you've thought about it," Elise said softly, touching Charlie's cheek.

Charlie nodded.

"You asked your mother about birth control pills."

Charlie nodded again. "I knew she'd tell you."

Elise smiled. "Your mother loves you, honey. She wants the best for you. She was worried. That's why she told me."

"I hadn't even met Rick when I asked her about the pills."

"Then why did you ask her?"

"I don't know. Well, you know . . . some of my friends are doing it, and I . . . I just *wondered*."

Now it was Elise's turn to nod. "Honey, please wait a while. Really, you're too young to make a wise decision about this. I know you're curious, and you want to do what the other kids are doing, but I don't think *all* the girls your age are having sex, are they?"

Charlie sighed. "No, not all of them."

"Honey, things change between a man and a woman after they start a physical relationship. They either go forward, or they go backward. And you said it yourself, Rick's too committed to his future to go forward. So that leaves backward."

"You mean after we had sex, he'd get tired of me, and eventually dump me?"

"Something like that."

Abruptly Charlie leaned forward and kissed Elise's cheek. "Thanks," she said. "I think you just helped me make up my mind."

Elise hugged her close.

"Don't tell Mom, okay?" Charlie said as they broke the hug.

"I won't tell her, but I want you to promise me something."

"What?" Charlie sounded wary.

"If you *do* decide you want to have sex with Rick, or anyone, for that matter, talk to me first, okay? I . . . I'll talk to your mother."

"Okay." Charlie hugged her again. "I love you," she whispered. Then she ran into the house.

At one o'clock Tuesday afternoon Elise crumpled up the wrapper from the cheeseburger she'd eaten for lunch, finished the last of her glass of milk and stood. She and Frieda were the only two workers in the lounge. "Well," she said, stifling a yawn, "I'd better head on downstairs. Meg wants me to get that mailing out today."

Frieda grimaced. "Lucky you. I hate stuffing envelopes. I'm actually glad I have a dentist appointment."

Elise gave a mock shudder. "Personally I'd rather do *anything* than go to the dentist."

After a few more comments, Elise left Frieda and headed toward the main office workroom, which was right across the hall from Meg's office. When she entered the room, she saw that all the materials for the mailing were sitting on a large worktable: the printed letters, all signed; the envelopes; the labels; the brochures that would accompany the letters; the gadget she'd use to moisten and seal the envelopes; and the postage meter. Meg had said she'd send someone else in to help, but no one was there yet, so Elise sat down and began folding letters and inserting brochures inside them. Soon she was absorbed in the work and her mind drifted between thoughts of Dev and thoughts of Charlie.

She hadn't let Charlie see how really disturbed she was by her confidences concerning the magnificent Rick. Charlie was so young. Too young to begin having sex. Yet Elise knew many girls her age already had an active sex life. It was a frightening thought.

Elise wanted more for Charlie. Charlie had such promise, so many things ahead of her. And even though she was mature and sensible, she still had a lot to learn before she would be capable of the kind of judgment necessary to make good decisions when it came to men, and sex.

Of course, Elise mused, are we ever mature enough to be objective about these things? Don't all women, *and* men, for that matter, too often allow themselves to be blinded by their physical attraction to a person?

She tried to tell herself she was not one of those people, that what she felt for Dev was much more than physical attraction. But deep in her heart she knew that the physical attraction between them was very powerful, and it had probably colored her thinking.

But I'm thirty-one years old. I know that my actions carry consequences. I'm not sure Charlie does.

Yeah, well, she answered herself, you're going to be just as devastated as Charlie would be if things don't work out with your white knight.

"Hi, Elise!"

Elise jumped. A smiling Marguerite stood in the doorway. She looked darling today, Elise thought, in a cute red shorts outfit and her buttery hair tied back with a red ribbon. "Hi, Marguerite."

"Judy said to come and help you stuff envelopes," the girl said.

"Oh, good. I can use some help."

For the next ten minutes, the two worked silently. Then Marguerite said, "I've been wanting to ask you something."

Oh, no. I hope she doesn't want to talk about sex, too. "Ask away."

Marguerite bit her bottom lip, her expression troubled.

Elise stopped stuffing envelopes. "What is it, honey?" she said softly.

The teenager turned, her lovely green eyes earnest. "My mom and dad are divorced, and I haven't seen my mom in a long time. My dad, well, he's mad at her."

Elise suppressed a sigh. Honestly, people screwed up their lives so terribly. And so many kids suffered because of it.

"He doesn't want me to have anything to do with my mom, but, well, I . . . I miss her."

"Oh, honey... I'm sure you do. In fact, I think I know exactly how you feel."

"You do?"

"Yes," Elise said. "I grew up without a father, so I understand."

"Were your parents divorced, too?" Marguerite asked.

"No. They... they were never married. I never knew who my father was."

"Oh, how sad!"

"Yes, it *was* sad." Elise smiled. "But later, just a few years ago, in fact, I found him. And it was one of the most wonderful days of my life."

"Ohhhh..." Marguerite said with a sigh. "That's so romantic, isn't it?"

Elise smiled. "I guess in a way, it was. And, well, it did something for me. I had never realized how much I needed to know my roots. Meeting my father, getting to know him and the rest of my family, well, it helped me understand who I was. Now I feel like a complete person."

Marguerite's eyes widened. "That's it! That's what my dad doesn't understand!" Her face took on a beseeching expression. "Oh, if only I could make him understand. I... I'm thinking about writing to my mother."

Elise didn't know what to say. After all, she knew nothing about Marguerite or her family. For all she knew, Marguerite's mother could be a terrible person. Maybe there was good reason for her father not to want her to have anything to do with her. Fleetingly she thought of Dev and his experience. He certainly felt strongly about *his* daughter. "Why don't you talk to your father first, Marguerite? Tell him just what you've told me today. You can even use me as an example, if you want to."

Marguerite shrugged unhappily. "I don't know. I can't talk to him lately." She sighed heavily. "Oh, maybe I'll just forget about it. I don't want to make him mad."

Elise reached across the table and took Marguerite's hand. She gave it an encouraging squeeze. "Listen, if I can help... maybe talk to him or something?"

Marguerite shook her head quickly, something very like alarm widening her eyes. "No. No, that's okay. Really. You don't need to talk to him."

Elise smiled. Kids were so funny. So grown-up sometimes. And then other times, such as now, scared to even have their parents know something was bothering them. "Well, remember, if you ever need me, the offer's open."

"Okay. I'll remember."

They smiled at each other and began working again.

Chapter Twelve

Daisy chewed on her pencil, thought for a few minutes, then began writing.

Dear Diary,

Today I talked to Elise about wanting to get in touch with my mom. Elise was so nice—she listened, and everything, and I wanted to tell her all about my mother and my father, but then I realized if I did that, I'd have to explain to her who I really am. Then she'd know I lied to her and everything.

I wish I hadn't deceived her and everybody. I wish I'd been brave enough just to tell Dad that I had signed up at the shelter. I thought it would be easier to wait to tell him. But it isn't. Now it's going to be harder. Boy, I guess it's really true what they say about telling lies, how they just get bigger and bigger.

I don't know what to do. I want to be straight with

Dad and Charlie and Elise and everyone else at the shelter, but I'm really scared. I'm afraid Dad'll be so mad he'll really punish me, and I'm scared Elise won't like me anymore. I don't think Charlie will be mad at me, because she'll understand. I mean, she's keeping something from her mother since she hasn't told her about Rick yet. I guess maybe I'll talk to Charlie about this first. Maybe she'll know what I should do now.

Oh, I wish I had a mother. Well, what I mean is, I do have a mother, but I wish I could see her and talk to her. Like Elise said, each person needs to know her roots. I really *am* glad I talked to Elise today, even if I couldn't tell her everything, because I didn't know all that, about Elise's father and her mother, and how she grew up not even knowing who her father was except for his last name, and how Elise's father and his wife loved her right away, and how she went to live with them and everything. It's so romantic, just like the fairy tales I used to read when I was little, with a happy ending for everyone.

Gosh, maybe if I wrote to my mom she'd really want to see me, too. Maybe she thinks I hate her like Dad does. I wish Dad understood. 'Cause like Elise said, I *do* need to know my roots. That's what Dad doesn't understand. I know if I tell him I want to write to Mom, he'll think that means I don't love him, and I do.

Daisy laid her pencil down. She chewed on her lower lip and reread what she'd written so far. Then she sighed heavily, picked up her pencil and began writing again.

Okay, I've decided. I'm going to talk to Charlie tomorrow. Maybe she can meet me at the yogurt place near her subdivision pool. I'm going to tell her everything, and if she thinks I should tell Dad and Elise the truth, I will.

Daisy felt better now that she'd made her decision. She closed and carefully locked her diary, hid it in her underwear drawer, then climbed into bed. She snapped off the bedside light and closed her eyes. She would call Charlie first thing in the morning—as soon as her father left for work.

"So your name is really Daisy?" Charlie asked. She grinned. "How'd you come up with the name Marguerite?" She took a spoonful of her yogurt, rolling it around on her tongue. "Um, good."

Daisy twisted a strand of her hair around her index finger. "Well, I didn't. What I mean is, Marguerite really *is* my name, but everyone's called me Daisy since I was little."

Charlie ate another spoonful, then frowned. "That's kind of weird, isn't it? I mean, my real name's Charlotte, so Charlie's sort of natural as a nickname, but *Daisy?*"

"Well, Daisy's sort of natural, too. My dad explained it to me when I was old enough to understand. See, I was named after my great-aunt Marguerite Sloan. Because the word *marguerite* means *daisy,* she was always called Aunt Daisy, so that's what they called me, too." Daisy laughed. "Well, not *aunt,* but you know what I mean."

"Oh, that's kind of neat." Charlie ate more of her strawberry yogurt.

"Yeah, I used to think so, too. Well, actually, I guess I still do."

"So if you like your name, why'd you tell the people at the shelter to call you Marguerite?"

Daisy made a face. "I kind of thought it sounded more grown-up." She finished the last of her peanut butter yogurt and licked the spoon.

Charlie nodded understandingly. "Yeah, maybe you're right. Charlie sounds sort of babyish, too, don't you think?"

"Oh, no! I think Charlie's a great name. It's the first thing I thought when I saw you that first day. What a great name!"

"Really?"

"Really."

"Well, I think Daisy's a great name. So we're even."

They grinned at each other.

"So, do I now get to call you Daisy?" Charlie asked.

"Uh huh," Daisy said with a relieved sigh. "I felt awfully weird when people called me Marguerite. As if I weren't really me, you know?"

"Yeah, I think I do know. I mean, when my mom calls me *Charlotte Ann* in that tone of voice...you know the one I mean...that you've-done-something-I-don't-like tone of voice, I feel weird, too."

Daisy giggled. "Yeah, but that's 'cause you know you're in trouble!"

Charlie nodded sheepishly.

"So what do you think I should do, Charlie?"

"I think you should talk to Elise. Tell her the whole story, and see what she says."

"Oh, gosh, I don't know. She's gonna hate me."

"She won't hate you. She's great. She really understands when you talk to her, pro'bly because she's been through so much herself. I told you, I can tell Elise anything, even things I can't tell my mom, and she always understands. She certainly doesn't hate *me*." Charlie eyed Daisy thoughtfully, as if she were considering something, then said, "I even told her about Rick."

"You did!"

"Uh-huh. Monday night."

"Gosh . . . what did she say?"

Charlie shrugged, then grinned. "She said a lot of things, but basically she said *don't have sex*. The same thing my mom said when I asked her about birth control pills."

"You *didn't!* You didn't tell me that." Daisy couldn't imagine talking to her father about birth control pills. Why, he'd *kill* her. It must be wonderful to have a mother and an aunt, both of whom listened. "What did she say?"

"Just what I thought she'd say. No way!"

"Did that make you mad?"

"No. I knew she'd say that."

"Then why did you ask?"

Charlie rolled her eyes. "Daisy, don't you know *anything?* You gotta pave the way, for when you *really* want something, you know?"

They both laughed. "Yeah, you're probably right. Uh . . . Charlie . . . are you thinking of . . . you know . . . having sex with Rick?" Daisy asked shyly. She'd never even had a real date yet, and she'd only been kissed a couple of times, and that was in her old neighborhood. She wondered what it would be like to have a boyfriend and want to have sex with him. Part of her couldn't wait to find out. The other part of her was scared to death, but she didn't want to admit that to Charlie.

"Well . . . I *was* thinking about it," Charlie admitted, and she sounded shy, too. "But, you know, it's really strange, but when both my mom and Elise said that . . . it was kind of like . . . you know, I felt *relieved*."

"You *did?*" Daisy was amazed.

"Uh-huh." Charlie ducked her head, as if she were embarrassed or something.

"Why?"

"'Cause even though I sort of want to, you know, have sex, 'cause some of the kids I know are doing it, and I, well, I wanted to see what it was like."

Daisy swallowed. Yeah, she wondered what it was like, too. Being naked in front of a boy was a pretty scary proposition, though. Of course, maybe if she had a body like Charlie's, she wouldn't be so frightened.

"But...well...I'm kind of scared..." Charlie said softly, still not meeting Daisy's eyes.

"Really?" Daisy said. "I...I thought I was the only girl in the world who was...scared."

Charlie looked up. "You *are?*"

"Uh-huh."

They stared at each other, then a slow smile spread over Charlie's face. Daisy smiled, too.

"I'm glad you're my friend, Daisy," Charlie said at last.

"Me, too."

"And I *love* your name!"

Daisy laughed. "Me, too!"

On Wednesday night, Dev waited until he was sure Daisy was asleep before he phoned Elise. He couldn't talk freely knowing his daughter was within earshot.

"So what are you doing?" he said when Elise answered on the first ring.

"Lying in bed," she said softly. "Reading."

Dev gave a mental groan, the image of her the last time he'd seen her in bed so strong and vivid it caused an instant flush of desire. "Don't do that to me," he said, hearing the roughness in his own voice as his imagination kicked into overdrive.

"Do what to you?"

He grinned. She sounded honestly bewildered. He low-ered his voice, even though he knew there was no chance Daisy could hear his conversation downstairs when she was behind a closed bedroom door upstairs. "Remind me of what you look like in bed, that's what."

She laughed softly. "Oh, Dev. . ."

They talked for a while, then she said, "I'm going to be away for two days."

"When?"

"I'm leaving in the morning, coming back Friday night, probably late."

"Where are you going?"

"To Patinville with my father."

"What's in Patinville?"

She sighed. "My father's brother, René. He had a mild heart attack—well, at least we *think* it's mild—this morn-ing. My father called me, all concerned and upset. Any-way, he wants to go over and talk to Uncle René's doctors, and see for himself how his brother is doing. I didn't want him driving there alone, especially when he's so upset, so I said I'd go with him. Besides, I love my father's family. I'm dying to see them again."

Dev loved Elise's devotion to her family. He wondered what it would be like to actually have a family you admired and respected. "Is your stepmother going, too?"

"No. She wanted to, but she's torn. She's chairman of a charity auction that takes place tomorrow at her church, and she felt she had to be there. My father encouraged her to stay home, especially after I said I'd go with him."

"I'll miss you," Dev murmured.

"It's only two days," she said, but he heard the pleasure in her voice.

"Will you miss me?"

"You know I will."

"Can I see you on Saturday?"

"Well, you know I work all day at the shelter...."

"I know. I meant Saturday night." He had a sudden inspiration. "Do you like to dance?"

"I love to dance, but I'm not that good."

"That makes two of us, but still, dancing has a lot going for it. Like..." he chuckled "...I can hold you close in public and no one will think a thing of it. And afterwards we can go back to your place..." He let his voice drift off.

"Dev, you're incorrigible. I never would have thought you were like this, especially the *first* time I saw you."

Dev squirmed. He didn't like remembering the first time she saw him. "Am I ever going to live that down?"

"Probably not."

"What *did* you think I was like?"

"Oh...you know...stiff, boring, professorial... pompous..."

"Stiff, boring, professorial and pompous!"

At his outraged tone, she burst into a merry spate of laughter. "I'm just teasing you...."

"You wait'll I get you alone. I'll show you *teasing*. I'll make you beg for mercy...."

"Oh, you will, will you? Well, we'll just see about that."

They continued in the same vein, and when they finally hung up, Dev was still chuckling. Every day he discovered something new about Elise. First her commitment and idealism. Next her courage and strength and love of family. Then her passion and sensuality. Now her ability to tease him and have fun, even when the talk turned to their feelings and the wonder of their lovemaking.

He could hardly wait for the next discovery.

* * *

On Thursday, Daisy's bike had a flat tire. It took her longer to get it repaired, then pumped up, than she thought it would, and she was late for work. She raced to the shelter.

When she arrived, for some stupid reason, her lock wouldn't shut. "Oh, darn it, anyway, you dumb lock!" She kicked her bike, knowing it was childish, but she was so mad. Uneasily she eyed the bike, a new ten-speed her father had purchased for her after their move to Lafayette. She loved her bike, and she never left it unlocked.

But surely, just this once, it wouldn't hurt. Would it? As far as she knew, no one had ever stolen anything from the shelter. Still, her new bike . . .

Oh, why did everything have to go wrong today? Of all days? Just when she wanted to be cool and grown-up and calm—because she had planned to tell Elise the truth about herself—that would have to be the day when she was late, and hot, and sweaty, and now her dumb lock was acting up.

Finally she just wrapped her lock around her bike as she usually did so that anyone casually looking at it would think it was locked, then she marched off, muttering to herself.

Daisy couldn't believe it when she found out Elise wasn't going to be at work today. "But why not?" she almost wailed when Judy said Elise wasn't there.

"She had to go out of town on a family emergency," Judy explained. "She'll be back Saturday, though."

Daisy didn't work on Saturdays. There was no way she would have been able to explain a long absence to her father, so she only worked Tuesdays and Thursdays. Well, she thought dejectedly as she walked to the nursery, there went her good intentions to come clean with Elise. She guessed she'd just have to wait until next Tuesday.

When quitting time came, Daisy hurried outside. She never fooled around after working at the shelter, because she liked to make sure she got home before her father did. One time, she hadn't made it, and he'd asked her where she was. "Oh, I went to the library," she said, hating herself for lying. Because it really bothered her to tell him less than the truth, she tried not to get herself in that position more than she had to.

So now she walked swiftly over to the bike rack, which sat under a huge sycamore tree.

Her heart shot up into her throat, and she gasped. "My bike!"

Her bike was gone.

Frantically Daisy scanned the rack. Her beautiful new, bright red ten-speed was gone, and now that she looked closer, she saw her lock lying abandoned on the ground. Her heart pounding like a trip-hammer, she spun around, looking up and down the street. "Oh, God," she said, covering her mouth. She could feel tears forming in her eyes. "Oh, God, please God. Don't let my bike be stolen. Please, please, please..."

But her prayers were useless, and she knew it. Her bike was gone. Stolen.

What was she going to tell her father?

Dev whistled as he climbed the steps to his town house. All day today he'd thought about his conversation with Elise the previous evening. She *was* wonderful, no doubt about it, and very soon, he wanted to talk about the future with her. All the doubts he'd had when he'd first met her had vanished. He wasn't even worried about her work at the shelter any longer. Besides, hadn't she told him she wanted to get her master's degree? He wondered how she'd feel if he applied for a job at Tulane. She could work on her ad-

vanced degree there and still be close to her family. He
wondered how Daisy would feel.

Even if Elise decided she'd rather work at the shelter full-
time, well, that would be okay, too. There was bound to be
some kind of place for him in Lafayette. Maybe he could go
to work for the Acadian Society full-time.

They could work something out.

He unlocked the front door and stepped inside. The first
thing he saw was his daughter's stricken face—all puffy eyed
and red-rimmed. Alarm shot through him. "Daisy! Sweetheart, what's wrong?"

"Oh, Daddy," she wailed, bursting into tears, "please
don't hate me. Please..." She launched herself into his
arms, and he held her trembling body tightly.

"Honey, of course I won't hate you." He smoothed her
hair and tried to lift her chin so he could see her face.

She buried her face against his chest, refusing to look at
him. Her words, when they came, were muffled. "D—dad,
I'm...I'm s-so s-sorry...."

"Daisy, what *is* it? What's happened?" He couldn't
imagine what terrible thing had occurred to upset her so
badly. Obviously she was unhurt physically. So what could
it be?

"M-my bike was st-stolen." Her sobs got louder.

"Oh, honey, my God, is that all?" Relief washed over
him. Bikes could be replaced. He'd thought something *serious* was wrong. "Now, calm down. It's okay."

She finally stopped crying and hiccuped loudly. But she
was still shaking, and he held her and soothed her. "Baby,
really, it's all right. We'll get you a new bike. Now quit carrying on. Come on, let's go sit down." He led her into the
living room, sat her down on the sofa, then sat next to her,
putting his arm around her shoulders. Reaching down, he

lifted her chin. He smiled gently and kissed the tip of her nose. "Okay. Now tell me, was the bike stolen at school?"

Her bottom lip trembled and tears welled into her lovely green eyes again.

He tightened his grip on her shoulders. "Daisy, sweetheart, it's *okay*. Just tell me where and approximately when this happened, and let me take care of it."

"Th-that's the hardest part," she finally said. "I...please, Dad, promise you won't hate me."

He sighed in frustration. "Now, dammit, Daisy, I already said I won't hate you! What's wrong with you? Just tell me."

She dropped her gaze and mumbled. "It was stolen at the shelter."

Dev stiffened. "*What* shelter?"

"Th-the St. Jacques Women's Shelter." Her voice was so soft he had to lean down to hear her.

Shock arrowed through him like a bolt of lightning. "What were you doing at the St. Jacques Women's Shelter?"

"I...I work there two days a week." Now she looked up at him, her expression beseeching.

"You work there! Since when?"

"Oh, Dad," she cried, "I've been working there for weeks. I went down there the day after we talked about it, right after you were on the Johnny Hagan Show, but I...I was afraid to tell you. I'm sorry. I'm really sorry I lied to you. Please don't hate me."

Dev couldn't believe it. Daisy's revelation hit him just as if someone had walloped him in the stomach.

He stared at his daughter. He noticed how her eyelashes stuck together because of her tears. He noticed how rapid her breathing was, how frightened she looked.

"Dad, say something, *please*..." She swiped at her eyes.

Dev took a deep, steadying breath. The shock was subsiding, being replaced by something else: anger. He tightened his jaw. "I'm very disappointed in you, Daisy," he said finally. "I thought you trusted me enough to be honest with me."

"Oh, Dad, I do! I really do. I wanted to tell you. In fact, today, I tried to talk to Elise—"

"Elise!" Somehow, over the past few minutes, he had forgotten that Elise worked at the shelter. A stunning sense of betrayal flooded him. Elise. How could she have done this to him? How could she have sat there, listened to him talk about Daisy and not said anything? What Daisy had done was bad enough; Elise's duplicity was intolerable.

Pain, sharp and piercing, clutched his heart. He ignored it. "Just what does Elise have to do with all this?" he said.

"Nothing!"

"That's very hard to believe, Daisy. I find out you're working at the shelter, and the woman I've been dating—who also happens to work there—knows nothing about it. Hah!" He heard the bitterness in his voice, but he couldn't seem to help it. *The woman I've fallen in love with,* he cried silently. *The woman I thought had so much integrity, was so honest, and pure.* The pain felt like spikes being driven deeper and deeper, but Dev forced it back.

"Dad, honestly, I'm telling you the truth. Elise doesn't even know who I am."

"Oh, come on, Daisy."

"No, really. We . . . we don't use last names at the shelter, and when I went there, well, I said my name was Marguerite. That's all any of them know. Only Charlie—"

"Who the hell is Charlie?" he shouted, visions of some gangly boy filling his mind. "What the hell else is going on behind my back? Are you also seeing some boy?"

"No! Will you just listen for a minute?" Now she looked angry, too. "Charlie is a nickname for Charlotte," she said with dignity. "And she's my age, and she works at the shelter, too. Actually, she's Elise's niece, but until yesterday, she didn't know who I was, either. She advised me to talk to Elise about it, then tell you."

Dev was still mad. He still felt betrayed on more than one level, and he wasn't sure why. Maybe it was because it was so hard to believe that the woman he loved and the daughter he loved already had a relationship he knew nothing about. "You know, Daisy," he said slowly, "whether Elise knew who you were or not really doesn't matter. What matters is, I told you I didn't want you working at that shelter, and you disobeyed me. And on top of all that, you lied about it."

Daisy nodded unhappily. "I know, Dad, and you'll never know how really, really sorry I am. I know I did the wrong thing by going behind your back, but Dad, you were wrong, too."

"Oh?" he said through gritted teeth.

"Yes," Daisy said earnestly, "you were. Working at the shelter is wonderful. It really is. It makes me feel good to work with the little kids, and everything. If you'd just visit the shelter, you'd see what I mean. It's not what you think. It's not ugly or dirty or anything. It's really nice." Her eyes begged him to understand. "I wish you'd just go see for yourself."

"Oh, I fully intend to visit the shelter. In fact, I'll go Saturday."

"You will?"

"You can bet your life I will."

On the drive back to Lafayette from Patinville, Elise talked to her father, but her mind was on Dev. She'd missed him. She'd missed him a lot. It had been wonderful to see all the Patinville Cantrelles again, but she had kept thinking how much she wished Dev was with her. In fact, she'd decided to ask him to come with her to the welcome home party the Patinville branch of the family was hosting the following weekend. She was anxious to show him off.

She could hardly wait until tomorrow night.

On Saturday, only minutes after she arrived at the shelter, Kim came rushing into the office workroom. "Elise," she said in a stage whisper, "there's a *gorgeous* man outside who wants to see you!"

Puzzled, Elise looked up from her task of printing labels. "Who is he?"

"He says his name is Sloan Devereaux." Kim's blue eyes sparkled with curiosity. "He really *is* a hunk!"

Dev! What was *he* doing here? First surprise, then pleasure, surged through Elise. She stood and quickly walked out to the reception area. A rush of happiness filled her as she saw him standing outside the railing that separated Kim's desk from the waiting area. He looked wonderful, although...a disturbing feeling of unease gripped her as she realized how stern and uncompromising his expression was, how he wasn't smiling, even though she was. She could feel her own smile sliding off her face.

"Dev," she said quietly. "This is a surprise."

"Is there somewhere private where we can talk?" he said.

Elise's heart thumped heavily as she nodded. What on earth was wrong with him? She gestured toward Meg's office. "My boss is away. We can use her office." She opened the gate, and he followed her down the hall.

When they were settled in Meg's office, Elise perched on the edge of Meg's desk, and Dev standing stiffly a few feet away, she said, "What's wrong, Dev?"

"What's wrong is that on Thursday when I got home from work I discovered that my daughter—Daisy—has been working here at the shelter."

"What?" Elise frowned. She knew everyone at the shelter. And there was no Daisy. He must be mistaken. She shook her head. "That's not possible—"

"It's not only possible, it's true," he said, interrupting her. "She gave her name as Marguerite. Does that ring any bells?"

Marguerite! That sweet girl was Dev's daughter? Suddenly an image of Marguerite's eyes, the same color as Dev's—something Elise had noticed more than once—flashed through her mind. "I'll be darned," she said slowly. "I had no idea." She shook her head in wonderment. "Of course, now that you say so, I can see it so clearly. Her eyes are exactly like yours. But, Dev, why did she give a false name?"

"She didn't. Marguerite is her real name. We've always called her Daisy, though."

"Oh."

"I came here today because I wanted to see for myself if Daisy was telling me the whole truth when she said you had no idea who she was."

"Oh, Dev... of course, I didn't know. Don't you think I would have *said* something?" Elise was appalled that he would think she'd lie to him. Why, didn't he know *anything* about her?

He shrugged. "I hoped that was the case."

"Surely you believe me!"

"Yes, I believe you." Now there was some warmth in his eyes. "But you've got to understand something, Elise. Regardless of our relationship, or your feelings about this shelter, I do not want my daughter working here. I intend to forbid her to return."

"Oh, Dev, that's a mistake," Elise said without thinking. Instantly she recognized her mistake when she saw his jaw tighten.

"I realize you're doing good work here," he said, "but I don't want Daisy involved in it. I thought you understood that."

"But Mar... Daisy loves working here, and it's good for her. She's made friends here, and the work has given her a feeling of self-worth." Elise slipped off the desk and walked over to where he stood. She touched his arm. "Dev, think about this for a while. Don't do anything too hasty. You're angry with her now, but, believe me, your daughter is a lonely girl. She needs this. It's important to her. I think it would be a terrible mistake to forbid her to come back."

She could feel the rigidity in his arm when he answered. "Let's get one thing straight. I believe you when you say you didn't know who Daisy was. But now you do. Daisy is my daughter, not yours, so please don't interfere."

Elise could feel her heart crumbling. Despair nearly overwhelmed her. Obviously what she and Dev had shared meant little to him if he could dismiss her feelings and her opinions so easily. She dropped her hand. "All right, Dev. You've made your point. And now, if you don't mind, I think you'd better go. I have work to do."

She turned away.

"Elise, listen, I'm sorry if I sounded harsh, but—"

She turned slowly, met his troubled gaze. "It's okay. You've made yourself very clear, and you're right. Daisy *is* your daughter. It was very presumptuous of me to try to tell you what to do as far as she's concerned."

"Look, we can talk about this tonight—"

"No. Not tonight. In fact, I think it might be a good idea for us not to see each other tonight. I think we need a little time apart... time to think about things."

"You're angry."

She sighed. "No, I'm not angry. I'm just...I don't know...I guess I'm confused...." She looked deep into his eyes, trying to see what was there, if what she'd thought was there was real or an illusion. Wanting to be as honest as she could be, she added softly, "And I'm sad." She looked away as she felt tears well in her eyes.

The silence in the room seemed heavy with so many unsaid words. Finally he spoke. He sounded unsure of himself for the first time that afternoon. "I'll call you tomorrow, okay?"

She nodded, still not looking at him.

She didn't turn around when she heard him walk out the door. Instead she stood there, seeing nothing and wondering if she was destined always to pick the wrong man.

Chapter Thirteen

By Sunday afternoon Dev knew he'd blown it big time. For days Daisy had been walking around with a hurt look on her face, and just minutes ago, when he'd tried calling Elise, he'd gotten an answering machine. An answering machine!

He'd stood there, holding the receiver, in a state of disbelief as he listened to the recorded message: *Hi. Sorry I can't take your call just now. At the tone, leave a message and I'll get back to you.*

When had she gotten an answering machine?

Probably when she decided she didn't want to talk to you anymore.

He didn't leave a message. He would try again in an hour. Dispiritedly he walked back to the kitchen. He opened the refrigerator. He wasn't really hungry, but eating was something to do. But after staring inside for a while, he saw nothing that appealed to him. Finally he pulled a can of root beer from a six-pack, popped the top and took a long swallow.

Why had he been so harsh with Elise? He really couldn't fault her in this situation, so why had she made him so angry when she urged him to let Daisy continue her work at the shelter? He still didn't know why he'd reacted as he had.

"Dad?"

Dev whirled around. Daisy stood into the doorway, a hesitant expression on her face.

"Dad, can we talk?" She walked slowly into the kitchen and pulled out a kitchen chair, then sat.

"Sure." He sat across from her. She looked as if she hadn't been sleeping well, with dark smudges under her eyes. Guilt smote Dev, although why he should feel guilty about Daisy—after all, *she* was the one who'd lied to him—he didn't know.

"Daddy, please, please let me go back to work at the shelter!"

"Daisy—"

"I...I was so miserable here before. I *hated* it. I didn't have any friends, and I didn't have anyone to talk to. And then I went to work at the shelter, and everything changed. Now I have Charlie and Elise and a bunch of other really nice women. And I love the little kids." Her voice softened as she mentioned the children. "That's what I do mostly...work in the nursery with the smallest children...and they're so sweet." Her eyes implored him to understand.

"I didn't know you were miserable. Why didn't you say so?"

"What was the point? What could you have done about it? Go back home?"

Dev cringed at the adult resignation and weariness he heard in her tone. And he knew Daisy was right. What *would* he have done about it? Wouldn't he have just encouraged her to make friends? To go to the pool?

"What about Shelley? I thought you liked her." Shelley was the girl who lived three units down—the one who'd invited Daisy to the concert.

"She's okay, but..." Daisy shrugged. "I don't know. She's so *different.*"

Dev sighed. "Honey, I'm sorry, but you'll make other friends. Regular school will start soon, and until then there are other things you can—"

"Dad! You're not *listening!*" She looked about to cry again. "I know I was wrong to go behind your back, but..." She made a sound of frustration. "But I *found* something really special at the shelter. It's just not *fair* of you to take it away from me!" She jumped up. "It's just not fair...." She turned to go, giving him one last beseeching look. "Will you at least think about it?"

Dev sighed. "Okay. I'll think about it."

She seemed about to say something else but didn't. Shoulders slumped wearily, she left the kitchen, and he could hear her slowly climbing the stairs to her room.

He listened as she reached the upstairs landing, followed her progress as she walked down the hall, imagined her walking into her room.

And when he heard her bedroom door close, he felt just as alone as if she'd closed the door to her heart.

Elise stayed away from home all day Sunday. After brunch with Justin and Lisette, she drove to Lianna's, and the two of them went to a movie—Charlie had other plans, so declined their invitation to accompany them—then went back to Lianna's to spend the evening.

She knew she was being a coward, but she simply didn't want to talk to Dev. Not yet. Not until she got over her hurt feelings. Not until she was thinking clearly and objectively. Otherwise, she might do or say something she'd later regret.

"So, are you going to tell me about it or do I have to guess?" Lianna finally asked. They were sitting in their favorite place around the kitchen table.

Elise smiled ruefully. "That obvious, huh?"

"Honey, it couldn't be plainer. Your face has been a picture of dejection the entire day." Lianna's soft eyes were filled with sympathy. "It's Dev, isn't it?"

"How'd you know?"

"Only a man or a child could make a woman look so miserable. And since you haven't got a child, presto, it's gotta be a man."

Elise sighed heavily. Then she related the previous day's scene at the shelter. She finished by saying, "And I'm just not sure where we go from here, Li. I mean, he said he was sorry, but I'm not sure that's good enough. Because, unfortunately, I think his reaction reflects the way he really feels down deep, and I'm not sure I can live with that."

Lianna nodded. "You're right. It certainly doesn't bode well for the future."

"The trouble is, I . . . oh, shoot, I might as well admit it! I'm in love with him. He . . . he makes me feel so *special*. I . . . I just don't know if I can walk away from that." She swallowed against the sudden lump in her throat. "But if I don't walk away now, I know I'm risking getting hurt even more. Because I'm not sure Dev can change. He's so bitter and hard and uncompromising when it comes to everything to do with his past."

"And the women who have hurt him," Lianna said softly.

Elise nodded. "That's it, of course. I know that he's scared to let me in too close, to let go of the little bit of control he has over his life, but I also know we can't really build a lasting relationship...at least not the kind of relationship I want...unless he does. I don't know what to do. Do you have any suggestions?''

Lianna was silent for a few moments, then said slowly, ''Is what you have with him worth fighting for?''

Elise didn't have to think at all before answering. ''Yes.''

''And aren't you a fighter?''

Elise stared at her cousin and friend. The only sound in the kitchen was the gentle hum of the refrigerator and the muffled bark of a dog outside somewhere. ''Yes,'' she said again, more thoughtfully this time.

Lianna smiled and reached across the table to touch Elise's hand. ''Well, then, I think you've answered your own question, haven't you?''

Dev wasn't surprised when Elise didn't show up at the lake on Monday. He'd always known he would have to make the next move. And he also wasn't surprised when she didn't answer her phone Monday evening.

On Tuesday morning he was waiting in the shelter's parking lot as she pulled in. She didn't see him until she got out of her Toyota, and when she did, she stopped. They stared at each other across the sunny pavement. Then he walked slowly toward her; after a second or two, she met him halfway.

He looked down at her.

She looked up.

Something inside Dev curled into a hard knot as he searched her lovely, expressive dark eyes. There were so many things he wanted to say, and he wasn't sure where to begin. ''I was wrong Saturday, and I'm sorrier than you'll ever know. Can you forgive me?''

When she smiled, it caused an ache around the vicinity of his heart. ''Yes,'' she said.

Dev felt as if a great weight had been lifted from him, and he smiled now, too. He took both her hands in his, lifted them and kissed their backs. "Would you have time to show me around the shelter?"

Her eyes widened. Her smile became brilliant, and her voice vibrated with happiness as she said, "Oh, Dev, I'd love to."

For the next hour, she gave him a careful tour. She explained what each area was used for, introduced him to all the personnel and all the women they encountered. She quietly told him some of their stories.

"Abby's husband routinely molested their two little girls, and when Abby realized what was happening, she tried to leave him. He beat her so badly, he actually frightened himself and called 911. Then, when the emergency team arrived at their house, he tried to lie his way out of it by saying Abby had fallen down the steps."

Dev knew he'd always remember the woman called Abby and her two small daughters. Their sad, doe eyes would haunt his dreams for months to come.

"Zelda's husband used a more subtle form of torture than simply beating her. He systematically put her down, every chance he got, but he really loved doing it in front of other people. He had her convinced she was totally worthless and stupid and unable to do anything unless he did it for her. Zelda needs a lot of counseling, but we're all hopeful she's going to make it."

Dev listened to the stories and studied the faces of the women. He watched Elise's expression and listened to her voice as she talked. He also saw the kind of women who worked at the shelter. They were different from what he'd imagined. There wasn't a Joelle in the bunch. No fanaticism shone from their eyes. They were just a normal bunch of women: kind, compassionate, hardworking and cheerul. The cheerful part really surprised him. His past experience with women who were involved in women's rights—which, admittedly, was pretty much limited to Joelle and her friends—had prepared him for humorless women who thought it was a sin to smile or tell a joke, especially at their own expense.

But these co-workers of Elise's—and Daisy's—were a bright, relaxed bunch who laughed and joked and made fun of themselves and their surroundings. When he commented on this phenomenon, Elise smiled. "I know. That surprised me, too, but you know, Dev, we're surrounded by such misery. These women, the ones who come here, have had so little laughter in their lives. They feel so hopeless. We try to show them by our example that life doesn't have to be that way. We particularly try to show them how good it is to have women friends."

Finally they were back where they'd started, outside the building. "I'm glad you came," Elise said softly.

"I'm glad I came, too." He hesitated, then said, "Listen, I've changed my mind. I'm going to tell Daisy she can continue to work here."

"Oh, Dev, that's wonderful!" She reached up, drew his head down and gave him a quick kiss. He was so startled, he didn't react soon enough, and then the kiss was over. Her eyes were shining as she stepped back. "I've got to go in now."

"When will I see you again?"

Still smiling, she squeezed his hand. "Call me tonight."

With the memory of her smile warming his heart, he drove to the university. He knew he'd taken a step toward a different life today, and his heart was filled with hope for the future.

* * *

"Daisy! Daisy! Aren't you ready *yet?*" Dev impatiently looked at his watch. He'd promised Elise he'd pick her up no later than nine o'clock, because she'd said the homecoming celebration for her cousin Desiree, which was taking place at her relatives' home in Patinville, would be in full swing by noon today. It was the Friday after his visit to the shelter.

He'd grinned when she said her family would make a weekend celebration of Desiree's homecoming. "A whole weekend?"

"Hey, I thought you were part Cajun," she teased. "We like any excuse to party."

"I'm coming, Dad," Daisy called, and a few seconds later, she raced down the stairs. "Do you think I look okay?" she asked.

He studied her: her fresh face with a minimum of makeup, her shining hair tied back with a green ribbon, the green-and-white shorts outfit and white sneakers. He grinned. "You look perfect."

She grinned back. "Thanks."

Their relationship had undergone a one-hundred-and-eighty-degree turn in the past few days. Daisy seemed radiantly happy, and that, combined with his reconciliation with Elise, made Dev feel as if nothing in the world could ever get him down again. He smiled, thinking about his reconciliation with Elise, especially the one that had taken place Tuesday night. He would have liked to relive every moment, right now.

He shook the thoughts away, though. There would be many more nights with Elise—hopefully for the rest of his life—and many more memories to savor.

Twenty minutes later the three of them were on their way to pick up Charlie Nicholls, Daisy's new best friend and

Elise's niece. Elise had explained to Dev that Charlie's mother, Lianna, ran a catering business and couldn't afford to take both today and tomorrow off. "She'll drive over tomorrow morning, but it would be a shame for Charlie to miss out on the fun today."

Dev immediately liked Charlie, who was a bright, peppy teenager with lively eyes and a pretty smile despite her braces. He enjoyed listening to the banter between the two girls in the back seat. During the drive over to Patinville, he and Elise exchanged amused glances several times.

Elise. He slanted a look her way. She looked incredible today, he thought. It was the first time he'd ever seen her in the color red. If he'd thought about it beforehand, he would have said red wouldn't suit her—too bold and brash for her personality and demeanor—but he would have been wrong.

Red certainly *did* suit her.

Her outfit consisted of a red T-shirt combined with red-and-white striped shorts. She'd tied a wide red ribbon around her head to hold her unruly hair back from her face. She looked fresh and young—almost as young as the teenagers in the back, he thought. Her slim, tanned legs looked tantalizing in the sunshine, and he wished they were alone so he could touch them. His heart beat heavily as he studied the swell of her breasts under the T-shirt, the roundness of her hip so close to his, the enticing curve of her neck and the delectable fullness of her lower lip.

She was some kind of woman, all right. Even more than he'd imagined her to be when he'd first seen her and spun his fantasies around her. He smiled, thinking of those days only scant weeks ago. They seemed to be in another lifetime.

"Why are you smiling?" Elise asked quietly.

"Just thinking about the first time I saw you."

A faint pink tinged her cheeks, and she shot a covert glance over her shoulder. Charlie and Daisy were giggling together, obviously not paying any attention to him and Elise.

He kept his voice low, though, for her ears only. "I was thinking how the reality of you is even better than the fantasy." He watched as her eyes softened. Now he gave in to his urge and reached across the dividing gears to touch her warm, golden thigh. He let his hand rest there only a moment, but it was long enough for an unspoken message to pass between them.

She smiled at him then—that bewitching, sweet smile he'd come to love—and Dev knew he'd remember this moment for the rest of his life.

"This is my uncle René," Elise said, guiding Dev over to where a surprisingly strong-looking man with lively color sat in a chair at the edge of the lawn. "He's chomping at the bit," she added laughingly, "because the doctors have said he can't dance today. He's recuperating, you see."

René Cantrelle looked up at Dev. His dark eyes assessed him, and Dev hoped he'd passed muster. "I'm ver' glad to meet you, Dev," he said with a thick, Cajun accent. "And you better take ver' good care of this sweet thing, 'cause we're all mighty fond of her." He smiled up at Elise, and she bent down and kissed his cheek. "Is he takin' good care of you, *chère?*"

Elise blushed and nodded. "Yes, Uncle René. He's taking good care of me."

"Good, good. Now you two young people, you go have some fun. Don' think you have to stick around an old man like me."

Laughing, Elise led Dev off to meet more of her relatives. There were uncles and aunts and dozens of cousins, the names soon becoming a jumble in his mind: André, Dennis, Lucién, Armand, Phillip and Beau. Corinne,

Tammi, Joan, Suzette, Robin and Heather. Toby, Harry, Neville and Matt. Missy, Nadine, Darlene and Alaina.

"Stop!" he protested, laughing. "My head is going around and around. I'll never keep them all straight."

"I've saved the best for last," Elise said. "Oh, don't get me wrong. I love them all, but I'm particularly close to my uncle René's family."

So Dev met her Aunt Arlette, René's wife, a motherly woman with kind eyes; her cousin Denise, René's oldest daughter, a lovely dark-haired, dark-eyed woman; Denise's husband, Jett, a quiet man who obviously adored his wife; their children, Justin and Jeannine; René's youngest son, Norman, a big, open-faced, friendly man who seemed to be about Dev's age, and who, Elise explained, was an amputee, "But you'd never know it." Then there was Norman's pretty blond wife, Alice, who had the most understanding eyes Dev had ever seen, and their four children—Jimmy, Lisa, Norman, Jr. and Annie, the baby.

Then he was introduced to René's oldest son and his wife, Neil and Laura Cantrelle. Dev and Elise were staying with them this weekend, Elise had explained earlier. "I love Laura," she said as they approached the couple. "From the first moment I met her, I knew we were soul mates." Her dark eyes met his for a moment. "She told me that she felt exactly the same way. You see, Laura was an abused child.... Maybe that's why we made such an instant connection."

Dev studied Laura carefully when Elise introduced her. Yes, he could see how Elise would be drawn to the slender blonde with the incredibly beautiful blue eyes. Her husband, Elise's cousin, Neil, was the perfect foil for her with his dark intensity. And it was apparent, to anyone watching the two of them together, that they were deeply in love. There was a kind of aura around them, as if they were enclosed in a special place all their own, Dev thought, almost embarrassed by his thoughts. Neil was very protective of his wife, but as the day wore on, Dev decided Laura was a pretty strong woman, for all her outward fragility. He grinned as he watched her chasing what looked to be twin boys.

"They're not twins," Elise said. "But they *were* born only eleven months apart. They're adorable, aren't they?" Her face took on a yearning look as she watched Laura and Neil with their children.

Dev found himself wishing he could give her a child. The thought startled him, and to cover his sudden qualms over the speed in which pleasing Elise seemed to be the dominating force in his life, he asked, "How old are they?"

"Almost three and almost two. Their names are Jason and Joshua." The yearning look remained.

"How about the blond girl? Is she theirs, too?"

"Uh-huh. She's about six, I think. Her name's Celeste. She's precious, too, don't you think?"

Dev thought the question really didn't require an answer.

About two o'clock there was a great commotion with the arrival of some newcomers. Elise jumped up, her face lighting with joy. "Oh, it's Desiree, finally!" She dashed toward the car, and Dev followed more slowly. He watched as she flung herself at a young woman who had just emerged from the front seat. The two women hugged and kissed and hugged again, laughing and talking at once. Finally they drew apart; and, as he moved closer, he couldn't believe how alike they were. The only apparent difference between them, at least on the surface, was the roundness of Desiree's figure under her loose top. He remembered that she was pregnant with twins. Elise had told him, of course, of the startling resemblance between her and her cousin, but he hadn't realized how stunning the reality of that similarity would be.

It disconcerted him momentarily to shake hands with this laughing-eyed and just a bit more colorful and animated version of Elise. "So you're Dev?" Desiree said, her voice lower than Elise's and tinged with amusement. She gave him a sassy look. "Your fame has preceded you, you see." Dev followed her gaze to Elise. Desiree laughed when Elise blushed. "He's gorgeous," she said, and Elise blushed even harder.

Desiree turned back to Dev. "And this is my husband, Jack Forrester." A tall, tanned, sandy-haired man with a strong handshake and very blue eyes smiled at Dev as they acknowledged the introductions.

Just then, an adorable minx with blond hair and dark eyes climbed out of the back seat, and before Desiree could say a word, ran off shouting, "Celeste, Celeste!"

"That was Aimee, our daughter," Desiree said ruefully. "Obviously she has more important things to do than mind her manners."

While she'd been talking, Jack Forrester had reached into the back seat. Dev could see him releasing another child from a car seat. "This is Alan, our son." Desiree beamed with pride as her husband lifted the toddler out and into his arms. Dev could see the strong similarity between the two males. Alan had inherited his father's blue eyes and his mother's dark hair, but he looked like his father.

Elise reached out her arms. "Oh, let me have him, please."

Alan struggled against his father's arms. "Down, Daddy, down!"

Desiree grimaced when Alan immediately toddled off to join his sister. "I guess he doesn't want to be hugged. I'm sorry, Elise."

Elise smiled. "That's okay. I'll get him later." The smile turned to a chuckle. "I'll sneak up on him!" She tucked her arm into Desiree's. "Boy, you're going to have your hands full with two more on the way!"

Desiree shook her head. "Don't I know it! But Jack's really wonderful with the kids, aren't you, honey?"

Jack rolled his eyes, a do-I-have-a-choice look, if ever Dev saw one. He and Dev smiled at each other, and Dev knew he could really like this man.

Desiree was still laughing and eyeing her husband. "You know, the more independent and hard to get they are, the harder they fall, Elise, remember that...."

Jack swatted his wife's rump, and she retaliated, her face flushing as he caught her hands, tugged her close and kissed her soundly. "*Now* will you behave yourself?" he said, love and amusement mixed together in his voice. "Or do I have to keep kissing you to keep your mouth shut?"

"They're wild about each other," Elise confided sotto voce.

"We *are not!*" Desiree exclaimed. "He's a brute! Did you see the way he smacked me?"

"You better watch it," Jack warned. "Or I'll find myself a more agreeable woman." He made a face. "One who appreciates me."

"You just try it!"

Elise looked at Dev. "They're great, aren't they?" she said happily.

He nodded. He could see how much Desiree and Jack and their children and all the rest of her big family meant to Elise. The love between all of them was wonderful to watch. It also made him envious, an emotion he didn't enjoy. Elise had so many people who loved her. She didn't need him the way he was beginning to realize he needed her.

It was a sobering thought.

Chapter Fourteen

Elise and Laura stayed up talking long after Neil and Dev had gone to bed. Elise kissed Dev good-night after sharing an amused glance with him over their sleeping arrangements. Quite obviously, Laura was taking her role as chaperon seriously, for she'd set up a folding bed for Dev in the little room she called a study on the first floor, and she'd put Elise in Celeste's room—moving Celeste in with her little brothers temporarily—on the second floor. Daisy was staying with Charlie at Neil's brother's house.

Now, with their men and Laura's children off to their respective beds, Elise and Laura sat over a cup of coffee in Laura's cozy kitchen.

"I love yellow kitchens," Elise said, looking around. "You don't see that many of them anymore. Everyone seems to want blue."

"Years ago I decided I only wanted to be surrounded by warm colors," Laura said, a soft smile curving her lips. She wrapped her slender fingers around her coffee cup and took a sip, eyeing Elise over the rim. "So... is it serious between you and Dev?"

Elise met Laura's gaze. She nodded. "I think so. I hope so."

"I like him." Laura smiled. "Neil likes him, too."

"Knowing Neil, that means a lot." Elise admired Neil tremendously. He and Laura had both overcome a lot of adversity in their lives. Also, Neil was a shrewd judge of character—as an ex-cop, he'd had a lot of experience.

"What does Uncle Justin think of him?" Laura asked after awhile.

"He hasn't met him yet," Elise admitted. "In fact, that's the only thing about tomorrow I'm a little apprehensive over." Her father and her stepmother were driving to Patinville early in the morning, so they would meet Dev tomorrow.

"Don't worry about it. Knowing your father, all he really wants is for you to be happy. And if Dev makes you happy, I'm sure Uncle Justin will love him."

Justin Cantrelle watched his beloved daughter dancing with Sloan Devereaux. He frowned.

"What is it, *cher*?" Lisette said, placing her hand on his knee. "You look so worried."

Justin sighed as he glanced at his wife, "Oh, it is perhaps nothing, *ma chère*."

Lisette gave him one of her loving, knowing smiles.

After a moment, Justin smiled back. "Oh, you know me too well." He looked once more at Elise and her professor. They were dancing close together, as were all the couples—to a seductive, slow song Justin didn't know the title of—and Elise's arms were locked around the professor's neck. She looked very happy. Very much like a woman in love.

And that was what worried him.

For Justin wasn't certain this Professor Devereaux was right for his daughter. "What do you think of our daughter's professor?" he said.

When Lisette didn't answer immediately, Justin turned toward her, studying her thoughtful face. Finally she said, "I sense that he is a man who has not known much love in his life."

Justin shook his head. His wife would never stop amazing him. They had been married for what seemed to be forever, and she still had the power to take him off guard with her uncanny ability to see into the heart—and very often the soul—of a person.

"Do you think he is right for our Elise?"

Lisette's serene dark gaze met his. "I'm not sure. I think he is a good man, and if he can let go of whatever it is that troubles him, perhaps. If not, well . . ." She gave an eloquent shrug. "He *could* break her heart."

"Yes," Justin said. "That is exactly what I am afraid of."

Dev couldn't remember when he'd had so much fun. "What's the name of that song?" he asked. It had a driving beat that was contagious and the musicians, four energetic Cajuns, had really thrown themselves into it. The woman at the washboard was dancing along while she played, and Dev grinned at her antics.

"I think that's *'Ma 'Tite-Fille.'* Great, isn't it?" Elise smiled. "Do you want to try it?"

"Do you mind if I make a fool of myself?" he countered.

"Not if you don't!"

When she laughed at him that way, the urge to kiss her was so strong, he wasn't sure he could withstand it. Since arriving in Patinville he'd gotten exactly one kiss—that peck she'd given him last night—which didn't count as a real kiss. His feelings must have been evident in his eyes, because the laughter died on Elise's lips, and she swallowed.

"C'mon," he said gruffly, "let's dance before I do something else to make a fool of myself!"

Much later, after stuffing themselves with more food than Dev had ever seen gathered together in one place, they sat in lawn chairs under the shade of one of the tall pines ringing the backyard of René Cantrelle's home.

Elise sighed contentedly. "Look at those kids," she said. "Don't you wish you had half their energy?" She laughed delightedly as she watched the two little boys who belonged to Laura and Neil chasing each other around the yard. When the littlest one collided with a dancing couple—falling backward, then bursting into tears—Elise sprang up and ran over to pick him up.

Carrying the weeping youngster, she disappeared into the house with him. Dev took a long swallow of his icy beer and let his gaze wander. He smiled as he spied Daisy, laughing and talking animatedly, surrounded by an exuberant group, which included Charlie and a dozen or so Cantrelle cousins and hangers-on.

"May I join you?" a quiet voice asked.

Dev looked up. Elise's father stood a few feet away. "Of course," he said.

Justin Cantrelle seated himself carefully, the way old men do, and for a few minutes he watched the noisy crowd. Dev studied his profile. Elise's father was an impressive man—small in stature, but with a commanding presence. He had shrewd eyes and a thoughtful way of speaking. Dev knew he had been a very successful lawyer before his retirement, and that early training was evident in the way he seemed to analyze everything. As he watched him, Dev wondered what he was thinking. After a moment, Dev said, "I owe your daughter a debt of gratitude, Mr. Cantrelle."

Justin's dark gaze slowly turned toward Dev's. "Oh? In what way?"

"Well, when she invited me here, I didn't realize I would learn so much that would be useful in my research."

"Ah, yes. Elise did explain to us what your assignment is. A year-long study of Cajun culture, is that not so?"

"Yes. That's correct."

"So," Justin said, an amused smile curving his lips, "you are studying the natives in their natural habitat, eh? Is that the only reason my daughter issued the invitation? To help you with your work?"

Dev felt like smiling himself, but he didn't. *Wily old fox.* "I don't think that was the main reason."

"No," Justin said. "I don't, either." He turned to face Dev fully, his face now devoid of amusement. "Let's not play games, Professor Devereaux. I know that you and my daughter are seeing each other. From what I have observed today, the relationship has progressed far beyond friendship."

Dev eyed his adversary, for adversary the old man was, there was no doubt of that. "Yes, that's true."

"I want to make a couple of things clear," Justin continued, his dark gaze pinning Dev's. "I have made many mistakes in my life, one of which was not attempting to find my daughter until just a few years ago. I feel a great deal of remorse for that. Elise is very important to me, Professor Devereaux. Her happiness is very important to me. She has had too much unhappiness in her short life, and I do not want her to have any more. I do not want to see her hurt...ever again." His jaw hardened. "Unfortunately I am afraid you *will* hurt her."

All Dev's amusement in the clichéd situation—father warning off prospective suitor—vanished, and a hot rush of anger replaced it. But as quickly as the anger formed, it disappeared. After all, Elise's father only wanted to protect his daughter, just as Dev himself had always wanted to protect Daisy. "I won't hurt her, Mr. Cantrelle," he said quietly. "I promise you that."

Justin studied him for a few more moments. "Very well. But know this—if you do, I'll come after you."

Dev shifted uneasily. Although the situation definitely had its amusing aspects—such as how a small, seventy-two-year-old man could do bodily harm to a man of Dev's age and size—Dev knew Justin was deadly serious.

Later, as Dev and Elise sat talking with Desiree and Jack Forrester and Desiree's sister, Denise Hebert, Dev, out of the corner of his eye, saw Justin watching them intently. Dev turned, and for just a moment, locked gazes with the old man. *I'll honor my promise,* he said silently. *Don't worry.*

For the next couple of weeks, Elise was happier than she'd ever been. Every aspect of her life seemed to have fallen into place: school, her work at the shelter, her finances and her relationship with Dev. Although so far, they had not had a serious talk about their future, she knew he was thinking in terms of something permanent. He gave her hint after hint.

She didn't mind that he had not yet "declared himself," as her stepmother would have put it. Elise was content to wait. She had married Derek after only knowing him a few weeks. It turned out she hadn't known him at all. Now Elise was cautious. She knew it was important for her and Dev to take their time, to see each other in many different situations, and most importantly, to resolve anything from their past that needed resolving before going on to something new.

Elise was encouraged by the gradual changes she saw in Dev—his growing trust and ability to open up with her. He'd softened his attitude toward Daisy, too, and that was also encouraging. In fact, Elise had been amazed when he'd actually permitted Daisy to go on a double date with Charlie and two school friends of hers. Elise grinned, remembering it. Dev had insisted on driving the kids to and from the party, so he hadn't *completely* relaxed his vigilance. Of course, she thought, in today's times, it paid to be a careful parent. There was a lot of scary stuff happening nowadays. Still . . . she was happy for Daisy.

Her budding relationship with Daisy was a source of great happiness, too. Elise loved Daisy. She thought she would have loved her just as much even if Daisy hadn't been Dev's daughter. The fact that she was . . . well, that was just icing on the cake. Elise felt sad for Daisy's mother—never knowing such a delightful child, one who wouldn't be a child much longer. Her mother had missed so much. Daisy had a fine mind. With intelligent, gifted parents, though, that was no surprise to Elise. The kid also had a good heart and a lot of common sense. When she worked with the small children at the shelter, she exhibited a grown-up compassion and empathy that continually surprised Elise. It was rare to see that kind of understanding in one so young.

Elise sighed. Who knew? Maybe if Daisy'd had a standard upbringing, with two more or less normal parents, she would not have turned into the person she was.

And she was a wonderful person. Elise would be proud to claim her as her own, just as she would Charlie.

Another great source of satisfaction was how well things had gone the previous Sunday. Laying her head back against the arm of the love seat, Elise allowed her thoughts to drift to the dinner party her parents had hosted, and to which Elise had invited Dev and Daisy.

Elise had arrived earlier than Dev because she wanted to help her stepmother with the preparations. They'd only been working a short time when Lisette warned her that Justin was concerned about her involvement with Dev.

Elise sighed as she whipped the potatoes that would accompany the rack of lamb roasting in the oven. "Please tell Papa not to worry," she said.

"Yes, *chère,* I *have* told him not to worry, but you know your papa. You are the most important person in his life. How could he *not* worry?"

Elise laid down her wooden spoon and stared at her stepmother. "Lisette, I am *not* the most important person in Papa's life. You are!"

Lisette shrugged. "Perhaps. Perhaps not. But that really don' matter." She turned, giving Elise one of her sweet smiles. "We both love you so much, *chère.* Justin, because you are the flesh of his flesh. Me, because you are a lovable person, but more than that, because you have brought my Justin such happiness in his sunset years." A poignant expression flitted across her lovely face. "It is the great sorrow of my life not to have given Justin any children." She smiled again, sadly. Her dark gaze swept Elise's face. "But I could not love you more if you were my own."

"Oh, Lisette . . ." Tears pooled in Elise's eyes, and she hugged her stepmother close. "I love you, too. More than I can ever tell you."

Lisette gently disengaged herself and with a great show of efficiency, lifted the lid of the pot containing fresh green beans, then poked at its contents. "Enough emotion, already. We have work to do."

Elise smothered a smile. Lisette was a gem. But Lisette's disclosure about her father's concerns worried Elise a little. She hoped he hadn't taken an unreasonable dislike to Dev. Surely not, she thought. Her father was a fair man, a man who didn't make rash judgments or statements. He always adopted a wait-and-see attitude, something he'd encouraged her to do on more than one occasion.

Later, as they all sat around the table and moaned about how stuffed they were, Elise's vague anxiety ebbed. Her father and Dev were engaged in a relaxed conversation—her father probing into Dev's work with sharp and intelligent questions—and Dev was obviously enjoying the stimulating exchange.

And Daisy. Daisy fairly shone with well-being. Lisette had fawned over her from the moment Daisy entered the house, and Daisy was blossoming under the attention. Elise grinned at her own inadvertent allusion to Daisy as a flower, which, now that she thought about it, fit.

In fact, she thought, charmed by her flight of fancy, Daisy resembled the flower after which she was named. Her green eyes were like the leaves and stem, her hair was like its sunny center and the rest of her was like its petals. And her emerging self-confidence and happiness was exactly like a flower opening its face to the world.

That night, as Elise prepared for bed, she relived the day just as she was reliving it now. A great hope filled her heart, for it seemed as if everything had finally settled into place. Dev seemed more and more willing to share Daisy with her, and even solicited Elise's opinions about the care and upbringing of his daughter from time to time. And she felt sure that Dev would eventually win over her father, if the dinner party was any indication. She also felt—and this was the best part of everything—that she and Dev would be able to work out their remaining problems.

Yes. She hugged herself. All was right with the world. She couldn't imagine what could possibly go wrong now.

* * *

Everything had gone wrong today. Daisy remembered what her dad had once told her about Murphy's Law, which sure seemed appropriate this day. First thing this morning Daisy had gotten her period. She hated getting her period. She always had cramps the first day, and that made her cross, and then, the next two days, she was miserable and didn't feel like doing anything.

And she'd had a ton of things to do today.

She sighed, wearily pedaling her new bike—the one her dad had given her to replace the one that had been stolen— up the last block before she reached their town house. She saw the mail truck when she turned the corner. It was parked next to the rows of mailboxes for her complex.

"Hi, Mr. Elvin!" she called as she braked to a stop beside the truck.

"Hi, Daisy. How're you doin' today?" Mr. Elvin, red nose even redder than usual, poked his bald head out of the truck. "Ain't seen you around lately."

"Oh, I've been really busy."

"Well, here, I ain't put your mail in your box yet, so you might as well have it." He handed her a thick batch.

Daisy leafed through the mail. Maybe there'd be a letter from Maura. As she fingered the last envelope, her heart stopped. Then it banged against her chest.

Daisy stared at the envelope. It was addressed to her in a thick, bold script, and it had been forwarded from her New York address to this one. But that wasn't what had her so stunned her mouth had gone dry. What rooted her to the spot was the name in the left-hand corner of the envelope—Joelle Flanders—and under it a post office box address in San Francisco.

Her mother. Daisy's hands trembled as she held the long white envelope. She stood there, under the hot sun, sweat trickling down her neck and between her breasts, and forgot all about Mr. Elvin and her cramps and everything else in the world except the realization pulsing through her.

Her mother had written to her. She was holding a letter from her mother.

Afterward, she never remembered getting back on her bike or riding to her unit or putting her bike away in the garage or going into the house, or anything.

All of a sudden, she was just there, standing in the middle of the kitchen, still staring at the envelope. Heart racing, she tore it open and took out the single folded sheet of paper. With a growing sense of being in the middle of a dream, she read the typed words.

Dear Daisy,

I know you're probably quite surprised to hear from the black sheep of your family—your errant mother. I have been thinking about you quite often lately. At first I wasn't sure if you'd be happy to hear from me. Then I thought, why not? After all, you're emerging into womanhood now, and you ought to be able to deal with some of the realities of life, one of which is that not all women are born to be mothers.

I'm not sure what your father has told you about me. I am sure, though, that none of it was good. We had a, shall we say, acrimonious divorce—if you don't know what the meaning of acrimonious is, look it up! However, I decided to chance your possible scorn and contact you. I'm not sure why. Maybe it's that I'm beginning to feel the passage of time. Maybe it's that I really *do* have some motherly instincts, hard as that may be for me, as well as you, to believe. Or maybe it's simply because I've grown up some myself and know that I have things to make up for.

All this brings me to the point: I would like to see you. I could come there, but I'd prefer you to come here. I will be at home for the next few months and hope that maybe, before the summer ends, you might come for a visit. A week, maybe two? Talk to your father about it, and if you want to, and he's agreeable, please call me collect. I will, of course, pay all your expenses. Just tell me when and where, and I'll make the arrangements.

I hope your father will agree to let you come. I think it's time we got to know each other. You may not like me at all when you meet me, but you *do* have a mother, and you should know who and what she is.

Your mother,
Joelle Flanders

Daisy read and reread the message. Finally her heart slowed, and she sank into a kitchen chair. She wasn't sure how she felt. Excitement, curiosity, elation and fear were all mixed up inside her.

The letter was dated two weeks earlier. It had taken awhile to reach her. The summer was almost gone. School would start in ten days. There wasn't much time to go out to San Francisco, even if her father would let her.

Talk to your father about it, her mother had written. Daisy chewed on her lower lip. If only she could. Could she? Oh, gosh, she could just imagine his reaction. And things were going so well between them. He was beginning to treat her the way she wanted to be treated. How would it affect their relationship if she asked him if she could go to California to see her mother and he said "No"?

Because he *would* say "No." Daisy knew it as well as she knew her own name. He would not only say 'no,' he would probably say "Hell, no." He would get very, very angry and forbid Daisy to have any contact with her mother. He would say all kinds of nasty things about her mother, such as, how come her mother had waited all these years to contact her if she cared about her so much? And, why would she even want to see her mother when her mother had ignored her very existence for nearly twelve years? Then he would get this hurt look on his face and make Daisy feel bad, as if she had let him down or something.

Maybe she should just forget all about the letter. But, oh, she wanted to go out there. She needed to go out there. Just as Elise had said weeks ago, it was important for Daisy to know her mother so that she could eventually know herself.

Okay, so was she brave enough to broach the subject with her father?

No way.

Daisy sighed heavily and laid her head down on her folded arms. She thought for a long time. Finally she raised her head. She knew what she was going to do.

"Oh, Elise, I can't believe it! She wants to see me! She wants me to come out to California and spend a couple of weeks with her. Of course, I couldn't go for that long, not this late in the summer. But she told me to call her and she'd make arrangements for my airline tickets, and everything. Isn't it wonderful?"

Elise frowned, trying to absorb the surprising information that Dev had given in to this request so easily. He'd certainly never given her any indication that his attitude toward his former wife had softened so much. She nodded slowly. "Yes, that's great, Daisy. I just can't believe your father has actually said you can go, but that's wonderful."

Daisy's eyes widened, and her face paled. "He doesn't know anything about it! And you can't tell him! Elise, you wouldn't tell him, would you? I told you in the *strictest* confidence.''

''Daisy—''

''I remember what you told one of your groups. Remember? That day I sat in on your session? You told those women that a woman has to be strong. You said they had to learn to make their own decisions, right or wrong. You said it was wrong to depend on any man too heavily. I heard you.''

Oh, God, please help me say the right thing. ''Daisy, I was talking to adult women who have been abused. You're twisting what I said to fit—''

''I'm *not* twisting what you said!'' Daisy's own face twisted. ''I'm doing exactly what you said to do. I'm making my own decisions. And if you tell my father, it'll just *ruin* my life! I'll never forgive you if you do—not as long as I live!''

If the situation hadn't been so serious, Elise would have been amused by Daisy's dramatics and her sweeping statements, but the situation *was* serious. Elise knew Dev would be absolutely furious with her if he thought she'd known something like this and hadn't told him—and rightly so. And yet, how could she destroy the trust Daisy had placed in her? Talk about being between a rock and a hard place. Elise fleetingly wondered if she had tempted fate when she'd thought, so smugly, that nothing else could possibly go wrong between her and Dev.

Quietly she said, ''Daisy, you have to tell your father. You know that. That's the way to be strong, by being honest. Tell him how you feel, how important this is to you and that you want to go. Emphasize that you love him, and that you will always love him. Be straight with him. Remember what happened when you didn't tell him about working here at the shelter?''

Daisy's eyes filled with tears, and she looked away. "I'm scared, Elise."

"Sweetie, I know you are. But your father is changing. He really is. He might be mad at first, but I think, if you really talk to him, he'll come around."

"You think so?"

"I do. Trust me, honey, okay?"

"I don't know..." Daisy's forehead creased as she frowned. "I'm not sure he's changed *that* much." Her beseeching gaze met Elise's. "If he won't let me go, will you talk to him?"

Elise opened her arms, and Daisy came into them. As she held the girl she'd come to love, she stroked her hair, saying gently, "You know I will."

Chapter Fifteen

"You what?" Dev couldn't believe he'd heard his daughter correctly.

Daisy's bottom lip trembled, but she raised her chin, saying defiantly, "I said I got a letter from Mom yesterday. She...she wants me to come out to California and visit her, and I want to go." Two bright spots of color stained her cheeks.

Dev stared at her. How dare Joelle do this without contacting him first! What gave her the right to think she could just pop back into Daisy's life as if she'd never left it? Where did she get off thinking she had any rights at all? And Daisy! He couldn't believe she actually wanted to go out there. After everything they'd been through together, after all the years he'd devoted to her, all she'd had to get was one letter and it was as if all those years had counted for nothing.

Hurt and fury churned in his gut. Added to the painful knowledge that Daisy wanted to go to California was the knowledge that she'd gotten the damned letter yesterday and hadn't told him. Last night, all through dinner and afterward, she hadn't said a word. Not one blasted word.

Through gritted teeth, he said, "No. Absolutely not. I forbid it!" He yanked open the refrigerator, rummaged around in it, then extracted a small can of vegetable juice. Angrily he popped the top and took a large gulp. His head felt as if someone was hammering at it—not an auspicious start to the day—especially one where he was scheduled to give a progress report to the Acadian Society Board of Directors.

"Dad! You can't just—"

Dev spun around. "I can do anything I damn well please, young lady. I happen to be your father *and* your legal guardian, and don't you forget it!" He drained the last of the juice and flung the empty can into the wastebasket. He glared at her.

Her eyes were suspiciously shiny. "Dad, can't we talk about this? There're things that, well . . . that you don't understand."

If she thought tears were going to work and give her her own way, she was sadly mistaken. He was tired of being manipulated, tired of being told he didn't understand. He understood a hell of a lot more than Daisy did. He understood that Joelle was a woman who thought only of herself. If she wanted Daisy to come out there now, after all these years, there had to be some ulterior motive. He had no intention of allowing her to exploit Daisy. To hurt her. Or to try to steal her away from him. "Nothing you can say will change my mind. This is a forbidden subject. You are not going, and that's final, and I don't want to hear one more word about it." He bit off the words, trying to hold on to his temper, trying to keep from saying things he'd regret.

Daisy stared at him, her chest heaving. Then, in a strained voice, she said, "I told Elise you hadn't changed, but she was so sure you'd listen if I talked to you. I should have known better." She tossed down the knife she'd been using to spread mustard on the sandwiches she'd been making for their lunch, and without looking at him again, rushed from the kitchen.

He heard her footsteps as she hurtled herself up the stairs and clomped down the hall into her room. He winced as the door slammed shut.

Dev stood there for a few minutes, her last words reverberating in his mind.

Elise. Elise had known about this, too. He had talked to her last night, and she'd said nothing. Not one peep. Now the hurt exploded into excruciating pain pressing into his temples. He rubbed them, closing his eyes, trying to think, trying to get some relief. Then slowly, like an old man, he walked over to the cabinet where he kept the aspirin and downed two. He eyed the abandoned sandwiches, then methodically finished making them. After that, he packaged his and Daisy's lunch, then put hers into the refrigerator. He gathered up his briefcase, found his sunglasses, then put everything on the kitchen table.

He walked upstairs, pausing for a second outside Daisy's closed bedroom door, then raised his fist and knocked. "Daisy?"

No answer.

"Daisy?" he said again, louder this time.

Still no answer.

He tried the doorknob. It was locked. He rattled it. "Dammit, Daisy! Open this door. I want to talk to you."

"Go away." The words were muffled.

Dev counted to ten. "Look, I don't have time to stand here and beg you. If you want to stay in there and pout, fine.

We'll talk when I get home tonight. Your lunch is in the refrigerator.''

He waited a second, thinking surely she'd relent and open the door, but he heard nothing from inside. "I'm leaving now, and you just remember what I said." He walked away, her silence fueling his anger.

Five minutes later he pulled out of the garage and pointed his car in the direction of Elise's apartment.

Daisy lay facedown on her bed. As soon as she heard her father leave, she let the tears come. "I hate him. I hate him," she wailed. "Why does he have to be so impossible? Why can't he understand?" She cried for a long time. When her tears were finally spent, she got up, went to her dresser, opened the bottom drawer and extracted the letter.

She read it one more time.

Then, letter clutched in her hand, she unlocked her bedroom door, walked down the hall to the spare bedroom and headed toward the upstairs phone.

She picked up the receiver.

Elise had just emerged from the shower when her doorbell chimed. She grabbed for her terry-cloth robe. It chimed again, then again, as if someone was angrily or impatiently punching the button.

"Okay, okay," she called as she hurried into the living room. She made sure her belt was securely tied, then peered out the peephole. Her heart lurched when saw Dev standing outside. She let the chain off, then unlocked the dead bolt.

"Dev! What're you doing here at this hour of the morning?" she said as she yanked open the door. Her smile died on her face as she saw his expression. Suddenly she knew exactly why he was there. She wet her lips. "Come on in."

He stalked past her, walked halfway into the living room, then turned around. His jaw looked like granite, and his eyes like cold jade—all the golden glints gone.

Elise wished she'd had time to dry herself, to dress and to put some makeup on. She felt vulnerable and at a disadvantage in her near-naked state, water dripping off her onto the rug. She could just imagine how she looked, and that knowledge did nothing for her self-confidence.

When he spoke, his voice was just as cold and hard as his eyes, and each word was like a needle pricking her heart. "I can't believe you encouraged Daisy in this scheme of her mother's to undermine my relationship with my daughter."

"Dev—"

"What really gets to me is that I told you *everything*. I cut myself open and bled myself dry. You knew *exactly* how I felt, yet you still encouraged Daisy to believe I'd let her go to California."

"I didn't encourage—"

"Don't lie to me, Elise," he said. "Don't lie to me on top of everything else. Daisy told me exactly what you said."

Elise knew she was going to cry. He looked so cold and forbidding—as if he *hated* her. "Dev, Dev," she pleaded. "I know you're upset. But you're being so unreasonable. Just listen to yourself." Fear clogged her throat, but she forced herself to go on. "I swear to you…I didn't encourage Daisy to go. All I did was advise her to talk to you! She…she was planning to just leave. Not even tell you, just go out there, and I told her she couldn't do that to you."

Her heart began to pound as his face flushed an angry red. "I don't believe you!" he said. He closed the distance between them in two long strides and grabbed her by the shoulders. "Daisy wouldn't do that!"

Alarm, fear, shock, anger, disbelief: all these emotions and more first stunned her, then galvanized her. "Get your hands off me," she said, shoving them away.

He backed up, his face draining of color.

Hands on her hips, she glared at him. "Don't think you can push me around the way you push Daisy around. I let one man do that, and I'll never let another push me around again!"

She could see she'd shocked him. Uncertainty and bewilderment crossed his face. Fear flared in his eyes. "I...I'm sorry, Elise," he stammered. "I...I wasn't thinking. I know you didn't lie to me, I..."

A great coldness engulfed Elise. She felt frozen and heavy, as if a huge block of ice had been dumped on her, erasing all feeling. "I just want you to leave, Dev." After all they'd been to each other, if this was how little he respected her, how little he understood her, how little he believed in her—there was no hope for them.

No hope at all.

The knowledge nearly flattened her, and it was all she could do to keep from sinking to the floor and crying her heart out.

"Elise, please. I really *am* sorry. I know I was out of line, but I wasn't thinking. I just got so mad at the idea that Daisy would even think of doing something like that behind my back. I...I had to lash out at someone. Can...can we talk about this?"

She shook her head. "I'm tired of talking, Dev." She couldn't look at him. The ice was beginning to thaw, and she knew that soon, very soon, she would be engulfed by all those emotions that would hurt her so much—emotions like unbearable disappointment and heartbreak and the death of dreams.

"Elise...love...please look at me."

She raised her head slowly, finally meeting his now frightened gaze. Her throat hurt from the tears she was fighting so hard to suppress. "*Love?* Dev, I don't think you know the meaning of love. Love isn't possessiveness. Love isn't controlling people and bending them to your will. Love isn't molding someone into the kind of person you want them to be."

"I—"

"Love is honesty and trust and acceptance and understanding." She bit her lip to still the trembling. "I want you to go, Dev," she whispered brokenly. "I want you to go."

"But—"

"Just go." She squeezed her eyes shut. She felt the heat of her tears behind her eyelids, the crushing pain that lurked nearby, waiting to claim her.

"Will I . . ." He cleared his throat. "Will I ever see you again?"

"I don't know." Her hands shook as she opened the door. "I don't see much point, do you?"

When the door closed behind him, Dev sagged against it. What had he done? Not only had he said unforgivable things to the woman he loved, but he'd also manhandled her. He couldn't believe he'd done that, especially to Elise who had suffered so much brutality at the hands of another man—one who had supposedly loved her, too.

He staggered down the outside steps. In a daze, he looked up at her window, the one that overlooked the parking lot. The closed slats of the miniblinds stared back at him. *Elise, Elise,* his heart cried. *Please forgive me.*

He got into his car, started it. He wished he could just go home, try to make things right again—somehow. Show her he knew he'd acted like an unreasonable jackass. He hit the steering wheel. *What the hell is wrong with you?*

If only he could start the day over. If only he could go back to Elise's apartment. Maybe if he got down on his knees and begged, she'd listen.

He couldn't, though. He had that meeting this morning, and he couldn't skip it. And this afternoon he was interviewing a local Acadian historian—an interview that had been very difficult to get. It would be after four before he would be free to go home and talk to Daisy. Tonight before he could try to talk to Elise again.

Why had he told Elise he didn't believe her? Down deep he knew she was telling him the truth.

You had to believe she was lying to you, otherwise you'd have had to admit that Daisy is unhappy.

Oh, God, was that true?

Hell, yes, it's true, and you know it. Why don't you come clean with yourself for once? You accused Elise of lying, but you're the one who's lying—to yourself.

Dev drove unseeingly as his mind churned. Had he been lying to himself?

Of course, you have. You know damn well that once you admitted to yourself Daisy needs something more than what you can give her, you'd be admitting you'd failed. Again.

Dev swallowed. He had never cried, not once in his life. Not when his mother had left. Not when his wife had left. Never. But he felt like crying now.

Come on, be a man. Admit it. You failed as a son. You failed as a husband. And now, you've failed as a father. You've failed at every personal relationship you've ever had. It's no wonder Elise kicked you out. She probably never wants to see you again.

The admission terrified him. How could he bear it if Elise refused to see him again? And Daisy... *was* he a failure as a father? Is that why she wanted to go out to California to see Joelle? What if she wanted to live with her mother?

Yeah, well, now we get to the heart of the problem, don't we? That's what you're afraid of. That's why you got so mad at both Daisy and Elise. You had to blame somebody for something, didn't you? Because you're scared out of your mind that if Daisy goes out there, she might never come back.

Dev pulled into the faculty parking lot, found a slot and parked the car. He turned off the ignition and leaned his head against his arms on the steering wheel.

How could he let Daisy go? What if she *did* want to stay out there, permanently? Live with Joelle?

That's a risk you've got to take, because if you don't let her go, she'll hate you. And Elise will hate you. Because Elise was right, and you know it. You can't control everything, no matter how much you might want to.

Wearily Dev climbed out of his car and locked it. He headed for his office.

For the rest of the day he operated on automatic pilot. He went through the motions, did all the things he was supposed to do: gave his report, interviewed the historian, answered questions, asked questions, said the right thing in all the right places, but his heart wasn't in it. His heart was with Daisy and Elise, Elise and Daisy—the two people he loved most in the world.

He hoped they'd each give him another chance.

Elise wasn't scheduled to work at the shelter, but after her classes were over, she couldn't face going home. She thought about going to Lianna's, but she couldn't face that, either. Lianna would take one look at her face and know something was dreadfully wrong. And Elise didn't think she could talk about what had happened—not yet, anyway.

She thought about going to the shelter. There was always work to do and never enough hands to do it. But she didn't think she could deal with anyone's problems today.

So she went to a movie. An anonymous theater where she could sit in the dark and stare at the flickering images on the screen and think.

She thought about her life with her mother.

She thought about her life with Derek, and everything she'd overcome since then.

She thought about her discovery of her father and his family.

She thought about her work at the shelter and all her friends there.

She thought about Lianna and her friendship, about Charlie, and about Daisy.

She thought about meeting Dev, and all the times they'd spent together. She thought about the things they'd shared, the things they'd talked about. She thought about making love with him and how special he always made her feel.

She thought about never seeing him again.

Apprehension slowed Dev's footsteps as he stepped from the garage into the kitchen. He knew Daisy was home because her bike was parked in its usual corner, and he wondered what kind of reception he'd get. He hoped they could sit down and talk. Maybe if he explained how he felt and allowed Daisy to explain how she felt, they could come to an acceptable compromise. Maybe—he cringed at the thought—Joelle could come to Louisiana.

"Daisy?" Usually, when he walked in the door, he immediately knew what Daisy had planned for their dinner. Tonight, though, there were no pots on the stove, no oven light beaming red, no evidence of any food preparation at all.

He tossed his briefcase on the table and walked through the kitchen in the hall. "Daisy?" The house was silent. Surely she wasn't still locked up in her room? He leaned over the banister and called upstairs. "Daisy! I'm home!"

Silence. She must be asleep. He walked to the foot of the stairs, intending to go up and check on her, when he spied the note. It was sitting on the small table in the entryway, the one where she always put the day's mail. It was propped up against the cloisonné vase he'd bought when he and Daisy vacationed in London two years ago.

He ripped the note open, irritated that she'd gone out. He was completely unprepared for the contents of the note.

Dear Daddy,

I'm sorry, but I just *have* to do this. I've gone to California to see my mother. I hope you can try to understand, because I don't want you to hate me. I'll call you when I get there.

I love you,
Daisy

Oh God! What did she *mean*—she'd gone to California? How? Panic, thick and terrifying, paralyzed him for a moment. How had she gone? By bus? Dev knew Daisy couldn't afford the cost of a plane ticket, but she *did* have about a hundred dollars in her savings account. Would that have been enough to get her a bus ticket?

Dropping the note, he raced up the stairs two at a time. He barreled into her room. He knew where she kept her personal things. He'd never before violated the privacy of her room, but desperate times called for desperate measures, he told himself, as he yanked open the bottom drawer of her dresser. It was empty. He searched the other two large drawers, then the two small ones. Her passbook was gone.

He looked at the clear glass piggy bank on top of her bureau. She'd even emptied that!

What should he do? He looked around frantically. Then he remembered the cop he'd met through Gerald Eggleston—the cop who belonged to Gerald's chess club. He'd know what Dev should do. What the hell was his name? He couldn't remember!

He ran from Daisy's room into the spare bedroom where he'd had their upstairs phone installed. With shaking hands he dialed Gerald's number and prayed he would find him home.

"Calm down, Dev," Gerald said. "I'll call Russ, then we'll both come over. In the meantime, don't you think you should call your ex-wife?"

Joelle! Of course. How stupid of him. "You're right. I'm not thinking straight."

"Well, that's understandable, old man, under the circumstances. Now you try to get her, and I'll get a hold of Russ. And don't worry. We'll find your daughter."

As Dev called San Francisco information, he prayed Gerald was right. God, he was scared. It was a dangerous world out there. And who knew what a kid would do if she was unhappy enough? What if she had hitchhiked, or something? The thought turned his blood to ice. *Please, God. Don't let her do anything stupid.* Surely she had taken the bus. But even then, Dev thought, there were a lot of unsavory people hanging around bus stations.

He closed his eyes. *Please, God, let her be all right.*

Because if anything happened to Daisy, nothing in his life could ever be all right again.

Chapter Sixteen

This is Joelle Flanders. At the tone, leave a message. I'll get back to you.

In frustration, Dev slammed down the phone. God, how he hated answering machines! They were so damned cold and impersonal. Then he heaved a heavy sigh and picked up the phone again. He should have left a message.

Drumming his fingers impatiently, he listened as her machine kicked in and repeated its short message. When the tone beeped, he said, "Joelle, this is Dev. Daisy's gone. She left a note saying she was on her way to California. I need to talk to you the minute you come in." He left his number, then hung up.

He stared at the phone. He felt so helpless.

What if Daisy tried to call Joelle and got that damned machine? What if she'd tried to hitchhike? What if...? Unspeakable thoughts churned around in his brain, thoughts he tried to bury. Panic clawed at him, and he knew if he gave in to it, he would go crazy. "Daisy, Daisy, Daisy," he whispered. What would he do if something happened to her?

Don't think the worst, he told himself. She's a smart kid. She's always been sensible, at least she was until we moved here. And even here in Lafayette, she really hadn't done much that he could complain about. In fact, until she'd gone to the shelter behind his back—

He broke off the thought, realizing for the first time that Daisy might have called Elise. "Elise! Of course! Why didn't I think of that before?"

He snatched up the receiver again. He dialed the familiar numbers. The phone rang and rang and rang. "Please, Elise, be there. Answer the phone. Please." Why wasn't her answering machine turned on?

It continued to ring. No one answered. Finally he hung up. What to do now? He ran his hands through his hair. *Think! Who else would she call?*

Charlie. Yes! Charlie. The two girls had gotten as tight as those biker shorts they both loved so much.

He hunted for the phone book. There wasn't one upstairs. He bolted out of the room and sped downstairs. It took him a few minutes to find the phone book, and a few more minutes to locate Something's Cookin', Charlie's mother's catering service.

A minute later he was impatiently waiting for someone to answer.

"Something's Cookin'."

"Lianna?"

"No, this is Roxanne."

"Is Lianna there?"

"No, I'm sorry, she's not."

Damn. He kept hitting blank walls. "Well, is Charlie there?"

"Neither one is here, sir. They're on vacation this week. Can I help you, sir? I work for Lianna once in a while, and I'm fillin' orders this week."

His heart sank. "No, I'm afraid not. It's personal."

"In that case, I'll be glad to take a message."

If they were away on vacation this week, Daisy couldn't have talked to Charlie. "No. Thanks, anyway."

He hung up, wondering what he should do next. Just then his doorbell rang. It was Gerald.

"Russ is on his way," he said, squeezing Dev's shoulder in a silent gesture of sympathy. "Listen, old man, I'm truly sorry."

They waited in silence after Dev brought Gerald up-to-date on the calls he'd made. Dev's mind refused to shut down, continuing to conjure up every horrible image it could: Daisy kidnapped, Daisy the victim of a sexual attack, Daisy afraid for her life. . . .

He paced up and down the room. This was all his fault. If he hadn't been so stubborn, so pigheaded, so stupid. If only he'd listened to her. If only he'd listened to Elise. If only it weren't too late to make things right again.

Daisy, Daisy. Where are you? Please be all right.

Finally the doorbell rang again.

Russ Aubrey was a big, quiet man with thick auburn hair and freckles all over. He exuded confidence and intelligence, and he immediately made Dev feel better.

"Now don't you worry none, Professor Devereaux," he drawled. "I've dealt with hundreds of runaways, and I know just what to do. I'll just need to get a little information from you, and then I'll get right to work."

So Dev described Daisy, rooted out a picture of her and told Russ briefly what had happened. Then Russ disappeared into the kitchen to make phone calls, saying, "You all just sit in here and give me a half hour or so, y'hear?"

Dev chewed his nails.

Gerald sat and watched him.

Twenty minutes later—a twenty minutes that seemed like hours—Russ came back to the living room to report on his progress. "I've got people checkin' the bus depot, the trains and the airports. Another buddy's callin' the cab companies. They'll let us know what they find out." He smiled reassuringly. "Then we'll go from there."

He had no sooner finished relaying this information than the phone rang. Dev jumped up to answer it, heart pounding.

"Dev? This is Joelle."

"Joelle! Thank God. Have you heard from Daisy?"

"Yes, Dev. Calm down. She's here with me, and she's perfectly fine."

"She's there!" Relief such as he'd never known before hit him like tornado force winds. His knees suddenly felt like water, and he sank into a kitchen chair. His hands were shaking, and he felt absurdly close to tears.

"Yes. She called me this morning, and I was able to get her a reservation for a noon flight. I just picked her up at the airport, and we just got home."

"Oh, thank God," he said. "I was scared out of my mind. I didn't know where—"

"You mean you didn't know where she'd gone?" Joelle sounded amazed.

"I knew she was heading out to see you," he said in a calmer tone of voice, his heart beginning to slow to normal speed. "She left me a note. But I didn't know how she planned to get there. I was so worried—"

"I'm sorry you were worried," she interrupted. "But believe me, she's fine. Do you want to talk to her?"

"Yes."

He heard a muffled conversation, then, "Dad?" Daisy's voice sounded small, unsure, and very young.

"Daisy? Sweetheart? Are you okay?"

"Uh-huh." Her voice broke. "Oh, Dad, I'm sorry I scared you. Are you mad at me?"

"No, honey, I'm not. Not anymore. Listen, I'm coming out there. I want to talk to both you and your mother."

"Okay."

"Put your mother back on the phone."

When Joelle came back, he said, "I'm coming out there. Either tonight or tomorrow. Depends on when I can get a flight out. Give me directions to your place."

Later, after Gerald and Russ had gone home—both of them assuring him they hadn't minded being called and that they were just glad everything had turned out all right—Dev began to pack. He hadn't been able to get a flight out that evening, but he was booked on one first thing in the morning. With the time difference in California, he'd be in San Francisco before ten tomorrow.

Once he was packed, he thought about calling Elise again. Elise. He hadn't had the luxury of thinking about her since his discovery of Daisy's absence, but now…God, he wished he could talk to her. Hear her calm voice. He wanted . . .

No. Better not. First things first. He needed to get things straightened out with his daughter, and then he needed to straighten himself out. His life was a mess. He was afraid Elise had been right. He needed to think about the things she had said. Then he needed to figure out where he was going from here.

It was probably a good thing he would see Joelle again, too. Maybe seeing her would allow him to put the past to rest.

Then, and only then, could he call Elise.

* * *

Elise finally went home about nine o'clock Friday evening. She spent a tearful, sleepless night. The next morning she had a giant headache and puffy, swollen eyes. She looked terrible.

She called the shelter and said she wouldn't be in. Then she moped around her apartment, periodically staring at her silent phone. She *did* finally turn on her answering machine Saturday afternoon, but there were only a couple of calls throughout the day—none of them important.

The call she was waiting for didn't come.

She had hoped—prayed—that Dev would call and say he'd changed his mind. That he'd gone home, talked to Daisy and realized he was being unfair. That he was allowing Daisy to go out to California.

Obviously her hope had been in vain.

Obviously he had not had second thoughts.

Obviously his earlier apology was only for his roughness when he grabbed her shoulders—not because he thought he was in the wrong.

Oh, Dev, how did this happen to us? How did something so beautiful turn so ugly? She blew her nose. Was it all over then? Was this going to be it? This feeling of desolation and abandonment?

Please, God. She had had to rebuild her life once. She wasn't sure she could do it again.

She wished with all her heart she could help Dev understand. She had thought she could, but now she knew the only person who could help him was Dev himself. No matter how much she loved him, he had to come to his own self-realization. And the only way he was going to do that would be to bury his bitterness and anger. He had to put all of the bad stuff behind him, just as she'd had to.

And that's a tough thing to do, especially for someone like Dev. She sighed, staring at the walls of her silent apartment. She wondered if Dev would ever be willing to do what it took to understand himself and the others in his life. Elise knew he had to be willing to accept what was and not try to make it be something different.

She remembered their conversation about letting go of their anger, how he'd disdainfully said that was a woman's concept. She wished she could tell him what she'd thought of later, that there was a difference between forgiving and letting go—that letting go was what she'd done.

Letting go was what he had to do, too.

Until he could do all that, there was no future for them.

Now dry-eyed, she lay in bed Saturday night and watched the shadows moving across her ceiling, reflections from the lights outside. She thought about how those shadows were actually reflective of life with its ever-changing patterns.

Why are we humans asked to endure so much?

She felt empty.

And so alone.

When the cab pulled up in front of a handsome, narrow, Spanish-style house midway down Lombard Street, Dev wasn't surprised. He knew Joelle was probably making a lot of money, and this kind of environment had always been one she aspired to. She'd always liked nice things.

He guessed that now she could afford them.

He paid the cabdriver, hefted his overnight bag and walked slowly up the short walkway to a wrought-iron gate. He opened the gate and entered a tiny, flower-filled courtyard with a fountain tinkling merrily off to the left side.

Hibiscus and bougainvillea fought for dominance in the courtyard, and their jeweled colors were a feast for the eyes. He stepped into the shaded doorway and pressed the buzzer.

The door opened immediately. A jeans-clad Daisy said, "Dad!" She rushed out and flung herself into his arms.

He hugged her tight.

When they pulled apart, he saw tears in her eyes—tears that he knew were mirrored in his own eyes.

"Dad, I'm sorry—"

"Daisy, I'm sorry—"

They both spoke at once. Then they both laughed. Then they hugged again.

Daisy took his hand. She grinned up at him.

He thought how beautiful she was in her bare feet, faded jeans and bright yellow sweatshirt. "Come on in, Dad," she said. "Mother's upstairs. She said she knew we'd want to talk alone first."

Joelle was showing a surprising sensitivity, Dev thought. Maybe she'd changed.

Daisy led him into a bright, high-ceilinged room furnished with gaily colored sofas and chairs and rough-hewn tables. The floor was a highly polished one of terra cotta tiles dotted with woven rugs. There was an enormous framed photograph over the mantel of Joelle and a former president shaking hands and dozens of others strategically placed around the room.

Daisy sat on one of the sofas, and he sat next to her. "Are you mad at me, Dad?"

He shook his head. "You shouldn't have left like that, honey, but I'm not mad. I'm just thankful you're all right. I know this was mostly my fault. Can you forgive me?"

"Oh, Daddy..." She leaned closer, and he put his arm around her. "I love you. Of course, I forgive you. I...I was so afraid you'd never want to see me again."

"Nothing you could ever do would make me not want to see you again," he assured her.

Just then he heard footsteps and looked up. Joelle—older but still a knockout—stood in the doorway. Her blond hair was braided in one thick plait which fell over her left shoulder. She was wearing some kind of loose black pants and a matching belted top in a silky, flowing material. There was a thick choker of gold around her neck and gold sandals on her feet.

"Hello, Dev," she said. "It's been a long time."

He stood. "Twelve years."

She walked closer. "You're looking very well. I always knew you'd get more handsome as you got older."

He smiled. Same old honey-tongued Joelle. "So are you."

She arched her head to the side, and her big gold earrings swung. She smiled, too. "Well, did you and Daisy get everything straightened out?"

Daisy got up and walked over to him, sliding her hand in his. "Yeah," she said. "He's not mad."

"So," Joelle said, "can I get you something to drink? Scotch? Vodka? A beer?"

"A beer."

"Daisy?" she said. "Do you want a Coke or something?"

"I'll get it," Daisy said.

A few minutes later, they were all settled in the living room—he and Daisy back on the sofa they'd been sharing earlier and Joelle sitting across from them in a matching love seat. She tucked her long legs under her and said, "Are you going to let Daisy stay?"

Still blunt and to the point, Dev thought. He looked at Daisy. She had gone very still as she waited for his answer. The only indication that she was nervous was the way she bit her bottom lip.

"Do you want to stay?" he asked softly.

She nodded.

He sighed. "Yes, she can stay."

Daisy exhaled, then grinned, her face lighting up.

Joelle smiled.

"But only for a week. I don't want her to miss the start of school."

"Oh, Dad, thanks," Daisy said. She looked at her mother.

"Sure," Joelle said. "A week's fine. Actually that probably suits my schedule better than a longer visit, anyway."

"In the future, if you want to continue to be a part of Daisy's life—and she wants you to—I won't give you any trouble," Dev continued. "We can set up a regular schedule of visitation."

Joelle's smile was speculative. "You've changed, Dev. I never thought I'd see it happen."

Elise finished her shift at the shelter Tuesday afternoon and listlessly retrieved her purse and umbrella from her locker. The weather forecast had predicted rain today, and when she'd looked outside earlier, the sky had darkened.

She walked out through the reception area.

"Bye, Elise," said Kim.

"Bye."

With no reason to hurry and nothing to look forward to, Elise walked slowly out the front door and down the steps. She looked up. The lowering clouds threatened rain at any minute. The air smelled moist and heavy.

A gray day to match my gray mood, she thought.

She turned left.

She lifted her gaze.

Her heart zoomed up into her throat.

"Dev." The word was a whisper, a prayer, a sigh.

He stood under the sycamore, the one that shaded the bike rack.

Elise swallowed hard. She stood motionless.

They stared at each other.

Thunder rumbled in the distance. A fat raindrop landed on her nose. Her heart was going *boom, boom, boom*.

Still unsmiling, he moved. Elise's mind registered his pleated khaki pants, his burgundy cotton shirt, the loafers on his feet. Her heart registered the familiar curve of his jaw, the dark sheen of his hair, the remembered feel of his mouth.

It seemed to take him forever to reach her.

She couldn't have moved if she'd wanted to. Everything in her was frozen in place—waiting.

She was afraid to think.

Afraid to hope.

Afraid.

He touched her shoulder. "Elise . . ."

She looked up. Another raindrop landed on her cheek. She didn't care. Her umbrella slid to the ground as his other hand touched her other shoulder.

Her heart was no longer booming. Now it was zinging wildly. She wet her lips. Several raindrops wet her face.

"Elise," he said. "You were right about everything. Can you forgive me?"

"You . . . you didn't call." She knew she sounded stupid and thick, but she felt so confused.

"Oh, God, I have so much to tell you. I . . ."

Lightning cracked, and they both jumped. Thunder and rain burst around them. "Let's go sit in my car," Dev shouted. He picked up her umbrella, grabbed her hand and they raced a few feet to the Mercedes, which Elise hadn't noticed until now. A few seconds later, wet to the skin, they were inside the car with the sky falling around them. Rain pelted the roof of the car. The noise echoed the chaos in Elise's heart.

She turned to Dev.

He began to talk.

Elise listened, first with shock as he told her about Daisy going to California. She lived his fear with him as he described his panic. "Oh, Dev, I wish I'd known," she said.

"I *did* try to call you Friday night, but there was no answer."

She remembered how she'd sat in the movie theater for hours. "So you went to California?"

"Yes." He described his reunion with Daisy, his conversation with Joelle.

Elise felt the first real stirring of hope as he said, "When she said I'd changed, I realized I had. And I realized that you had played a large part in that change." He smiled tenderly and touched her cheek, pushing back a strand of wet hair. "I wanted to come home that instant, but I knew I had to do a lot of thinking before I could. So I booked a room at a small hotel overlooking the ocean and I spent Saturday and Sunday and yesterday holed up there or walking around on the streets. I thought and thought and thought. About everything in my life, and then about you."

Elise's pulse fluttered as his eyes softened and his hand caressed her cheek.

"You've taught me so much, you know."

"I have?"

"Yes. About warmth and love. About trust." He smiled again, this time ruefully. "I couldn't believe how blind I'd been. Especially when I thought over what you'd said about acceptance. You know, accepting the things that I couldn't change. Learning from them."

"Growing from them . . ." Elise said.

"Yes, exactly." His hand settled on her neck, and he tugged her closer. "I knew I *had* been trying to control everyone around me. I guess because so many of the things that had happened in the past were uncontrollable."

"I know," Elise whispered. "Really, Dev. I *do* know. We all need to feel some measure of control over our lives, but—"

"But not to the point where we let it become the focus of our lives," he finished. "Not to the point where we try to control everyone else."

Their gazes locked, and what Elise saw caused a great rush of joy to permeate her body. She knew Dev was finally a whole person again.

And when his arms enclosed her, and his lips finally met hers, she could feel her own splintered self become complete. They kissed deeply, telling each other with their lips and tongues how much they'd missed each other, and how much they wanted and needed and loved each other.

The rain fell in torrents around them, but they were lost in their own private world.

Finally Dev lifted his head. He stroked her cheek, looking deeply into her eyes. "Elise, I love you. Will you marry me?" He kissed the tip of her nose. "If you will, I promise to find a permanent job in Louisiana."

"I'd marry you even if it meant going halfway around the world," she said, so happy she wasn't sure she could bear it.

"I don't deserve you." His eyes looked like dark pools of spring water.

Elise grinned. "True. But you can work at it!"

A surprised laugh erupted from him. "I can't think of anything that will be more fun."

Then he kissed her again.

And again.

And again.

A long time later, when the rain had slowed to the tempo of a ballad instead of a march, Dev said, "Let's go home. I want to make love with you."

And so they did.

Epilogue

He loved everything about her.

Her hair. The way she'd arranged it high on her head, with her frothy pink hat forming a halo around it.

Her head and the way she held it. Chin up, so that she looked like a proud young queen walking before her subjects.

Her graceful movements in perfect synchronization with her father's as they glided to the soul-stirring strains of Purcell's "Trumpet Voluntary."

And as she drew closer, and the sunlight streaming through the stained-glass windows captured her in its jeweled rays, the luminous look of joy in her dark eyes and the soft smile curving her lips.

As Justin placed Elise's hand in his, Dev looked down at the beautiful woman who would soon be his wife. Elise had given him so much already, and now she was going to give him even more. He took her hand, and just before they turned to face the altar, his gaze met Daisy's.

She grinned. Face full of mischief, she gave him a thumbs-up sign, which she tried to hide behind her bouquet.

Dev grinned back, then slowly turned his attention to his bride. Elise looked up, and as their gazes met, his heart filled with a great rush of happiness, and along with it, the knowledge that he was the luckiest man in the entire world.

*   *   *   *   *

Silhouette

SPECIAL EDITION™

It takes a very special man to win

That **SPECIAL** *Woman!*

She's friend, wife, mother—she's you! And beside each Special Woman stands a wonderfully *special* man. It's a celebration of our heroines— and the men who become part of their lives.

Look for these exciting titles from Silhouette Special Edition:

April   FALLING FOR RACHEL by Nora Roberts
Heroine: Rachel Stanislaski—a woman dedicated to her career discovers romance adds spice to life.

May   THE FOREVER NIGHT by Myrna Temte
Heroine: Ginny Bradford—a woman who thought she'd never love again finds the man of her dreams.

June   A WINTER'S ROSE by Erica Spindler
Heroine: Bently Cunningham—a woman with a blue-blooded background falls for one red-hot man.

July   KATE'S VOW by Sherryl Woods
Heroine: Kate Newton—a woman who viewed love as a mere fairy tale meets her own Prince Charming.

Don't miss THAT SPECIAL WOMAN! each month—from some of your special authors! Only from Silhouette Special Edition! And for the most special woman of all—you, our loyal reader—we have a wonderful gift: a beautiful journal to record all of your special moments. Look for details in this month's THAT SPECIAL WOMAN! title, available at your favorite retail outlet.

New York Times Bestselling Author

Sandra Brown

Tomorrow's Promise

She cherished the memory of love but was consumed by a new passion too fierce to ignore.

For Keely Preston, the memory of her husband Mark has been frozen in time since the day he was listed as missing in action. And now, twelve years later, twenty-six men listed as MIA have been found.

Keely's torn between hope for Mark and despair for herself. Because now, after all the years of waiting, she has met another man!

Don't miss TOMORROW'S PROMISE by SANDRA BROWN.

Available in June wherever Harlequin books are sold.

INTIMATE MOMENTS®
10TH
Anniversary

Celebrate our anniversary with a fabulous collection of firsts....

The first Intimate Moments titles written by three of your favorite authors:

NIGHT MOVES	**Heather Graham Pozzessere**
LADY OF THE NIGHT	**Emilie Richards**
A STRANGER'S SMILE	**Kathleen Korbel**

Silhouette Intimate Moments is proud to present a FREE hardbound collection of our authors' firsts—titles that you will treasure in the years to come, from some of the line's founding writers.

This collection will not be sold in retail stores and is available only through this exclusive offer. Look for details in Silhouette Intimate Moments titles available in retail stores in May, June and July.

WHERE WERE YOU WHEN THE LIGHTS WENT OUT?

S I L H O U E T T E

SUMMER Sizzlers '93

This summer, Silhouette turns up the heat when a midsummer blackout leaves the entire Eastern seaboard in the dark. Who could ask for a more romantic atmosphere? And who can deliver it better than:

**LINDA HOWARD
CAROLE BUCK
SUZANNE CAREY**

Look for it this June at your favorite retail outlet.

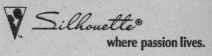

Silhouette®

where passion lives.

SS93